BIG HARD
Stick

SYLVIA PIERCE

BIG HARD STICK
by Sylvia Pierce

Paperback ISBN: 978-1-948455-02-2

CHAPTER ONE

First day of summer, eight in the morning, and one thing had just become abundantly clear: Rob "Roscoe" LeGrand was going to need a bigger set of balls.

"Knock it off, sixty-one," he called out across the rink. "You too, thirty-four! Helmets stay on at all times."

Fuckface. He'd said that last bit in his head, because cursing out kids less than half his age was a surefire way to end up on the wrong end of the publicity train. The Buffalo Tempest had done enough of that already, and as team captain he'd promised Coach Gallagher and the suits he'd help them turn it around, whatever it took.

Make himself available for more interviews and photo shoots than he could stomach? No problem!

Donate a fuck ton of money and signed merchandise to Children's Hospital? Happy to!

Spearhead the team's new youth hockey clinic? Bring

it on!

Yeah… He probably should've read the fine print on that last one.

Because now he had less than half an hour before the PR manager—Chief Executive Ball Buster, as the guys affectionately called her—showed up with the photographer, which meant less than half an hour to organize this rabble into some semblance of a team, complete with newspaper-worthy smiles.

"This is a shit idea," Roscoe grumbled, not for the first time that morning.

Henny, his right winger and second-in-command for this community enrichment fiasco, tapped his stick on the ice and shrugged. "No worse than getting caught on camera licking whipped cream off a woman's—"

"Hey. That was a completely consensual licking. Gallagher's overreacting."

"Doesn't matter." This from Alex Kenton, Roscoe's best defensemen and co-whipped-cream-licker. "We did the crime. Unless we want Gallagher up our asses all season, we're doing the time."

Crime? Technically, Roscoe hadn't done *anything*. It was just a bachelorette party at Big Laurie's—the pub Henny's girl Bex owned—a few months back. A bunch of pretty, perky bridesmaids were looking for a few laughs with the hockey players, and Roscoe and company obliged. Despite the whipped cream, a few shared drinks, and autographs on various body parts, Roscoe had gone home alone that night, same as always. Next morning, he'd woken up solo, wearing nothing but a feather boa and red lace bra, phone blowing up with the news that some fanboy had caught the whole thing on video and uploaded it to YouTube. Shit went viral. Gallagher went ballistic.

That video, coupled with the Tempest losing the Cup this spring after last year's big win, was the reason Roscoe had stepped up this summer. He respected his coach, loved his team, and there wasn't much he wouldn't do to boost their sinking rep in the community, including sacrificing his summer vacation to manage Gallagher's latest pet project. Alex Kenton, Sven Jarlsberg, and Dimitri Kuznetzov—his bachelorette party partners in crime—had lined up to help, right along with Henny, whose only crime was being a damn loyal friend.

The boys had spent a few weeks planning their strategy while PR handled the marketing and media crap. It was supposed to be a cakewalk. Neighborhood kids, pro athletes, fun times on the ice? Guaranteed positive press.

"Settle down over there," Roscoe shouted at the kids now, "or you're all going in the box."

Ignoring his lukewarm threat, two kids chased each other around the net while another entertained himself by spitting in the air and catching it on the way down.

Nice photo opp. PR's gonna love this.

"They need to find a way to channel that into the game," Henny said. "I'd kill for that kind of energy."

"Yeah?" Roscoe chuckled. "Pretty sure Bex would kill for you to have that kind of energy too, old man."

That earned him a punch in the arm.

"They're not even human," Roscoe continued. He was certain of it. Twenty minutes into the practice, and he still couldn't get most of them to pay attention. Only one kid—number forty-four—seemed like he wanted to be there. The kid stood a little bit apart from the rest, eyes on Roscoe and Henny, tracking their moves like he was taking notes in his head.

But one decent kid wasn't enough to make up for the rest of the bunch.

Roscoe shook his head. "Have I mentioned this is a shit—"

"Idea? Once or twice." Henny laughed. "Thought you loved kids, Mr. Sunshine."

"Used to. Until about twenty minutes ago." Besides, all of the kids in Roscoe's life were under the age of ten, a whole brood of adorable nieces and nephews still young enough to think he was cool. The punks on the ice today were teenagers, and judging from the scowls on their faces, Roscoe's coolness factor was at an all-time low.

It wasn't supposed to be like this. He was supposed to win them over, inspire them to greatness, all that jazz.

But they'd barely paid attention to his intro speech, didn't even cheer when he and Henny showed off some of their best tricks. Roscoe was starting to feel like a glorified babysitter.

"Maybe I should go Russian mafia on them," Kuznetzov deadpanned. He'd spent the morning trying to talk to the kids about the importance of stretching and warming up, but all they wanted to know was whether he'd ever taken a shot to the nuts. "My accent can be pretty scary."

"Your *face* can be pretty scary, Kooz," Jarlsberg said.

Kooz cocked his head and smirked. "Not according to your mother, my friend."

"Knock it off, children," Roscoe told them. "Or you're going in the box, too."

"My offer is still on your table," Kooz said, the accent making him sound like every Russian mobster in every Russian mobster movie Roscoe had ever seen. "I will tell them of my Uncle Yuri. Yuri is in Siberian prison since I was small boy."

"You're full of shit," Jarlsberg said, laughing. "So is Uncle Yuri."

Kooz raised an eyebrow and lowered his voice. "Do you know what happens to man who calls Uncle Yuri full of shit?"

Roscoe sighed, dragging a hand through his hair. Tempting as it was to let Kooz put the fear of God into these kids, he gave the idea a pass. Ultimately, turning this sinking ship around was his responsibility. He was the team captain. The leader. And, according to his teammates and family and basically everyone who'd ever spent more than five minutes with him, a nice fucking guy.

Probably explained why he kept going home alone at night. *Too* nice, they all told him. Even the women themselves.

Especially the last one, right before she packed up and bailed, two nights before he'd planned to propose.

It'd been a few years, but he'd only just gotten rid of the ring. He'd kept the damned thing locked in a box in his closet all that time, like some old relic to happier days.

Roscoe took a deep breath, shook off the funk. What did he have to complain about now? He had great friends and a big, closer-than-close family. Loved his city, his job. Got to spend his days on the ice, teaching kids how to shoot and score and charge down the rink. That's what it was all about.

"Thanks, Kooz," he said. "I'll take it from here."

"Sure you're up for this, Mr. Sunshine? Or would you rather go get a manicure?" Henny nailed him in the shoulder, but real concern flickered in his eyes.

"Got one last week. Hasn't even chipped yet." Roscoe wriggled his fingers in Henny's face, his mood brightening. Yanking his helmet into place, he knocked it once and said, "Let's roll."

Roscoe and Kooz scooted down to the net, zooming around the cluster of kids gathered in front of it, herding them like cattle into a tightly packed group. Henny and the D-men fell in line behind them with a puck, the five of them passing it back and forth, showing off some stick work.

But damn, those kids were a tough bunch.

"What about us?" one of them shouted, and the others nodded along. Number sixty-one again, Roscoe noticed. The alpha. Every group had one, and Roscoe knew from experience with his nephews that kids like that would set the tone for the whole pack. "When do we get sticks?"

"Not yet." They weren't ready for gear, that was for sure. They hadn't even mastered the basics yet; most hadn't even paid attention during the safety drill.

"Come on," sixty-one whined. "We came to play hockey, not watch from the sidelines. Let us make a move here, Feathers."

Feathers?

Before that moment, Roscoe hadn't realized teen boys could actually *giggle*.

Before that moment, Roscoe hadn't realized his teammates could giggle, either, but Henny and Kenton were quickly challenging that assumption.

Roscoe looked over his shoulder at Henny. "Did he just call me—"

"Feathers?" Henny could barely contain himself. "Yeah. Yeah he did."

"What is American saying?" Kooz asked. "If your feather bra fits?" Bastard really got the kids going with that one.

That's it.

Ignoring his boys, Roscoe skated up to the kid who'd just given him his new moniker. "Name?"

The kid sniffed, jutted out his chin. "Nick Harper."

"So you've spent some time trolling me on YouTube, Nick Harper." Roscoe said. "That where you learned your stand-up routine, too? Pretty amateur, if you ask me."

"At least I don't wear a bra, bro."

Everyone laughed at that, even Roscoe. Damn, these kids didn't miss a beat.

"That a fact?" Roscoe asked, keeping his tone light. Teasing was all part of the game, and as long as they all kept things good-natured, he'd play along. "Seems to me, hanging out on the Internet all day doesn't leave much time to work on your weak-ass game."

The kid's cheeks turned red behind his face shield, but to his credit, he didn't back down. "I got plenty of game, Feathers."

"Yeah?" Roscoe got right up in his face. Smiled that

sunshine grin of his. And handed over his stick. "Don't keep us in suspense, sixty-one."

Nodding once, Nick took the stick, zoomed down to the blue line at the other end of the rink. Henny followed, passing the puck good and hard.

The kid actually caught it, right in the sweet spot of the stick. Kenton went after him, but Nick was quick, dodging and weaving, charging down the ice. Kooz positioned himself in the net, ready to block.

The rest of the kids were cheering Nick on, shouting as he slipped past Kenton and Henny. He got in position for the shot, wound up...

Out of fucking nowhere, another kid swooped in with a stick and stole the puck, right from under Nick Harper's nose.

"Who's that?" Roscoe asked, impressed.

"Forty-four," Jarlsberg said.

Roscoe pulled the roster from his pocket, scanned the list. Reggie Heinz. Fifteen years old—a year younger than Nick Harper. Fast as hell, too.

The kids on the sidelines went wild again, whooping and hollering as Nick and Reggie fought for the puck. They chased each other around the net, stealing and blocking, but their antagonism quickly morphed into mutual respect. Soon they were passing like real teammates, testing each other's skills and limitations, uniting together in a quest to get that puck into the net. It was a damn thing of beauty, and as the kids zoomed together toward the goal zone, Roscoe's heart warmed at the sight of it.

Nick got in position for the shot, catching Reggie's perfect pass. He arched his stick, took the shot hard and straight…

No dice. Kooz dove and blocked the puck—good thing, or Roscoe would've benched his ass for letting two kids beat him on the first day—but hell, Roscoe cheered anyway. These kids knew their stuff.

Holding out his hands for the sticks as they skated back toward him, Roscoe nodded at them, acknowledging their skills. "Alright, sixty-one. You've got some moves. You too, double-fours."

Both kids beamed.

"Damn straight we do." Nick punched Reggie's shoulder.

"I can teach you guys a few more," Roscoe said, "if you'll let me."

Roscoe stuck out his hand. Reggie shook right away. Nick hesitated only a moment, then reached out. Roscoe went in for the shake, but Nick fist-bumped, and Roscoe totally fumbled the follow-through.

Roscoe laughed. "Maybe you can teach me something, too, slick."

"We'll see about that, old man." Nick gave him another fist bump and a big, genuine smile. Reggie hadn't said a word, but he hadn't stopped grinning, either.

These kids were happy. No hiding it.

And just like that, the whole morning turned right around.

The kids just needed to play—to be kids. Let off some steam, expend some of that pent-up energy before they got serious with all the rules-and-regulations bullshit. Roscoe had his own reasons for being there, but for the kids, this wasn't the NHL. Wasn't a job.

"Alright." Roscoe clapped once, turning toward the rest of the group. "Everyone grab a stick. Let's play some hockey."

The kids erupted in cheers, damn near killing each other to get to the box where they'd stashed the rest of the equipment.

Since Nick and Reggie seemed to know their way around the rink, Roscoe paired them up with Kenton and Jarlsberg to help out some of the younger kids, then sent Kooz and Henny to scope out the rest of the crew, gauging their skill level and physical fitness so they could assign official positions before the photographer showed up.

Roscoe kept his eyes on his star players, Nick and Reggie. In their short time together on the ice, they'd already bonded, already had that connection that allowed them to communicate wordlessly in a game.

"Left winger and center, I'm thinking," Henny said. He'd left Kooz with the less experienced group and joined Roscoe in watching the standouts.

"You called it," Roscoe said. "Nick's got a bit more technical finesse, but Reggie's faster. His heart is all in, too. Kid like that was born to play."

They both watched in awe as Reggie sped past, demonstrating a move for the others. He skated a little too hard, undisciplined and rough around the edges, but he was definitely talented with the stick. He switched from the left side to the right, equally adept at both. And when he faked out Kooz and made a shot that some of Roscoe's own pro teammates might've missed, Roscoe wanted to weep with joy.

Not that he was the type to get weepy on the ice, but still. The shot was fucking beautiful. Kooz would catch hell for the miss later.

"Nice work, forty-four," he called out. Then, to Henny, "Let's send him through the special backward crossover drill."

"Eva's?"

"Why not?" Roscoe asked. Eva was their skating coach, the kind of woman who took a special pride in torturing Tempest players as often as she could. She was also engaged to Tempest starting center Walker Dunn; the two were currently island hopping in the Caribbean, scouting out wedding locations.

"You want the kid to quit on us?" Henny asked. "My legs are still screaming from the last time Eva worked me over."

"Dude. She's been on vacation for two weeks."

"My point exactly."

"Let Reggie try," Roscoe said. "I need to see how hard he's willing to push."

"You're the boss." Henny called out to Reggie, and the kid skated over to them, barely winded from all the hard work he'd already done.

"You up for a challenge?" Roscoe asked.

"Yes, sir." The kid squared his shoulders, nodding so hard Roscoe thought his helmet might pop off.

"You familiar with backward crossovers?"

"Totally."

God, he sounded so young. Young and enthusiastic.

"I'd like to have you try our special version," Roscoe said. "It's like the backward crossover, but with a twist."

"More like a kick in the balls," Henny grumbled. "With another kick in the balls right after."

Ignoring him, Roscoe explained the deal, then sent Reggie off to give it a try.

Kid fucking nailed it. Not only that, but he swung back around for two more runs.

"Is it weird that I wanna adopt that kid?" Roscoe asked Henny.

"Totally weird."

"Look at him," Roscoe said. "When was the last time you saw a fifteen-year-old kid with stamina like that? Not to mention stick control."

"You want a kid, pops? Make your own." Henny laughed and nodded toward the seats, where a few parents had gathered to catch the rest of practice. "Maybe one of the hockey moms will help."

Roscoe barked out a laugh. "Yeah, *there's* a brilliant idea."

"Glad you think so. Because here comes your future baby mama." Clamping a hand on Roscoe's shoulder, Henny jerked his head toward the tunnel, where a blonde woman was stomping toward the rink.

Even at this distance, Roscoe could see the anger in her eyes.

One of those kids was in serious trouble.

"Christ. I'd better take care of this," he said to Henny. "Can you help the guys out there? I want Nick on left wing, Reggie on center. See what the other guys think about the lineup. Then you need to get them calmed down for the photo opp."

"On it," Henny said. Then, just before he skated off, "Hey. I was just kidding about the baby mama thing, douche bag. Don't get any bright ideas."

Too late, though. One look at those plump, heart-shaped lips as she came out into the light, and Roscoe's head was *swimming* with ideas, each one filthier than the last. So much for being a nice fucking guy.

Now that *is a hockey mom I'd like to f—*

"I'm here to pick up my kid," she said, skipping right over the pleasantries. Her short blonde hair was wind-blown and wild, her face pink, her blouse pulled back off one shoulder, revealing a blue bra strap. "Reggie Heinz?"

"I, uh…" Roscoe blinked, forcing himself to pay attention. Reggie Heinz, his new starting center. Best kid on the team. And the one with the hottest mom he'd ever laid eyes on.

"There," the woman said, pointing to the ice. "Forty-four. Also known as Grounded for Eternity."

Oh, fuck. Roscoe hoped the eternal grounding didn't apply to hockey practice.

"Sure," he said. "We've still got about twenty minutes on the clock, though. We're waiting for the photographer."

"Photographer?" Her light brown eyes widened in shock.

"Didn't you sign the release? It should've been in the packet you filled out this morning."

At this, she laughed, sharp and cold. "No. No I didn't."

Roscoe waited for her to say something else, but she folded her arms over her chest, her jaw clenched.

"Are you okay to wait," he asked, "or do you

need to—"

"No. Now would be best." She forced a smile, but it wasn't real. Whatever Reggie had done, the poor kid was in deep shit. Like, wait-till-I-tell-your-father, you're-never-leaving-the-house-again kind of shit.

Nodding, Roscoe turned toward center ice and blew his whistle. "Double fours," he called out, waving. "Bring it in."

The kid looked up and skated toward Roscoe, then froze at the sight of his mother.

"You are in *serious* trouble." The woman took a step out onto the ice. Soon as her foot touched down, she lost her balance.

Roscoe saw it coming a mile away. He lunged forward and grabbed her arms, steadying her right before she went down. They were closer now, so close he could smell the faint scent of her shampoo, like lemons and sugar, cookies left out in the sun.

It took her a second to realize what had happened.

"Thank you," she finally said, a little breathless.

With a cocky grin, he said, "Not as easy as it looks, is it?"

"You can say that again." For a moment she seemed to forget about Reggie, whatever screwed-up thing he'd done to invoke her ire. She was clutching Roscoe's arms, looking up at him through dark lashes, her eyes sparkling under the arena lights. They weren't just brown, he saw now, but amber, ringed in dark honey and flecked with gold. She smiled at him—a real one this time—a little shy, a whole lot sexy, and absolutely worth the wait. It was easily the most beautiful smile Roscoe had ever seen; it took every ounce of brain power he possessed just to remember his own damn name.

"You okay now?" he asked softly.

"I… I think so. I'm not really a fan of ice rinks."

"I see that." He smiled softly. "Name's Roscoe LeGrand. I'm heading up the youth clinic."

"Reggie's mom," she said. "Um. Ally Heinz."

They were in their own little world now, all the sights and sounds of the arena fading into an indiscernible buzz as Roscoe continued to stare into her eyes.

"Nice to meet you," he said.

"You, too."

After a second that stretched out like an hour, he finally said, "Well, Reggie's mom, you're welcome to keep holding onto me, but eventually we'll need to go home, and driving like this could be a challenge. I'm up for it if you are, but—"

"Oh my God, I'm so sorry." The woman—Ally—blushed again, another smile appearing on her face. Roscoe could've stared at that mouth all day.

"Mom?" a small, desperate voice squeaked out from behind a face shield, breaking the spell between Roscoe and Ally. The kid's voice sounded nothing like the fierce player Roscoe had seen on the rink. "Don't freak out. I can totally explain."

Ally's smile vanished, ice rushing back in where the warmth used to be.

Game over.

She righted herself, straightening her shirt and turning all her attention on the kid. "You'll have plenty of time to explain later. Right now I want you to take off that helmet and apologize to Mr. LeGrand for wasting his time today."

Roscoe wanted to tell them both it was unnecessary, but if he'd learned anything from his years of summer vacations with his parents, four brothers, one sister, five siblings-in-law, and all his nieces and nephews crammed into a five-bedroom cottage and a couple of pup tents, it was this: never come between a mama bear and her cub. Especially when the cub did some dumb-ass shit to piss off his mama.

"We're waiting," Ally said.

"God. Fine." The kid took off the helmet, shaking out a head of long, honey-blond hair the same color as Ally's. "I'm sorry I wasted your time."

Roscoe stared into a pair of bright blue, tear-filled eyes, trying not to show his utter shock.

Reggie, number forty-four, the player he'd already pinned all his hopes on for the youth cup and for all the youth clinic summers to come, was a girl.

CHAPTER TWO

I am a smart, capable, strong woman. I am unafraid. I am the master of my destiny. I am a fierce warrior goddess standing in my power...

Ally Heinz had memorized the mantra from Savannah Hart's *You Glow, Girl!*—her favorite self-help podcast—and now she repeated it in her head, desperately trying to calm her nerves and, well, glow. Roscoe LeGrand might not have noticed the wild banging of her heart, but there it was, the constant drumbeat of her anxiety. Despite her warrior goddess efforts, and Roscoe's surprisingly calming presence, Ally was a nervous wreck, her mind swimming with thoughts about all the ways a person like her daughter could die on a hockey rink.

Hitting her head on the ice, crashing into the boards, getting stabbed with an ice skate, assault with a deadly flying stick, assault with a deadly flying puck, choking on a mouth guard, hypothermia...

Indoor hockey hypothermia was totally a thing, right?

Ally closed her eyes and took another deep breath, shaking off her morbid thoughts. She didn't have to worry about any of those things happening to Reggie, because Reggie wouldn't be playing hockey. Problem solved.

Clamping a shaky hand over Reggie's shoulder, Ally opened her eyes again. Feeling the familiar solidity of her daughter—whole and unbroken—reassured Ally in a way no podcast mantra ever could.

"I'm sorry," she said to Roscoe, ignoring the little spark of desire his intense hazel eyes sent through her body. "It seems my daughter thinks the rules don't apply to her."

"That's not always a bad thing." He winked at Ally, his smile accentuating the dimple on his left cheek. God, he was cute. Really, *really* cute.

Focus, Ally. Focus!

"It *is* a bad thing," Ally said, gripping Reggie's shoulder tighter and giving her a little shake, "for a fifteen-year-old who sneaks out while I'm at work, then schemes her way onto a hockey team by forging my signature and pretending to be a boy."

"Oh, there's no gender requirement," Roscoe said.

"Sorry if I gave that impression—your daughter just took me by surprise." He turned to Reggie, his face serious once again. "You can *skate*, kiddo. A few more years and you'll be giving the pros a run for our money."

Beneath Ally's firm grip, Reggie stood up a little straighter, and Ally's lips curved into a smile, totally against her will. She couldn't help it; seeing her kid impress the hell out of a big, strong NHL player filled Ally with a special kind of pride.

My girl is such a badass.

Unfortunately, all that baddassery was a danger to Reggie's well-being, not to mention Ally's fragile nerves. Ally hated the ice—she didn't even like walking on pavement in the winter, lest there be an invisible slick spot waiting to take her down. But here was Reggie, throwing herself right into danger.

Not to mention lying. Batting those baby blues may have worked on Reggie's dad more times that Ally cared to count, but there was no way Ally would let something like that slide, no matter how badass Reggie was.

"You're not the only one taken by surprise today, Mr. LeGrand," Ally said. "First week at a new job, and I get a phone call from your staff about my kid's forms." Ally glared at Reggie. "Here's a tip, honey bunch. Next time you decide to forge my signature, make sure you complete the back of the form, too. They called me to make sure your tetanus shot was current."

"And you forgot the photo release," Roscoe said with another wink. Ally bit back a smile.

Cute and *funny…*

And totally distracting her from the point.

"Reggie, what were you thinking?" she asked.

Reggie lowered her eyes, kicking the ice with the front of her skate. Ally didn't even know how the kid had managed to locate her old skating gear amidst all the boxes stacked in their garage, still waiting to be unpacked.

"It's not a big deal," Reggie said.

"Oh, I beg to differ," Ally said.

"I just wanted to get out of the house and *do* something for once. And you're the one who wanted me to quote-unquote get to know the neighborhood and give Buffalo a chance."

"Not by sneaking around." Ally blew out a breath, trying to reign in her anger. Reggie screwed up, but at least she was safe. Unharmed. In a softer tone, Ally asked, "How did you even get here?"

Reggie jutted out her chin, defiant till the end. "I took the bus."

"You took the bus?" Ally turned to Roscoe and threw her hands up, fresh anger surging through her. "She took the bus!"

Roscoe offered a sympathetic smile, but this was obviously not his battle. She'd kept him from his work long enough, and unlike Reggie, she was pretty sure the other kids had permission to be here.

"I'm sorry to keep you," she said to Roscoe, reaching into her purse for her car keys. "Thanks for... well, for taking care of her out there."

Roscoe held her gaze for a long moment. Ally didn't know him well enough to know what that look meant, but she was pretty sure he wasn't just being polite.

Her mouth went dry, and despite the chill in the air from the ice, sweat pooled in the small of her back.

She needed to grab Reggie and hightail it out of there.

But then Roscoe said, "Sure you can't stick around a few more minutes? Watch the end of practice? I'd be happy to answer any questions about the summer program, if you've got 'em."

Reggie jumped on the opportunity. "Can't I just show you *one* thing? Please?"

"I don't—"

"Come on, Mom. *Please*?" Reggie's eyes glazed with fresh tears, her voice full of fragile hope, and Ally's heart squeezed inside her chest. Ally hated seeing her daughter cry, especially over this. Between the two of them, they'd shed an ocean of tears together, taking turns holding each other during dozens of sleepless nights, whispering promises that they'd get through it, that things would work out. But these tears were different. These tears were Ally's fault. She'd put them in her daughter's eyes, all because she was too scared to let the girl live a normal life.

"It will just take a few minutes." Reggie pulled her helmet back on, tucking her hair up inside. She was still on the verge of tears, but behind her desperate sadness, Ally saw the same determination and competitiveness she used to see in her husband's eyes.

Her own eyes misted with tears, and she quickly looked away, unable to hold her daughter's gaze. "Oh, fine," she muttered. "You've got five minutes. And no—"

Reggie was a blur, shooting out to the middle of the rink before Ally had even completed her sentence.

"—running," she finished weakly. Automatically. It didn't make sense on the ice; it was just another one of her mantras. No running, no going outside with wet hair, no diving into the shallow end.

No getting hurt.

Ally pressed her lips together, inhaling the cool air through her nose as she and Roscoe watched Reggie in action. The kid zoomed out to the middle of the rink, then turned and gave one of the other coaches the thumbs-up. At her signal, he slapped a puck toward her —way too hard and fast for Ally's liking, but Reg caught it easily with her stick. Seconds later, she was off, speeding down the ice again, stick in hand, puck completely in her control. She wove effortlessly through a row of orange cones, then sped things up, charging toward the net at the other end of the rink, moving so fast it made Ally queasy.

When she got near the net, she pulled her stick back and smacked the puck, sending it sailing through the air just above the ice. There was no goalie manning the net, but it didn't matter; the shot was impressive any way you looked at it.

Ally's jaw dropped. How anyone Reggie's age and size could hit something with so much precision at such high speeds was completely beyond comprehension.

Roscoe let out a low whistle. "I meant what I said, Mrs. Heinz. Your daughter is incredibly talented."

Ally could only nod, struck mute by her daughter's courage. God, Reggie was fearless. Ally couldn't decide whether she felt more proud, scared, angry, or flat-out jealous. The warring emotions swirled inside, leaving her exhausted.

Hoping for a total reboot on their lives, she'd moved Reggie across the country last month, away from her childhood home in Denver, away from her school and friends and everyone she ever knew. So on one hand, she desperately wanted Reggie to make new friends, to get involved, to embrace their new life in Buffalo. And hockey misgivings aside, she also wanted to be the kind of mom who encouraged her child to follow her dreams, to be brave, to be bold.

More importantly, she wanted her daughter to be

happy, and hockey and ice skating were things that had always brought her joy when she was younger.

But these days it felt like there was another person living inside Ally, a dark shadow who refused to let her or Reggie truly live. Fear and anxiety were Ally's constant companions now. They stalked her every move, curled up with her in bed at night, followed her into her dreams. But unlike dreams and shadows, they didn't dissipate in the morning sun. They lingered, swirling around her head like smoke, never far.

Too risky, they whispered now. *Those helmets sure don't look very sturdy. And all those boys? You can bet they won't go easy on Reggie just because she's a girl. Look around, Ally. Do you see any paramedics here? Are any of these hockey players even qualified to administer first aid?*

Ally rolled her shoulders and silently repeated her warrior mantra, trying to release the tension. The trick didn't work.

What would Dan do in this situation, she wondered? She tried to ask him, tried to imagine him standing right here and talking to Roscoe LeGrand about their daughter.

But that was a pointless exercise. Dan was no help now.

The dead never were.

Desperate to keep her mind from sliding into total darkness, Ally turned to Roscoe and forced a smile.

"Soooo…. You play for the NHL? What do you guys do in the off-season?"

Master conversationalist, girl. Nice job.

If Roscoe noticed her complete inability to be normal, he was kind enough not to show it. "You're looking at it," he said. "This is the first year we're doing the youth clinic, but we've always got community relations projects going on. Fundraisers, media appearances, local stuff. Day-to-day we're still training, too. Lots of workouts. Early morning runs, weights. Can't get too comfortable, even in the summer." He laughed and patted his abs, and Ally couldn't help but wonder what he looked like under that fleece. Probably totally ripped. She suddenly wanted nothing more than to run her hands up under there, touch his hot, smooth skin…

Whoa. Where the hell did that *come from?*

She looked back toward Reggie, who was now skating backward, laughing as one of the other kids tried to catch up to her.

"I usually head up to Maine with my family for part of the summer," Roscoe continued, "but this year I'm sticking around to manage the clinic, keep an eye on these little beasts." He thumbed toward the boys at the other end of the rink and rolled his eyes, but his tone was so sweet and sincere it made Ally's throat tighten with emotion. He loved kids—that much was clear.

Just like Dan.

Suddenly she wondered what Roscoe had meant by "family." Parents? Brothers and sisters? Or was he talking about a wife and kids? Her gaze darted quickly to his ring finger—unadorned.

Hmm. Maybe he just didn't wear his ring on the ice.

Or maybe Ally shouldn't be checking out the NHL player like some kind of desperate, crazy, unstable, sex-starved maniac...

The thoughts jolted her back to reality. What was she *doing*? She'd come to the arena to put an end to this hockey business, not find a man. In fact, finding a man was the very *last* thing on her bucket list, right after skydiving and getting a double root canal.

"Well, thanks again," she said, waving for Reggie to come back from the rink. "Looks like she had a good time."

"Sure did," Roscoe said. Turning to face Ally, he said, "Are you sure there's nothing we can do to—"

"Roscoe!" One of the other players shouted. "Just got the text—the photographer is on her way. Let's go."

Roscoe waved at the guy. To Ally, he offered another fantastic smile as he stepped backward onto the ice, smooth and graceful and nothing like Ally's first steps out there. "I need to get the kids ready for the photo shoot, but if you change your mind, Reggie is welcome back any time. We meet Wednesday and Friday mornings, and the tournament is August twentieth."

"Tournament?"

"Big game against the youth team from Rochester. Should be a good time."

"I'll... I'll keep it in mind," Ally said, even though she knew she wouldn't. An actual tournament? That sounded even more dangerous than the clinic.

"Mom!" Reggie skated up to them, her cheeks pink from exertion, her smile broad and genuine. "Did you see me?"

"You looked great out there," Ally said, because that much was true. But it still wasn't enough to change her mind about letting her daughter play such a dangerous sport, and neither was Roscoe's smile, as much as she wished it could've been.

"Does this mean I can stay?"

Ally frowned. "We'll talk about it later."

"But—"

"Go get changed, baby," she said, hiking her purse up on her shoulder like a piece of body armor. "I'll meet you by the entrance." Then, with one more smile for Roscoe LeGrand and a final look across the rink, Ally took an icy breath and held it, knowing that it would be her last moment of peace for a long time.

CHAPTER THREE

"What were you thinking?" Ally demanded, tugging Reggie's seatbelt to make sure it was secure before starting up the car. "Does Aunt Clarissa know?"

Clarissa Finch was Ally's best friend and the only close connection they had in Buffalo—a woman whom Ally credited with keeping her alive during the darkest days of her life.

She was also the senior account manager at Seton Mack Associates, the firm that handled public relations for the Buffalo Tempest. Clarissa must've mentioned the hockey clinic in passing when she was over at the house a couple weeks ago, but Ally barely remembered—she'd been too focused on unpacking and getting their kitchen organized and trying not to freak out about the fact that she'd just moved across the country. She was pretty sure Reggie hadn't shown any interest, either.

Just proves how far out of the loop you are about your own kid…

"I don't know," Reggie finally said.

"Did you see her today?" Ally pulled out her phone, but there weren't any missed calls or texts from Clarissa; she would've given Ally a heads up for sure.

"She wasn't there. Just some volunteers in the morning, then us kids and the coaches, and a couple of parents who came at the end to support their kids."

Ally felt a little sting in her gut at that, but she dismissed it. It was easy to support your kid, to let her follow her heart right over all kinds of cliffs when you still believed there was a safety net at the bottom. Ally knew better.

"What if Clarissa *had* been there?" she asked, pulling out of the parking lot. "Did you think about how this might make her look? How it could affect her job?"

Another shrug. "I just wanted to play hockey again. It's got nothing to do with Aunt Clar."

"Reg, if you were interested in the clinic, why didn't you say anything to me sooner?"

"Why do you *think*, Mom?" Reggie folded her arms across her chest and turned her face away, staring out the window like she was looking for a good place to jump out. "God, you make a big freaking drama out of *everything*."

"This isn't everything. This is your health and safety

we're talking about. What if you'd gotten hurt out there today?"

"I didn't. Just like I never got hurt all the other times I played."

"But you *could* have."

"I *could've* had fun, too. But thank God you showed up in time to make sure nothing crazy like actual fun happened."

Actual fun? Ally barely knew the meaning of the phrase anymore.

Leaving the arena behind, she pulled onto the highway, merging into the afternoon traffic. Her new boss had been understanding about the family emergency, told her to take as much time as she needed. Ally had planned to drop Reggie at home and go back to work, but she didn't see that happening now. She didn't trust Reggie not to escape again, to wander into some other dangerous situation Ally wouldn't be able to protect her from.

Yes, she realized how overprotective and crazy she sounded.

But no, she didn't care. This was her daughter. Her heart. Her entire world.

After five minutes of silence, Reggie finally piped up again, and Ally braced herself for the next phase of the nagging campaign that was sure to come.

"You know that guy, Roscoe LeGrand?" Reggie

asked. "He's the starting left winger for the Buffalo Tempest. He's basically famous."

"Is that so?"

"If you weren't so busy flirting with him, you might—"

"I wasn't flirting with him," she said. *Was I?* She replayed their conversation in her mind. She'd definitely felt a little spark when he grabbed her arms on the ice, and yes, had a momentary lapse in judgment when she'd started fantasizing about his abs, but that was *not* flirting. "We were just making conversation. Mostly about you."

Ignoring this, Reggie said, "This is his first year as team captain, and he's in charge of all of us. He tied the league last year in assists with his right winger, Kyle Henderson, but they call him Henny. Walker Dunn is the center. He wasn't there today, but he's supposed to join up later. And there's a special skating coach that used to be in the Olympics—Eva Bradshaw? Now she works for the team, but I don't think she's doing any of the clinic stuff. Oh, and she's getting married to Walker. They have a daughter and a big dog, too. His name is Bilbo Baggins. Cute, right?"

Ally laughed. "How on earth do you know all of this?"

"Interviews and stuff. They were featured in *Sports Today* last year. But Roscoe LeGrand? He's, like, amazing. You should've seen this one shot he made today. Some of the asshole boys acted like they weren't impressed, but they totally were."

"Language." Ally sighed. This was Reggie's typical strategy—when her persuasion techniques failed, she moved on to the facts, proving she'd done her homework. Ally didn't bother asking for more details—Reggie would share every last one without prompting.

Too bad they wouldn't help. Not with this.

"He's really good, Mom."

"I'm sure Mr. LeGrand is great at his job, baby," Ally said, remembering his easy confidence on the ice, the lightning-fast reflexes that had saved her from an embarrassing fall. "That's not the point."

"What *is* the point?"

"Hockey is dangerous. And—"

"Then why did you let Dad take me all those times?"

Ally knew it was coming, but the mention of Dan still felt like an arrow to the heart.

He'd always been a huge hockey fan. He played in college—not for a career aspiration, but for fun. After they got married and settled down in Colorado, he'd gotten season tickets for the Colorado Wolves every year. As soon as Reggie was old enough, he'd started taking her to the home games, too. For the away games, the two of them had this whole ritual, dressing up in their team jerseys and lucky ball caps, ordering their "winning" pizza—half peppers and mushrooms, half ham and pineapple—camping out in front of the big-screen TV until the end.

Dan had bought Reggie her first pair of skates, as well as her last. He'd taught her everything he knew about the game, and they'd played together whenever they could, indoors and outside, even in the dead of winter. She'd even petitioned her middle school, with Dan's backing, to let her play on the boys' intramural team in seventh grade.

She'd been better than all of them.

But Reggie hadn't played in years. She'd packed up all of her hockey stuff the winter after Dan's death, and as far as Ally had known, hadn't picked up her stick since.

Clearly, Ally had missed something.

"I wish Dad was still around to play with you," Ally said gently, taking a chance and squeezing Reggie's knee, "but he isn't. I have to be both parents now, and that means making the best decisions I can—by myself. My first priority is to keep you safe and healthy, and I don't feel like I can do that if you're out on the ice with all those kids when I can't be there to keep an eye on you."

"Maybe you should've thought of that before you took that stupid job."

Another arrow, one Ally was certain would become a staple in Reggie's arsenal in the months and years to come. Ally had only been working full time for a three days—a marketing assistant and graphic design position in a boutique marketing firm Clarissa had connected her with when they'd arrived in town last month—and already Reggie resented her. Not that Ally could blame the kid. For her entire childhood, Ally had devoted herself to motherhood, to making a home and life for her husband and daughter, happily putting her art and design dreams on the back burner.

After Dan died, she and Reggie had slipped under the fog together, huddling close and hoping it would pass. Now that they were starting to emerge again, everything was different. New town, new house, new school for Reggie this fall, and Ally was entering the full-time workforce. It had to be hard for Reggie to adjust to their new reality, but what choice did Ally have? Dan's insurance money and the settlement they'd received from his company wouldn't last forever. And as much as it'd felt like the world ended when he died, it hadn't. Ally and Reggie had to keep on living. Keep on planning and saving. Keep on existing. And existing? It cost a lot of money, even when it sucked.

"You know I'd rather be home with you than anywhere else in the world." Ally squeezed Reggie's knee again. "Things are different now. We both have to make sacrifices if we want things to work out."

Reggie inched away, pulling the long blond curtain of

her hair in front of her face. "If this is your idea of things working out, I feel sorry for you."

Me too, kiddo. Me too.

Minutes ticked on as they scooted down the highway, Reggie staring out the window again, jaw clenched, arms locked across her chest like her own personal bulletproof vest.

The silence was so all-consuming, Ally thought it would swallow them both. But then Reggie tucked her hair behind her ear, turned those pretty blue eyes toward her mother, and said, "If you hate hockey, why were you flirting with Roscoe LeGrand, anyway?"

Ally clucked her tongue. "I told you, I was *not* flirting."

"Okay, cougar."

"*Cougar?*" Ally laughed, relieved to see Reggie crack a smile of her own. "I'm not older than him. At least not that much." She flicked her gaze up to the rearview mirror. So her eyeliner was a little smudged, and fine, maybe she had a few more lines around her mouth than she used to, a few more gray hairs—grays that had Reggie's name all over them. But she didn't look *old*. Did she?

"Well, how old is he, anyway?" Ally asked casually.

"Oh my God. Gross."

"It's just a question! You're the one who studied his bio."

"Like you care about his *bio*," Reggie said, her tone a little lighter. "I saw the way you were looking at him. Falling into his arms when you slipped on the ice—nice move, by the way."

"It was an accident."

"Mom. The entire time I've been alive, you've never once gone near the ice. Ever. You're, like, pathological about it."

"It's slippery!"

"Mmm-hmm." Reggie smirked. "But one look at Mr. LeGrand, and you're practically pirouetting out to him. You know what that's called, right? A meet-cute. You totally met-cute him, and soon you'll be drawing his name in your notebook with little hearts around it. Ally and Roscoe for *evah*!"

Ally cracked up at that, the tension in the car finally easing. She exited the highway and threaded through the stop-and-go streets that led to their neighborhood in North Buffalo, not far from the Buffalo Zoo. At the next stop light, she stole another glance at her daughter. Reggie was still looking out the window, but she'd finally relaxed her arms.

Progress.

"We should check out the zoo this weekend," Ally said. "See if we can track down that strange animal." They could hear it screeching late at night, when the windows were open and the rest of the neighborhood was asleep. The first night in their new house, they'd stayed up until three in the morning, sitting on the front porch in their bathrobes with hot ciders, counting the minutes between screeches. Reggie had wanted to sneak over to the zoo right then, peek through the iron gates with flashlights and binoculars.

"With your new boyfriend?" Reggie asked.

"Someone's been watching a few too many rom-coms," Ally teased.

"You're right, actually," she said. "Netflix is turning my brain to mush, not to mention ruining my eyes. I really should get involved in a sport or something."

"When did we get Netflix?"

"I signed us up a few weeks ago. Honestly, Mom, I'd rather be playing hockey. You know—getting some exercise, building team spirit, challenging myself. I'll totally cancel the Netflix subscription if you let me back on the ice."

Ah, so we're on to phase three of the nagging campaign: bargaining.

"You know I can't do that, honey bunch."

"Why?" Reggie's voice cracked, fresh tears choking her words. "And don't say it's dangerous. I could get eye strain and bulging disks from watching movies on my laptop. I could get murdered on the way to school. I could fall and hit my head in gym class. Or get attacked at the monkey house at the zoo. Or get heat stroke in this very car, or—"

"Regina Heinz." Ally clenched the steering wheel, her fingers turning white. "Are you *trying* to get yourself locked in your room until you're fifty?"

"Locked in my room? Mom!" Reggie put her hand to her heart, her gasp loud and dramatic. "What if the house burns down, and the firemen can't get to me because you locked me in? What kind of a mother would do that to her own flesh and blood?"

And just like that, their momentary peace evaporated.

"Forget hockey," Ally grumbled. "You should go to law school. You've got an argument for everything."

"I wouldn't need arguments if you'd just let me play like a normal person. You know that, right?"

Ally sighed, her entire body so suddenly weary, she wanted to close her eyes, let go of the wheel, and fall asleep for an entire year.

She didn't, though. Didn't let go, didn't collapse, didn't scream until her vocal chords gave out. She couldn't; as a mother, she didn't have the luxury of giving up.

Instead, she took a deep breath into her belly, channeled her inner calm, and pulled into their driveway. She let the car idle a moment, then shut off the ignition, reaching for her purse. Tucked inside was a framed photo of her and Dan with the last note he'd ever written her, its wooden frame small enough to fit in the palm of her hand. The picture was taken at the wedding of one of his colleagues a few months before he died, and the two of them looked so happy and carefree. It was her favorite picture, even more precious than her own wedding photos, because it captured the two of them so perfectly. She'd spent so many nights tracing her fingers over the glass that she could see the image without even looking, and now she closed her eyes and felt for the frame's hard edges through the leather of her purse, seeking strength. Guidance. Anything to get her through this.

In a soft voice she said, "I know you enjoyed playing hockey with Dad when you were younger—"

"Not everything is about Dad," Reggie snapped, but beneath her anger, the words lacked conviction. Everything *was* about him, and they both knew it. His death had shattered their family in ways they hadn't even begun to deal with. She could only imagine how it was for Reggie, but Ally couldn't go more than an hour without thinking of him, without something calling her right back to the gaping void he'd left behind: the picture, a song, a scent, a ringtone, the taste of his favorite ice cream, a single athletic sock with a hole in the toe showing up in the laundry as if it had been tucked away in a pocket until just that moment. Clarissa always said it was like Dan stopping by to say hello, to let them know he was with them. But Ally knew it was just coincidence. Just a collection of painful reminders that she and Reggie had lost the most important man in their life.

Ally opened her eyes, looking back at Reggie through a glaze of fresh tears.

"Please?" Reggie asked again, her big blue eyes yet another reminder of her father. "Can I just do this for the summer? I won't play during school. It's just a couple of months, and I'll never ask you for anything again. *Please?*"

Desperation laced her words, so deep and all-consuming Ally almost—*almost*—gave in.

But she couldn't risk it. Wouldn't risk it, even if it meant Reggie would hate her for the entire year. Ally would much rather have a daughter who hated her than a daughter in the cemetery.

Ally took another deep breath and dashed the tears from her cheeks, remembering something she'd read in one of her self-help books for young widows: *Death sure has a funny way of sucking the fun out of life.*

Ally reached over to tuck Reggie's hair behind her ear, her palm cradling Reggie's baby-soft cheek. When Ally spoke again, her voice was as weak and watery as her bones. "I'm sorry, Reg. But the answer is still no."

CHAPTER FOUR

"What's another word for hot mess?" Ally asked Clarissa, phone pinned between her shoulder and ear as she tried to fan the black smoke of a ruined dinner out the kitchen window. "Like, a hotter, messier word?"

Clarissa laughed. "Searching for a crossword clue?"

"More like a personal power word. It can really set the tone for the day," she said, doing her best impersonation of Savannah Hart, a shiny, happy, eternal optimist.

"God, we need to find you some new podcasts. You're doing New Age wrong, Ally."

"I'm doing *everything* wrong."

It was the day after the hockey debacle, and she'd taken a sick day from work to spend time with Reggie—risky, considering she'd taken yesterday afternoon off and she was still the newbie at the office—but the kid refused to speak to her. She hadn't uttered a single word in more than twenty-four hours. Ally had planned to serve up Reggie's favorite dinner tonight as a peace offering, but somehow she'd ruined the baked chicken enchiladas, too, nearly burning down the kitchen in the process.

"What's going on?" Clarissa asked.

She filled Clarissa in about Reggie's hockey shenanigans, leaving out the part about falling into the arms of Roscoe LeGrand, the memory of which sent a weird little jolt into her belly.

She also left out the part about how she'd since thought of a hundred more intelligent and charming things she could've said instead, and how she was secretly wishing they'd met under circumstances that didn't involve her daughter careening around on the ice at lightning speeds, and she *especially* left out the part about last night's not-so-G-rated dream about him, leaving her aching and unfulfilled and still half-dreaming about his impossibly strong arms...

But *anyway*.

"Reggie's been locked in her room ever since," Ally finished up. "Slamming things around and blasting that horrible emo music. I swear she's trying to put me in an early grave."

Clarissa stifled a laugh—Ally could totally hear that

through the phone, like it was a real struggle to keep it stuffed down inside. "Holy shit, Als. You sound like such a mom right now, it's scary."

"I *am* a mom. Just not a good one. Hence the hot mess."

"Why didn't you call me sooner? I must've just missed you guys yesterday—I was there for the photo shoot. No one mentioned anything about Reg."

"It's not your job to clean up our disasters."

"Ally. Come on."

"It's not a big deal," Ally said. It was a huge deal, actually, but she didn't want Clarissa to worry. Her best friend had already done so much for her—Reggie too— and she didn't want Clarissa to let this interfere with her PR work. "I handled it, brought her home, forbid her from playing. From leaving the house at all, actually."

"Hence the emo music and the slamming."

"Now you're all caught up."

"I can't believe she went out there on her own," Clarissa said. Ally swore there was a hint of admiration in Clarissa's voice.

"That makes two of us. Well, three, if you count the hockey guy."

"Which one?"

"The cute one with the clipboard. I think he's the captain?" Ally's heart did a weird little jump. *Annoying.*

"Ah. Roscoe LeGrand."

"Right. Anyway, she had everyone fooled pretty good. Roscoe says she's super talented."

"She always was," Clarissa said.

"No kidding." Ally opened the fridge, trying to find a way to salvage dinner. She hadn't had time to do a proper grocery shopping this week, and the pickings were pretty slim. She'd pinned all her hopes on those enchiladas.

Ally tried not to look at it as a sign.

"She didn't even ask me about it, Clar," she said. "Didn't even give me a chance to consider it."

After a long pause, Clarissa asked, "Would you have said yes?"

"That's not the point."

"Okay. I get that you're pissed about the lying and sneaking around—you have every right."

"Spit it out, sister. I can hear that 'but' coming a mile away."

"*But*," Clarissa said, "it takes a lot of guts to get out there on the ice with a bunch of NHL players and boys twice her size, and she was obviously serious about it, considering everything she did to get there. Sounds to me like it's pretty important to her."

"Hey. Who's side are you on?"

"Ally..." Another sigh and an extra long pause, and

Ally knew what was coming next. She braced herself for it, but no matter how many times Clarissa brought it up —no matter how gently and carefully she stepped around the land mines of Ally's heart—Ally was never quite prepared to hear the sound of her husband's name.

"She misses Dan," Clarissa said, and Ally winced, her eyes blurring with tears.

"So do I," Ally whispered.

"I realize that, hon. I just think this hockey thing could be a way for Reggie to connect with her dad in a more—I don't know—joyful way? To honor the good memories instead of focusing on the sad ones. Does that make sense?"

Ally shut the fridge door and rested her forehead against the stainless steel. No, it didn't make sense. Nothing in her life made sense anymore.

But deep down she knew Clarissa was right.

Rather than honoring her husband's life, Ally had spent the last few years obsessing over his death, over all the things she might have done to prevent it. What if she'd cooked breakfast that morning, making him five minutes later for work? What if she'd gotten him up and out the door five minutes earlier? What if she'd asked him to take the day off? Or to stop and pick up her prescription first? In any of those scenarios, he would've arrived at work at a different time. He wouldn't have gone down to the plant floor at that precise moment, wouldn't have been there right when the rigging for one of the conveyor systems broke loose. Wouldn't have noticed the man standing beneath it. Wouldn't have leapt to shove that man out of the way, saving the man's life while sacrificing his own.

Now Ally worried that all of their happy memories of Dan—family fishing trips to Rocky Mountain National Park, watching the snow fall outside their big bay window on Christmas mornings as Reggie tore open her presents, laughing at his horrible cooking, planning surprises together for Reggie's birthdays, helping him match his suits and ties—would eventually be tainted by this immense grief, the sharp pain of loss seeping into the past and poisoning it until all she could remember about him was the black hole he'd left behind. She wanted Reggie to be able to remember her father with a smile on her face, not with a broken heart. Ally hadn't been able to find anything in her life that reminded her of Dan without squeezing the air out of her lungs, but maybe Reggie still had that chance. Maybe hockey was supposed to be that thing for her.

And maybe Ally had no right to get in the way of that. Of her daughter's chance at peace and acceptance. At happiness.

"If anything happened to her," Ally choked out, "that's it. I would stop existing."

"You can't keep her in a bubble, though. She'll end up resenting you, and you'll lose her anyway."

What could Ally say to that? Once again, Clarissa was right on the money. Ally already felt it happening—the way Reggie spent so much time in her room, even when they weren't arguing. The noncommittal shrugs and mumbles whenever Ally tried to engage her in conversation. The compulsive attachment to her phone. Sure, part of that was normal teen stuff. A few little potholes on the long and winding road of mother-daughter relationships.

But the rest of it *wasn't* normal. It was the aftermath of the terrible storm that had ripped through their lives three years ago, and all the mistakes Ally had made since.

The mistakes she *kept* making.

"But hockey, though?" she asked. "Why does it have to be hockey? Or anything with ice, for that matter?"

"You know you're going to give in," Clarissa teased gently. "When have you ever said no to that girl?"

"Hmm. When she asked me to paint her new room black?"

"Ally. You bought the paint. It's sitting out in your garage."

"So? I haven't put it on the walls yet. I'm hoping she'll change her mind once she makes a few friends in town and sees that none of them have morbidly depressing black bedrooms."

Clarissa laughed, and Ally imitated her, forcing the sound through her lips. She wanted to laugh, too— wanted to make jokes and let stuff go and focus on the positive and find the joy in the small moments, just like all the podcasts preached. But every time she tried to let go, to let the light back in, she felt like a big, fat fraud. Who was *she* to make jokes? To forget her troubles? Her husband had been robbed of his life before he'd even hit forty, her daughter was miserable and lonely... Ally had no business being happy, no matter what the gurus and experts claimed.

"I still can't believe she showed up at the rink," Clarissa said, her voice taking on that same admiring tone. "How'd she like meeting the guys?"

Ally laughed, and this time it almost felt genuine. "They didn't even know she was a girl. You should've seen the look on their faces when she took off her helmet. They were totally speechless, especially that Roscoe guy. The captain, right?"

"Yep. Also the Tempest's most eligible bachelor, which you obviously noticed."

Bachelor? Good to know...

"He's an attractive man," Ally admitted, rummaging through the junk on the counter for the Pasquale's menu Clarissa had left for her. Then, as casually as if she were asking about the price of a large pepperoni with extra cheese, she said, "What's his story, anyway?"

"Don't even start with that tone, Ally."

"There's no tone. I'm just curious. What kind of star athlete bachelor signs up to entertain a bunch of rowdy kids all summer?"

"The kind that needs to look good on TV after a play-offs loss and a compromising video involving a can of whipped cream and some overeager bachelorettes."

"Oh." Ally's heart sank. It shouldn't have bothered her, but it did. He'd seemed like such a nice guy, down to earth, sweet.

No matter. Daydreaming about the hockey hunk was pointless anyway. Reggie wasn't going back to the youth clinic, and even if Ally wanted to start dating again— which she absolutely did *not*—the timing was all off. She needed to focus on making the right impression at her new job, on getting them settled into the house. And most importantly, on making sure Reggie survived the transition to a new school and new town with as little friction as possible.

A wave of emotion rose inside her, squeezing her throat.

"Am I doing the right thing, Clar?" Her voice cracked again, all thoughts of Roscoe LeGrand gone. "Keeping her away from this?"

"Oh, hon. I can't answer that for you. I know you're

doing what you believe is right to keep Reggie safe. You're her mom."

"What would you do?"

"Honestly? I don't know. I can't imagine being in that situation, and I think you're an amazing mother and the strongest woman I know, hands down."

"Okay, I'm *so* not either of those things. And I know there's another 'but' in there."

Clarissa laughed. "Here's your but, babe. You're strong, *but...* Reggie's pretty damn strong, too. Maybe you should give her a chance to show you."

Reggie didn't come down for dinner—wouldn't even open her door when Ally knocked with a plate of food for her.

Hours later, her own pizza cold and untouched on the kitchen counter, Ally finally mustered the courage to go to Reggie's room and check on her.

She opened the door a crack, careful not to let the light from the hallway spill onto Reggie's face. She was sound asleep, feet sticking out from under the sheet, a faded unicorn T-shirt twisted around her body, the dinner plate Ally had left outside the door sitting on the edge of her desk, littered with pizza crust.

In the corner across from her bed, her hockey gear was stacked up against the wall.

The scene was so normal, so *Reggie*, that for a minute Ally lost all sense of time and place. Suddenly she was back in Denver, waking Reggie up early one morning so she and her dad could head up to Montana.

The two of them had been planning their father-daughter camping trip all year, and they'd had the time of their lives. Reggie had talked about it for weeks after, telling Ally and anyone else who'd listen story after story. They'd had so much fun that they'd forgotten to take pictures.

It was the last big, special memory she'd ever make with her father.

The following month, Ally had been working in the garden behind their house when she'd gotten the call from Dan's boss. Her husband had been in an accident. No, they didn't have details, but maybe she could ask a neighbor to drive her there? Urgently?

She'd driven herself, doing close to ninety miles an hour the whole way.

It hadn't been fast enough.

By the time she pulled into the lot, Dan was already gone. She'd felt it—felt his soul leaving this life, leaving her heart, passing over her body like water she just couldn't grab hold of—even before she opened her car door, before she noticed his assistant and another staff person running toward her, their faces grim, mouths pulled tight to hold in the words no human being should ever have to say to another.

Your husband is dead.

A fresh wave of grief crashed over Ally now, the loss hitting her all over again. Dan's death had nearly destroyed her, had all but shredded her heart. In the three years since, the sharpness of that shocking pain had dulled to a constant but bearable ache, allowing her to get out of bed, to function again even when she really didn't want to. But when she thought about that camping trip again, the ear-to-ear grin Reggie had worn for days after, her heart nearly cracked in two. Her pain was for Reggie, for all the time she lost with her dad. For all of the things Ally couldn't do for her. For all of the promises she could never make to her daughter, could never hope to keep, because they should've been Dan's promises instead.

Ally blinked back her tears and looked around the bedroom again. Reggie had hung an old hockey poster on the wall above her dresser, an autographed one she and Dan had picked up at a Colorado Wolves game. *Skate hard, Reggie!* the inscription read. It was another reminder of what Ally had seen on the ice yesterday. Reggie was so passionate about the game, so intense. She really did love hockey.

Reggie's pretty damn strong, too.

Clarissa's words echoed. Yes, Reggie was strong. Stubborn, too—just like her father. Ally knew that even if she forbade Reggie from playing at the Tempest clinic, the kid would find another way to get back on the ice.

Ally sighed, dashing away the last of her tears.

Like it or not, there was only one right answer.

She just hoped Roscoe LeGrand had meant what he said.

CHAPTER FIVE

"Duck and cover, jack-offs." Henny skated up behind Roscoe and Kenton, knocking them both on their helmets. "Chief Executive Ball Buster, twelve o'clock."

"Fuck," Roscoe said. "I'm not wearing a cup."

"Then you'd better hold it," Henny said. "She's wearing a scowl with your name written *all* over it."

"Again? Splendid." Roscoe chugged the rest of his water and pitched the empty bottle into the players' box. He and the boys had just finished an early morning practice, and they had about twenty minutes before the monsters from the youth clinic showed up. Wednesday had ended on a high note, but today they had to work. Hard. He had no idea how the kids would handle it, and he definitely wasn't in the mood for a lecture from PR.

Clarissa Finch, however, seemed to thrive on lectures.

"Mr. LeGrand." Her voice echoed across the rink,

announcing her arrival seconds before she stomped out of the tunnel. "What have you got for me? Short version —I've got a meeting with Gallagher in ten."

Kenton let out a low whistle. "How can anyone so beautiful be wound up so tight?" he mumbled to Roscoe. "On a Friday, besides."

Clarissa flashed Roscoe her usual irritated glare, but Roscoe detected something else when she looked at Kenton—a little warmth in her otherwise icy demeanor. Before he could confirm, she was looking down again, face buried in her iPad.

He didn't know what was going on there, but for Roscoe, irritating the PR manager was one of the perks of the gig. "We're great, Clarissa," he said. "Thanks for asking! How's your day going so far?"

"What part of 'short version' did you not understand?" Her trendy black-framed glasses slid down to the end of her nose as she tapped and swiped her screen. Not for the first time, Roscoe wondered what the hell she was doing on that thing. Reading the sports page? Scanning YouTube for more Tempest indiscretions? Catching up on porn? Hell, he never thought he'd miss Eva and her simple, straightforward clipboard.

"We've got twenty-four kids on the team," Roscoe said. "Fairly experienced overall, only a handful of bench riders. We'll test them out in different positions today to get a feel for their specific skills."

"And the bench riders?"

"We'll figure it out. Put them through some more drills, see where we can improve." He had a few ideas, but he'd need to spend one-on-one time with each of them to do it right. For some of the kids, it was just a discipline issue, and once he earned their respect, he could get them in line. Others lacked motivation and drive, or they were afraid of the ice, just here to appease a pushy parent. A few had all the heart in the world, but were hopelessly uncoordinated. Still, Roscoe wouldn't give up on any of them.

"Everyone needs ice time, boys," Clarissa said. "No matter how lousy they play. One complaint from a hockey mom about her kid being left out, and this whole thing goes south."

"I'm on it," he assured her. "Every kid here will have a role in the tournament. That's what it's all about, right? Giving the kids a boost?"

"That's all I needed to hear." She flashed him a cool smile that made his balls shrivel. "Anything else?"

"It's only the second practice," Roscoe said. "Ask me again next week."

"I'm asking now, Mr. LeGrand. In case you've forgotten, I need to start booking TV spots. The sooner you can identify the kids with media potential, the better. I need to confirm with the parents, get these interviews locked down, and keep this thing running tight."

"Media potential? I thought we were done with all that."

Clarissa rolled her eyes. "One photo shoot is hardly enough. We need TV clips, action shots, captions. Meme-able backstories."

"What the fuck is a meme-able?" he asked.

"Human interest is always a good angle." She tapped the iPad again, her black bob swishing as she spoke. "Miraculous recovery from a terrible injury, underdog of the family, that sort of thing."

"Your compassion never ceases to amaze me."

At this, she rolled her eyes again. "My job is to make you knuckle-draggers look good on TV and convince this city that you're worth rooting for again. Compassion has nothing to do with it."

"Smart *and* beautiful," Kenton said. "I like it."

"Now you're just trying to piss me off." Clarissa flipped her iPad closed and looked at Roscoe. "I understand there was an issue with one of the teens yesterday. Regina Heinz?"

"How did you hear about that?" Roscoe asked.

"It's my job to hear about it, despite the fact that no one felt compelled to tell me at the photo shoot. What's the story?"

Roscoe scratched his stubbled jaw and shrugged. "If you're thinking of pimping the girl out to your media pals, forget it. She's off the team. Apparently she forged the parental release. Mom found out, showed up here all pissed off, hauled her kid home."

Clarissa made a grumbling sound in her throat, but didn't say anything.

"Shame, really," he went on. "That girl was our best player."

"I'll bet."

Roscoe could've sworn Clarissa was biting back a laugh, but since he'd never seen the woman truly smile before, it was hard to tell.

"If she comes back," Clarissa said, "I want her treated with total respect. The kids are here to learn hockey from the pros, no matter what their gender, and you guys need to lead by example. Got it?"

"Nothing to worry about there," said Roscoe. "Doubt we'll be seeing her again, anyway." *Or her gorgeous mother, which is a damn shame...*

"Regardless," she said, "It's good policy going forward. Actually, I'm thinking we need to revisit our outreach campaign for next year. We need to diversify, get on the radar for other girls who want to play hockey."

"I think that's a great idea," Kenton said. "Maybe you and I could get together after work, do some brainstorming."

Plowing ahead, Clarissa said, "Buffalo News wants to do another group photo shoot next week—we'll need to let the parents know. And keep me posted about those human interest stories."

"I could tell you some stories," Kenton said.

"Do I need to remind you boys what's at stake here?" Clarissa slapped her iPad closed and shot one of her patented death-glares at Kenton. "Stop screwing around and get with the program. None of you can afford another fuck-up, so you'd better start taking this clinic—and me—seriously."

Kenton nodded, apparently struck dumb by the take-down. Despite his silence, though, he was still smiling.

"We'll handle it," Roscoe assured her, but Clarissa was already gone, leaving them all shivering in her frigid wake.

"That was… special," Henny said.

"No shit." Roscoe slapped Kenton on the back, biting back a laugh. "So, how long have you been banging the Ball Buster?"

—————

CHAPTER SIX

"All good?" Henny asked, lining up the last of the orange cones for the clinic. Kenton had gone after Clarissa, dodging Roscoe's questions but chasing after her like a sad little puppy in need of some affection. Roscoe figured he'd be out of commission for the next half hour.

Not that Roscoe could blame him. At least *someone* was having a good morning.

Roscoe grabbed his stick with both hands and stretched it over his head. "Operating at eighty-four percent," he said. "Give or take."

"Damn. We'd better call Dunn," Henny said. "Boy's not allowed to take vacation anymore. You get weepy when he's not around."

"I do the same when you're not around, Kyle

Henderson." Roscoe winked at him, then followed up with a punch in the arm. "You ready to work?"

"Always. You?"

"Kids are my jam."

Overall, Roscoe felt like he had a handle on the situation now. He'd spent the last two nights since their inaugural meeting putting together what he thought was a pretty good training program, and he'd planned to lean on Nick to set the example for the other kids. But no matter how excited Roscoe was about working with the teens, he couldn't deny his disappointment about Reggie Heinz. He really hoped she'd be back again.

Along with her mother.

Thinking about the woman now made his head swim, which made no sense. Was he just lonely, picturing his family on vacation without him? Had Henny's talk of making babies set his biological clock to ticking? Forty was creeping up fast, and he'd already had one relationship crash and burn on him... How much time did he have left, really?

Christ, was he just going soft and mushy in his old age?

Roscoe hadn't a clue. All he knew was that of all the beautiful women he'd encountered in his adult life, none had managed to get inside his head like Ally Heinz—not even his ex. They'd only talked for a few minutes, really—

and not even about anything substantial. But something about her just *got* to him, working its way inside and grabbing on tight, refusing to let go. Was there a Mr. Heinz? Why was she so upset about her kid playing hockey? Did she like Italian food? What turned her on? What would it feel like to part those plump pink lips with his tongue, kissing her until he made her weak and wet with desire...

His cock strained against his pants, threatening to make a scene. It'd been happening on and off for two days straight; he hadn't been able to stop thinking about Ally since they'd met.

Fuck. Two days might not seem like an eternity to most people, but it sure was a long-ass time to deal with a perpetual hard-on.

What would the sweet, sexy hockey mom say if she knew the effect she had on me...

"Look alive," Jarlsberg said. "Here comes the cavalry."

The kids spilled down the tunnel and onto the ice like an oil slick. And there, at the very back of the line, came the woman who'd occupied most of his waking thoughts and all of his dreams. For a moment Roscoe thought he may have conjured her up, but the fact that she was fully clothed was a pretty good indication that this wasn't one of his dreams.

If this is a dream, please don't wake me up...

"Didn't expect to see you back here," he said casually.

Ally nodded, and again, he felt that same spark of aware-ness he'd felt at Wednesday's practice. His eyes were immediately drawn to her mouth, hoping for a smile.

"Change of heart," she said simply, some of that old shyness creeping in around the edges. "Is it okay if Reggie joins you guys today?"

The kid was all smiles, geared up and ready to go.

"Absolutely," Roscoe said. Then, to Reggie, "Go ahead and get into the lineup. Kooz will show you what we're working on today."

Reggie nodded once, then she was off, eager as ever to get in the game.

"What happened?" he asked Ally. "Things seemed pretty final the other day." Yeah, he was fishing for reasons to keep her there, even for a few extra minutes. He didn't know what the fuck was going on with him. Suddenly he was an awkward teenager again, no idea what to say, what to do, how to stand, how to hold his stick. All Roscoe knew was that he wanted to be near this woman. To find out what made her tick. To make her laugh.

To taste that sweet mouth.

"I'm sorry. I think we got off on the wrong foot," Ally said. "At least, *I* got off on the wrong foot."

Roscoe leaned in closer, like they were sharing a secret. "You *did* almost fall on your ass. Lucky for you, I have excellent reflexes."

"Don't remind me." Ally tucked her blond hair behind her ears. It was soft and shiny, falling in uneven waves that Roscoe wanted to run his hands through. Barely reaching her chin, the front of it wasn't quite long enough to stay put, and a lock slid forward again, brushing her cheek. "Anyway, I was hoping you'd give us—Reggie—another chance? I gave it a lot of thought, and it's possible I... well, I may have overreacted about all of this."

Roscoe cracked a grin. "Ah. She wore you down."

"You have no idea." Ally blew out a breath and laughed. "She ignored me for a day and a half—we're talking not a single word. Then she launched one of the most intensive nagging campaigns I've ever experienced, and believe me, I've heard them all."

"I've seen some of those campaigns in action."

"Do you have kids?"

"Nieces and nephews." Roscoe's heart swelled a little as he thought of them. Right about now, his oldest nephew Sammy was probably leading the pack of cousins out into the chilly Atlantic, devising contests for who could catch the biggest wave, who could hold their breath the longest, who had the best underwater hand-stand. The little ones would still be eating breakfast, but they'd be outside soon enough, filling their red plastic buckets with sea glass and dried crab legs as their parents stretched out on the sand with books and iced teas and bottles of sunscreen. He missed them fiercely; they'd Skyped last night, everyone taking a turn in front of the camera with Uncle Roscoe, but it wasn't the same as getting to hug them in person.

Out on the ice, the kids gathered around Jarlsberg and Kooz. They demonstrated a few light stretches, then led them through the warm-up routine. Ally watched her daughter closely, her eyes tracking Reggie's movements, her body leaned forward as though she might need to run out there and save her from some invisible assailant.

"You're not wrong to worry about your daughter, Ally," Roscoe said, his voice soft. "But she's safe with us. You have my word."

"She's… my world." Ally pressed her lips together, her brows knitting in concentration. Roscoe waited for her to continue, but whatever she'd meant to say next, she let it go.

The moment had turned unexpectedly serious. Roscoe knew all about that mama bear protectiveness, especially with kids who played sports. But there was something more there. Something darker and deeper flashing in her eyes, running through her voice, emanating from her entire body.

Ally was truly afraid.

"Is there anything I can do to make you feel more comfortable with this?" he asked. "Answer questions, give you a tour of the facility, introduce you to some of the other parents? Hell, I'm sure we've got a pair of skates around here that would fit you—you could even try it out for yourself."

"Me? On skates? No. No way." She let out a nervous laugh. "The one and only time I ever ice skated, I sprained my ankle and bruised my right butt cheek."

Roscoe cocked an eyebrow, and the woman blushed scarlet.

"I can't believe I said that out loud. Okay, moving on!" Ally looked away again, her smile fading as her gaze drifted back out across the rink. Roscoe couldn't hear what Kooz had said, but the kids were busting up laughing.

"She looks happy," Ally said softly. The words felt heavier than they should for such a casual observation.

"Kooz is goofy as hell," he said, trying to lighten the mood. "Teenagers like him because they think he's one of them."

"Hmm. And you're not?" Now she was smiling again, looking at him with those glittery brown eyes in a way that made his whole fucking day better.

"Nah. Someone has to be the grown-up around here. Set the example."

"Well, you *are* the captain. Setting a good example is probably second nature for you."

"Only when my boss is around," he teased. "The rest of the time I prefer to misbehave."

Ally blinked, her mouth parting, the blush in her cheeks deepening. He'd never wanted to kiss a woman so badly in his life.

But instead of staring at her mouth like a total stalker, he lowered his eyes and sucked in some cold air, counting backward from ten. He needed to get back to work, get those kids in shape, figure out the media stuff for Clarissa.

"Speaking of setting a good example," he said, "I should probably get back on the ice." *And stop thinking about what you sound like when you come...*

"Right," she said, her fingers curling around her purse strap. Her blouse gaped open again, giving him a peek at her smooth skin. He couldn't see the bra today, but that didn't stop him from obsessing over it.

Fuck, his cock was throbbing in his pants. He *needed* her to leave. To say her goodbyes, turn on her heel, and walk away.

But holy *fuck* he wanted her to stay.

"I guess I should head out, before I'm late for work," Ally said. "I just wanted to make sure it was okay for Reggie to stay. She's getting an Uber later, so she doesn't have to take the bus. And her helmet is a few years old. I looked up the model number online and it still meets all the safety guidelines. But maybe you could make sure it fits her properly? And let me know if not, so I can order a new one?"

"Of course."

"Thank you. That helps a lot."

"Ally," Roscoe said, leaning in close again. He took a chance, put his hand on her shoulder. Her skin was warm beneath her blouse, and Roscoe couldn't help but imagine the bare curve of her shoulder, the softness of it, the exact shade of her creamy skin against stark white sheets. If Ally was surprised or put off by his touch, she didn't show it. Instead, she leaned into it, and Roscoe could've sworn he heard her breath catch.

"You're sure there's nothing else I can do for you?" he asked.

She didn't answer right away—just held his gaze, searching for something he couldn't even guess at. She bit her lip, the silky strands of her hair shifting in the gentle wake of her breath.

"Actually," she finally said, "there might be something."

Take you home, lay you on my bed, strip off your clothes and fuck you with my mouth until you're screaming for mercy?

"Name it," he said.

"This might sound crazy, but do you have time to grab a coffee after the clinic? My treat? I could scoot back on my lunch break. I wouldn't take up too much of your time. I just... I think I'd like to take you up on that offer after all."

"Offer?" Roscoe's voice broke on the word. He hadn't said any of that stuff out loud, had he? About taking her home and—

"To ask a few questions?" she said. "About the program?"

"Right. Of course." Clearing his throat, he said, "I'd—"

"Roscoe!" Henny zoomed past, showering Roscoe in a spray of ice like a goddamn frat boy. "Get your head in the game. Kooz and I promised the kids we'd beat your ass out here today, and we do *not* want to let them down."

Ally laughed, the sound of it filling Roscoe with a deep longing that went far beyond physical attraction. "Well," she said, "don't let me keep you. I know you're busy. Seriously, if coffee isn't convenient—"

"Tell you what," Roscoe said, rubbing the ice out of his hair. "Make it dinner instead of coffee, *my* treat, and you've got yourself a date."

CHAPTER SEVEN

When the maitre d' led the impeccably dressed man to her table, Ally almost sent him away, certain he'd brought her the wrong dinner companion.

But then the man smiled, and that dimpled grin brought her right back to that moment on the ice when they'd first met, his strong hands firm around her arms, steadying her as he gazed into her eyes and set her mind spinning with fantasies she had no business imagining.

Roscoe LeGrand. In a suit. A dark blue number that fit him so well, she could see the outline of his muscled arms and thighs through the fabric, the distinct bulge of his—

Oh my God.

Ally grabbed her water glass, sucked down a long drink.

"I hope I didn't keep you waiting too long," he said,

sliding gracefully into his chair. They'd agreed to meet at seven at the restaurant he'd suggested, but she'd arrived at 6:40, too anxious to do anything but sit and wait. The alone time had done nothing to settle her nerves. Didn't help that the place was so nice, so intimate.

"It's okay," she said. "I'm usually early."

"Good to know."

Despite the awkward formality of meeting in a social setting like this, off the ice, the lights dim, ambient music floating on the air, Roscoe's hazel eyes glittered with a playful mischief that drew Ally in like a moth to a flame.

Keep it up, girl, and you'll get singed…

Remembering what Clarissa had told her about the bachelorette party video, she set her glass back on the table and took a deep breath. She wasn't here to ogle the man. She needed to stay on point.

"Thank you for meeting me," she managed, finally daring to look at him again.

Damn. Still smiling. Still all dimples and sparkle and brain-melting hotness.

"Oh, it's my pleasure," Roscoe said, leaning in a little closer. When he'd done so at the rink, she'd chalked it off to the acoustics; with all the kids goofing around, it was harder to hear. But here in the intimate space of the restaurant, there was only one reason to lean in. He wanted to be closer to her. "But I gotta admit—I wasn't expecting you to ask me out."

"Ask you... What?" Ally blinked rapidly, her cheeks going hot. Too late, she realized her mistake.

He thinks this is a date. Like, a romantic *kind of date.*

Then, immediately after, another realization dawned.

He thought I asked him out on an actual date... and he accepted.

Not only had he accepted, but he'd upped the stakes. When she thought about it now, she realized that technically, he'd asked *her* out. Coffee was one thing—safe, friendly, professional. Lots of people had non-date coffee. But dinner? In a place like this?

She looked around now as if for the first time, realizing just how romantic the restaurant really was. The decor was rich and elegant, shaded in deep browns and reds and burgundies, like dark chocolate and wine and those ridiculously lush canopy beds they kept in castles. White tablecloths adorned the tables, and in the center of each, a candle flickered in a glass jar. There were no children in the restaurant, no families, no business associates. Everyone here was paired off, sharing soft laughter or sweet little murmurs, heads bent close as they scanned menus or nibbled on a piece of chocolate cake.

Ally's skin felt hot and blotchy. She had been out of the dating game for decades, and even before that, she'd never had much experience. Dan was the only man she'd ever truly been with—physically *or* emotionally. All she had to go on now were the horror stories Clarissa had shared about her own dating disasters, and Ally wanted no part of that. Since her arrival in Buffalo, Clarissa had even tried to set her up a few times with "nice, normal" guys from her firm, but Ally had always turned her down, reasoning that if they were so nice and normal, why wasn't Clarissa going out with them?

"Not that I'm complaining," Roscoe said now, jumping into her thoughts.

Ally blinked, unsure how to respond. She tried to remember what the grief books had said about getting back into the social scene. They'd all talked about how grief was unpredictable and immense, how no one could say just how long the process would take because everyone dealt with loss differently. But they'd also warned her not to use her grief as a shield, or as an excuse to isolate herself. The books were just like the grief pamphlets the funeral director had given her, which were just like the podcasts, just like the websites. They all said the same things: Embrace your inner goddess! Speak your truth! Be confident and bold! Be brave!

But how could she be brave in the presence of this strong, powerful, incredibly gorgeous, and—if Reggie was to be believed—famous athlete? How could she embrace her inner goddess when this man's intense, piercing gaze was currently turning her insides into pudding?

She didn't know how to date, how to flirt, how to do... *whatever* Roscoe thought this was. She'd come here straight from work, still dressed in the same boring white blouse and navy slacks she'd had on when she'd dropped Reggie at the rink this morning.

She needed to get her head out of the clouds and hit the reset button on this night before she made any more of a mess.

"Mr. LeGrand," she said, summoning her courage, "this isn't—"

"Mr. LeGrand is what my PR manager calls me when I'm in trouble. Call me Roscoe. Please."

"Roscoe." She lowered her eyes, heat spreading from her cheeks down to her neck as Clarissa's warnings echoed through her mind again. Her upper lip felt sweaty. "I didn't mean to imply..." She gestured quickly between the two of them, nearly knocking over her water glass. Gripping it tight before it toppled into her lap, she took another steadying breath, ignoring the water that had splashed onto her hand. Being around this man robbed her of all coordination, and they hadn't even ordered dinner yet. "This isn't a date. I didn't—"

"Good evening, Mr. LeGrand." A waiter appeared at their table with a bottle of wine, uncorking it with ease.

"Hey, Jackson," Roscoe said. Then, to Ally, "He's brought my usual, and I'd love to share it with you. How do you feel about—"

"Great!" Ally grabbed her empty wine glass, thrusting it toward the waiter. "I mean, yes, please. I'd love some."

The waiter raised an eyebrow—Ally was certain she was breaking some fancy-restaurant, fancy-wine-tasting protocol—but he reached for the glass anyway, giving her a generous pour. She swirled the glass and took a big gulp, nodding her approval.

The waiter topped off her glass, then filled Roscoe's, before finally leaving them alone.

She was about to apologize—for the date misunderstanding, for her hijacking of the wine, for her awkwardness, for her very existence—but a perky hostess appeared at the edge the table, startling them both.

"Oh, no!" she exclaimed. "Your candle went out! I can fix that." She picked up the jar and relit the votive, setting it down between them before scampering off to another table to do the same. God forbid a candle go out somewhere, lowering the romance quotient in the room.

Ally coughed, buying herself some time, but Roscoe's smile stayed firmly in place, his eyes still glittering, never leaving hers for an instant.

"Okay, honestly?" she said, the wine giving her a momentary burst of courage. "I can see how I gave you the wrong impression. But I really thought this was just a... a meeting. To talk about Reggie and the hockey clinic, like we said?" She reached for the purse she'd draped over the back of her chair and dug out her note-book. "I wrote down a few questions."

Ally took a chance, glancing up from her notes to meet his eyes. The intensity of his gaze made her feel fluttery and off-balance. She tried to remind herself that he'd probably brought many women here, had probably shared his "usual" wine with them, had probably looked at them in exactly the same way he was looking at her now: like he might just skip the menu and swallow her up instead.

But it didn't matter. Ally's insides went right on fluttering. She was certain he could read it in her eyes—the tell-tale signs that she wouldn't mind being swallowed up by him.

Finally, just when she thought she'd spontaneously combust from the heat in his eyes, Roscoe broke their connection to glance at her notebook. The entire page was scrawled with questions and sub-questions, bullet points and underlines and arrows. Ally heard his intake of breath, but couldn't bring herself to look up again. She didn't want to know what he thought of her particular brand of neurosis—not yet.

Channeling her inner corporate marketing drone, she tapped her finger against the page and jumped right in with the first question. "Talk to me about the safety protocols. What happens if someone gets hurt on the ice?"

Seemingly undaunted, Roscoe said, "We have two onsite EMTs, and my team and I are all trained in emergency first aid."

"Wow. Is that typical?"

"No. A few years back, the Tempest did a public awareness event with some of the Buffalo first responders, and a bunch of us decided to take the course after that. Coach heard about it, thought it was a good idea for everyone. We make the new guys do it, too."

In the margin next to the first question, Ally made a little check mark. "First aid training. Okay. So if something happens that you guys *can't* handle, how quickly could you get someone to the hospital?"

"Ten minutes."

"Are the kids given safety training too?"

"That's part of our program, yes. We work with them on safe techniques for the game as well as on their general conduct. We also ensure they're wearing the proper gear at all times, and not doing anything that puts them or their teammates—or us, for that matter—at unnecessary risk."

Ally raised a brow. "So you're saying there's *necessary* risk?"

"Ally. It's a competitive sport. There's always some level of risk, but we do everything we can to minimize that."

"And how many incidents have you had in the past?"

she asked.

"Incidents? Like bruised butt cheeks?"

Oh my God.

"Well that, among other things."

"Like?"

His smile was maddening.

"Like, kids getting hurt at the clinic," she said. "Accidents, severed arteries, broken bones, concussions—"

"Zero. This is our first clinic." He sipped his wine, set his glass back on the table. "But they run these youth camps all over the country. They're no more dangerous than any other sport, and we've taken precautions for all scenarios."

"I've seen hockey games, Roscoe. Guys losing their teeth. Gushing blood. Getting carried out on stretchers."

"The clinic isn't the NHL. We don't let the kids play that hard, they're all wearing plenty of protective gear, and there are at a minimum four of us on the ice at all times to keep everything under control." Roscoe smiled. "Trust me. The only injuries I predict are all the bruised egos your daughter's gonna give those boys."

Ally couldn't help her smile. She could totally picture it—Reggie showing those boys how it's done. Not taking any of their crap. Giving her all, no matter what anyone else thought.

Total opposite of her mother, queen butt-bruiser and all-around scaredy cat.

Ally glanced down at her notes. "I'm crazy. That's all there is to it."

"Most parents are concerned about their kids, Ally."

Ally capped her pen and tossed it onto the table, letting out a sigh that made the candle between them flicker. "Do most parents interrogate you by candlelight in fancy restaurants?"

At this he laughed, deep and genuine. The skin around his eyes crinkled, his big smile immediately soothing her nerves. "This is a first."

Ally stuffed the notebook back into her purse. "I guess my track record for first impressions is pretty rocky."

"Rocky? Not the word I was thinking, no." He sipped his wine again, watching her over the rim of his glass, candlelight sparkling in the reflection of his eyes, the glass, the wine. When he spoke again, his tone was serious. "Ally, we care about these kids. I promise you that everyone on staff has done and continues to do everything in our power to ensure that the kids stay safe and have fun. Now, I'm happy to answer all of your questions, any time you want. But ultimately you're gonna have to make an actual decision here. It's not fair to Reggie or the rest of the team to keep wavering on this."

Nodding, Ally reached for her wine again, Roscoe's directness and the intimacy of the restaurant pressing in on her from all sides. Why hadn't they just gone to Starbucks like she'd initially planned? She'd buy him a dark roast, perch at the counter without even setting her purse down—that's how quickly it would be over. She'd let him know that Reggie needed a little extra encouragement and care, a little more attention. That she might appear fearless and tough on the ice, but she was still just a little girl.

A girl who'd lost the one man in her life who'd promised he'd always be there for her, no matter what.

"I'm sorry," she said, blinking away the tears that glazed her eyes. "I guess I didn't really think this through."

Roscoe didn't say anything. He pressed his lips together, brow furrowed in concentration, probably wondering why the hell she'd wasted his time. She was about to blurt out another pathetic apology when he finally said, "With the right training and a little encouragement, she could be really great."

Ally frowned. "And you're the one to train her?"

"I can certainly get her started. After the clinic ends, I can recommend some top-notch private trainers. Our skating coach is another great resource—she used to teach figure skating, and she knows a lot of dedicated people in both fields."

"Eva Bradshaw," Ally said, remembering the names Reggie had rattled off that first day. "The Olympic medalist."

"You've done your homework."

"Reggie did it, actually. It was all part of her appeal process."

"She probably knows more about my team than I do." Roscoe laughed.

"Look, I know she's talented, Roscoe. But right now I just want her to enjoy herself. Maybe make a new friend or two. She's had a hard time..." Ally trailed off. She hadn't meant to go down that road—not like this. But the longer she waited for Roscoe to ask another question, to redirect the conversation back to Reggie's hockey skills, the more she realized she had to be honest about this. "I don't know if Reggie has shared anything personal with you, but she's been through a lot. She hasn't been the same since... since..."

Ally's throat tightened, choking off her words. No matter how many times she'd let the words run through her mind, she just couldn't make them come out of her mouth.

Her father died. My husband. No warning, no goodbyes. One minute he was here, tugging on her braid and kissing her cheek as he rushed out the door for work, and then...

God. What had she been thinking? That she'd just breeze through dinner with this man—this stranger who'd thought he was in for a romantic night out—and drop all of this dead husband business in his lap?

Honestly, Ally. You are so obtuse.

"Hey. You okay?" Roscoe's kind voice broke into her thoughts.

When Ally met his eyes, she found only compassion, only concern.

Ally offered a tiny smile.

"There you are," he said. His voice was soft and low, his smile intimate and sweet in a way that made everything else in the room—in the whole wide world—disappear.

They sat in silence, gazing into each other's eyes, suspended in a perfect moment outside of which nothing else existed. Time stopped. The clink of silverware, the uncorking of bottles, the soft murmurs that had only moments ago surrounded them suddenly faded.

Roscoe reached for her hand beneath the table, finding it in her lap and squeezing it tight. Every hair on her arm stood on end, and a warm current ran down her spine.

I'm safe with him.

The thought came unbidden, but not unwanted. Ally couldn't find words to describe what she felt; logically, it made no sense. She didn't know the man. Not even his middle name or where he lived or whether he was a dog or cat person or maybe a lizard person. But there in his eyes she felt it—something real and sweet and kind and, yes, safe.

A calmness washed over her, a warmth that flickered

low in her belly and radiated outward like the flame between them.

The moment was so pure, so beautiful. So intense.

Until the fear rushed in.

She slid her hand out from under his touch, grabbed her wine glass again, and forced a laugh. She *had* to laugh, or she'd burst into tears.

What the hell was *that?*

"Sorry," she stammered, raising the glass to her lips. If there was an award for greatest number of sorries issued in a single outing, she was pretty sure she'd win.

Despite her awkwardness, Roscoe hadn't moved. Hadn't looked away. Even as she sipped her wine, his eyes never left hers.

The waiter returned to take their order, and by the time they'd finished picking out appetizers and main courses, the intensity in Roscoe's eyes had finally dimmed.

Ally ignored the disappointment churning in her gut. She had no right to miss that intensity.

"Why are you so determined to keep my daughter on the ice?" she asked, wanting—no, *needing*—to get back on track.

"She's the best player on the team. Skates circles around boys twice her size. Knows all the drills, fights hard to nail every single one of them, and she's not afraid of the puck. I don't say this often, and I don't say it lightly. She's got real potential."

"So what happens once school starts and she doesn't have time to play?"

"If she wants it badly enough, she'll make time. Lots of kids do sports in school or through intramural programs. Right?"

"Not me." Ally laughed, remembering her own mortifying high school career. "I spent all my free time in the art room drawing skull tattoos on my skin and painting pictures of dead birds and rotten fruit."

"Skull tattoos?"

"It's true. I was voted Most Likely to Marry a Vampire. And that was years before vampires became cool, so that just shows you what a freak I was."

Roscoe grinned. That dimple was going to be the death of her. "You little rebel, you."

"Not anymore," she assured him. "Now I'm a mom, and way too practical to fall in love with vampires." *Or hockey players...*

"Nah. I bet you still have a wild side." His teasing smile split into a full-on grin. "A few skeletons. Maybe some *real* tattoos, not just the Sharpie ones. Right?"

Ally brought the glass to her lips and downed a big gulp of wine. Roscoe did *not* need to know about her tattoos.

"And there it is." He tipped his glass toward her face. "A blush is as good as an admission, Ally Heinz."

"What about you?" she asked. "Let me guess. All-star jock, debate team, varsity everything, teacher's favorite."

"That would be my three oldest brothers. Me? I was a terror. An absolute terror. I passed high school by the skin of my teeth, mostly because the teachers loved my brothers so much, they felt sorry for me."

"Wow, three brothers?"

"Four, actually. One is younger. I have a sister, too."

"Are you close with them?" Ally didn't have any siblings. She was fascinated by large families. Secretly, she'd always longed to be part of one—a big, noisy, messy bunch.

Roscoe nodded, but sadness clouded his eyes, the first she'd seen his smile truly fade all night. "I don't get to see them much, though. We live in different states, and they're all married with kids. My sister just had a baby girl. Haven't met her yet."

"They're all in Maine right now, right?" she asked, remembering what he'd said the other day about his family vacations.

"Yep." Roscoe reached for the phone inside his pocket. "Can I be that guy? With the pictures? Doesn't count as annoying if they're not my kids, right?"

Ally laughed. "It totally counts, but I'd love to see them."

He scooted his chair closer to hers and held the phone between them, swiping through a series of photos that must've been taken on the family's last vacation. There were at least a dozen kids running around the beach, each one more adorable than the last, all of them carefree, the very embodiment of summer. There were a few shots with Roscoe, too—one where they'd buried him in the sand, leaving only his head and feet exposed as they climbed on top of him for the photo. Another where he was dressed in an apron and chef's hat, a lobster clutched in each hand as he chased one of the little ones down the beach.

"Maddox," he said, pointing at the boy running off in the distance. "Six years old in this shot. He always asks me to do the lobster voices, but then he gets totally freaked out."

"Excuse me," Ally said. "You have lobster voices?"

"Doesn't everyone?"

Ally laughed, suddenly wishing she'd ordered the lobster instead of the prime rib.

As Roscoe narrated the rest of the photos, she snuck a glance at his face, wondering what she might find there. Was he lonely without them? Bitter that he was missing this year's vacation in order to manage the hockey clinic?

But all she saw was genuine happiness, the same unadulterated joy reflected in the smiles of all of his nieces and nephews.

"They're really sweet," Ally said. "Thank you for showing me."

"It's all part of my master plan." Roscoe slid the phone back into his jacket pocket. "You said this wasn't a date, but I've already introduced you to the family. See how I did that?"

"Very smooth, Uncle Roscoe," she admitted.

Roscoe returned her smile, but then his mouth sagged into a grimace. Pinching the bridge of his nose, he closed his eyes and groaned. "Did I really just show you my family vacation photos? Who *does* that?"

"You, apparently."

"I bet this is the worst first non-date you've ever been on."

"Oh, totally. But to be fair, it's the *only* first non-date I've ever been on, so you're kind of setting the bar."

Their laughter faded, silence drifting between them. It wasn't awkward, though. In the short time they'd been together, Ally was realizing how much she actually enjoyed his company.

How much she trusted him.

The waiter finally delivered their food, a mouth-watering feast of epic proportions, and when Roscoe looked at her and said, "Don't forget to save room for dessert—the turtle pie here is killer," Ally was pretty sure she could spend the rest of her life with him. Or at least the rest of the evening.

"Ally?" he continued. His voice was suddenly soft and low, so sexy it made her thighs clench, and when she looked up into his eyes again, she saw that same glittering intensity from before. "Let me take you out again."

Electric tingles ran up and down her spine as Roscoe held her gaze, waiting for her answer. God, she wanted to say yes. To believe that the look in his eyes was real—was only for her.

"I've already decided to let Reggie play hockey," she said, playing it cool. "And I promise not to show up at the practices and—to quote my daughter—make a big freaking drama out of everything. So you don't have to—"

"No." Roscoe shook his head. "This has nothing to do with Reggie. I want to take you on a proper first date—a real one. Tomorrow night."

His voice was so sincere, so hopeful. Everything in her was screaming for her to accept the offer, despite the rattling of her nervous heart. But how could she?

First, there was the obvious risk—falling for a man in the spotlight, only to wake up one morning to a million messages from Clarissa about yet another YouTube sex scandal starring Mr. Dimples over there.

But beyond that, the idea of letting someone in again, even for a little while... God, what if she started to really like him? What if she started to feel truly happy again, and then the universe swooped in and stole him away?

No. She couldn't risk something like that. Not again.

Ally sighed. "I'm flattered, but—"

"I promise I won't take you ice skating, even though that would make an amazingly romantic first date, complete with matching fuzzy hats, hand-holding, and hot cocoa in a thermos, but I know how you are about skating, and I certainly don't want to be a—wait for it—" He wriggled his eyebrows, making her crack up. "—pain in your ass about it, but—"

"You went there. You really went there." Ally shook her head, trying to hold back a fresh wave of laughter. "I shared my private butt pain, and you mocked me."

"You're right." Roscoe pressed a hand against his chest. "I'm sorry. Please allow me to make it up to you by taking you out on a date."

"Roscoe…" She opened her mouth to say no, to make an excuse, to put an end to this before it went any further…

Do something that scares the hell out of you. How else will you know the true depths of your courage?

The voice floated suddenly through her head, something she recalled from her *You Glow, Girl!* podcast. She wasn't sure if dating was quite what Savannah Hart had in mind with that advice, but to Ally, dating a man like Roscoe definitely qualified as a top-ten scary experience.

Especially now that she'd agreed to let Reggie play hockey. Forget the universe stealing him away. If things went bad with Roscoe, Ally wouldn't be able to bury her head in the sand and avoid him without hurting her daughter in the process.

But all she could think about now were those hazel eyes, that smile, that desirous gaze lighting her up from the inside. He'd made her feel entirely wanted, and Ally couldn't deny that she'd enjoyed it. One smile from him had her heart pumping again, her body humming in ways she hadn't felt in years.

Call it the calm after the storm, a bit of normalcy in a world that had been utterly turned upside down, but Ally wanted this. She wanted to go on dates, to feel desired by another man. Maybe even to feel the fluttery excitement of a first kiss again.

And right now, this man—charming, funny, drop-dead sexy Roscoe LeGrand—wanted to give that to her.

Courage, girl. Get it together.

"All right, Roscoe LeGrand," she said. Saying yes to her desires despite her fears felt like a personal victory, albeit a small one, and her face split into a grin as she held up her wine glass. "But one condition—I want to hear your lobster voice."

Roscoe grinned and picked up his glass, touching the rim to hers. "And I want to see your tattoos, so I say we negotiate a trade."

CHAPTER EIGHT

Two hours.

That's how long it'd taken Ally to decide on her official first date outfit—a tasteful yet sexy black dress that dipped low in the back, paired with dangly silver-and-turquoise earrings and black peep toe heels.

She'd spent another two hours on makeup and hair, and now, staring at herself in the mirror, she was *this* close to scrapping the whole ensemble and starting over.

How was one supposed to dress for a night out with a professional athlete? Was black too morbid? Too formal? Was her short wavy hair too messy? She'd skipped the bra and gone a little bold on the lipstick... Was all that sending the wrong message?

Did she even *have* a message?

"Clearly I have no idea what I'm doing," she said. "*There's* my message."

She should've called Clarissa for fashion help, but she couldn't—Clarissa was out with Reggie, supposedly to give Ally some uninterrupted time to unpack the rest of the boxes in the kitchen. It's not that Ally had lied to them; Clarissa had called in the morning, offering to scoop Reggie up for a girls' day and a sleepover. Clarissa had assumed Ally could use a night off, and—well—that much was true.

Ally would come clean eventually, but she wasn't quite ready to admit to her best friend or her kid that she was going on an actual date. With an actual man. Especially since Clarissa and that man had a professional relationship that Ally did not want to interfere with, and Reggie was playing hockey for him. Besides, this wasn't a *thing*. It was just a date. Guys like Roscoe weren't into *things*. If she needed a reminder, all she had to do was click over to YouTube and search out that video—something she'd promised herself she wouldn't do, despite her curiosity. She didn't need to sift through his past. This was just a simple little date.

So why was Ally getting so worked up about how she looked?

"This is insane." She stuck her eyebrow brush into the cup on her dresser and went back to fiddling with her hair. Fifteen minutes until Roscoe LeGrand was due on her doorstep, and she had no idea what to do.

Was she supposed to keep him waiting? Or respect

his time? Should she meet him outside, or invite him in for a drink and some chit-chat? Should she have made appetizers? Was there some text or app thingy she was supposed to know about, some new dating-in-the-internet-age ritual she had yet to discover? The idea of figuring out this complicated dance filled her with the same kind of dread she'd felt seeing Reggie zoom around on the ice that first day.

It was too much, and all her doubts rushed in again. She never should've accepted his invitation, never should've allowed herself to be charmed by those hazel eyes. Who was she trying to fool? She'd been married for most of her adult life—she didn't know how to date casually, let alone date a man like Roscoe.

Do something that scares you? No thanks, Savannah.

Ally didn't need to explore the depths of her courage. For her, courage only went as far as the shallow end of the pool, and that's just the way it was.

Ally grabbed her phone. She was about to call the whole thing off, when she spotted the black SUV rolling into the driveway, gleaming like it had just been washed and waxed.

For me?

Her heart skipped, sending a bolt of nervous energy straight to her stomach.

From her bedroom window, Ally watched Roscoe climb out of the SUV, all muscle and grace, even as he ducked down to check his reflection in the car window. He spent a few seconds running a hand through his hair, flipping it around several times before finally settling on a look. He did the same thing with his tie, loosening the knot, then tightening it, then changing his mind altogether and tugging it free from his shirt, ditching it in the car. When he shut the driver's side door again, Ally noticed a bouquet of bright yellow flowers in his hand.

Ally smiled. He looked so sweet, so earnest. So... normal. She couldn't turn him down now. Besides, it was just a casual night out. It didn't have to—*couldn't*—turn into anything serious. Assuming she could keep her crazy nerves in check, maybe it would even be—what was that phrase Reggie had used? *Fun.* Actual fun.

By the time she opened the front door and saw him standing there with those flowers, the nerves in her stomach had turned to butterflies. The good kind.

"Hi," she said, smiling so big her cheeks hurt. He smelled like spices and fresh cut wood and endless summer nights and holy *hell* he was delicious. He was dressed in dark jeans and a silvery blue dress shirt that made his eyes look even more intense. The top buttons were undone from when he'd ditched the tie, and now his sleeves were rolled up a bit, showing off his muscled forearms.

Ally wondered how she'd feel with those strong arms wrapped tightly around her waist. Or maybe pinning her to the bed, his mouth covering hers, both of them panting and gasping for air...

Stop it. That's not happening.

A kiss was one thing, but for Ally, that's where she had to draw the line. Anything more getting attached, and that was not part of the deal.

"Hi," Roscoe said. She felt her cheeks warming under his gaze, but she didn't break eye contact. She was more certain than ever that the connection she'd felt with him was real; it was even more intense now than it had been at the restaurant.

You're still not getting into these panties, Roscoe LeGrand...

After a moment, he finally handed her the flowers and leaned in to kiss her cheek. His lips brushed her skin, breath warm as he lingered a few extra seconds. In a low growl that made her thighs clench, he said, "God, you're beautiful."

"I... Thank you." Again Ally felt the uncertainty creeping in, but she dismissed it. Doubt was for serious things, for commitments, for emotional entanglements. Not for a casual, no-strings date. Not for this.

So after a quick trip to the kitchen to put her flowers in water, she grabbed her purse, and they were off.

CHAPTER NINE

"Are you going to tell me what we're doing tonight?" Ally asked as Roscoe exited the highway in Williamsville, not far from where she worked. The suspense was basically killing her.

"Right. About that..." Roscoe's tone made her stomach swoop again, and not in the good way. Her fingers dug into the purse in her lap. Darting a quick glance her way, Roscoe said, "How do you feel about sharing?"

"Depends," she said, trying not to show her relief. "I can be pretty territorial when it comes to burgers and tacos. Chicken wings, too."

"How about when it comes to *me*?"

"Sharing *you*? Like... a threesome?" Ally forced out a laugh. He had to be kidding. Right? *Right?* Oh, God. Maybe she should've watched that YouTube video after all. She figured he was a bit of a playboy, but… multiple women? At the same time?

Her heart rate skyrocketed, and Ally immediately crossed her legs, feeling herself close up. They hadn't even kissed yet, and now they were talking about sex? With someone else?

"I promised a friend I'd help him out." Roscoe shrugged as if the idea of it had no effect on him one way or the other. "And yet… As much as I'd love to let this joke play out for maximum enjoyment, I *really* don't want you to jump out of a moving vehicle, which is clearly what you're thinking about doing." Turning again to offer her a dimpled smile, he said, "It's not what you think, Ally. We're in for a G-rated evening, I promise."

"G-rated?" She blew out a breath and uncrossed her legs, willing her heart rate to slow down again.

"Well, maybe PG-13. The ladies of Wellshire can get a little saucy, especially if they bring their flasks."

Roscoe left Ally hanging after that, the silence stretching on for a full five minutes. Just when she thought she'd burst from the suspense, he navigated his SUV into the parking lot of a white building surrounded by trees and gardens. *Wellshire Place*, the sign out front said.

"This looks like some kind of eldercare facility," Ally said. "What are we doing here?"

He unclicked his seatbelt and pointed at her, his smile stretching huge. "Bingo!"

Ally narrowed her eyes. "Bingo what? I don't—"

"No, we're literally here to play bingo. With Walker Dunn's mother."

"Walker... from the team?"

"The one and only. His mom lives here. We go way back." Roscoe nodded toward the entrance, where an older woman in a light blue cardigan and glasses waved excitedly, a smile lighting up her face. "Walker usually plays bingo with her, but he and Eva are stuck in the Caribbean a few extra days with a flight delay. They asked me to swing by instead. I took a risk, thought it might make a fun pre-date. We can head out whenever you want."

"Fun? It sounds amazing." And much less scary than a threesome.

They headed inside, where a couple of aides dressed in bright-colored scrubs greeted Roscoe with waves and warm smiles. Ally got the impression he'd been here more than a few times.

Mrs. Dunn was small and wiry, with pretty salt-and-pepper hair pulled back into a low ponytail. Up close like this, Ally guessed she was in her late sixties—a little on the young side to be living in a facility like this, Ally thought.

The woman wrapped Roscoe in a huge hug,

squealing like a kid as Roscoe lifted her off her feet and give her a little spin. Once she was back on solid ground again, she looked out into the parking lot and said, "Where's Walker? Is he still at school? I think he had that geometry test today—I know how worried he was about it. Poor kid stayed up half the night studying."

School? Geometry test? Ally's heart squeezed as the realization dawned. She recognized the signs of dementia—her own mother had died of early onset Alzheimer's several years ago. Ally glanced at Roscoe, seeing a familiar struggle play out across his features: *Do I explain this to her, or do I let it ride?*

She reached for his hand, gave him a gentle squeeze.

Ally felt a gentle warmth as Roscoe squeezed back. Without missing a beat, he said, "Walker's just fine. I talked to him earlier—he said he'd call you later tonight. In the mean time, you're stuck with me tonight. And I've brought a friend I'd like you to meet."

"Oh." Karen scrunched up her face in confusion, but then her eyes seemed to clear just as quickly, and she smiled up at Roscoe once again. "Well, I'm glad for anything that gives me a chance to spend some extra time with my favorite hockey player. Don't tell him I said that."

"Mum's the word."

"Now, who's this beauty? Aren't you the sweet-est." She opened her arms to Ally for a hug. Her embrace was warm and kind, so comforting and motherly it almost brought tears to Ally's eyes. "It's about time Roscoe started getting out of the house and socializing," Mrs. Dunn said, pulling back and giving Ally a wink. "It's no good letting all that charm go to waste. We've been telling him that ever since—"

"I couldn't agree more," Roscoe said quickly. Ally wondered what Mrs. Dunn meant by that "ever since" comment, but now was not the time to let her mind run away with her.

Still holding Ally's hand, Roscoe kissed Mrs. Dunn on the cheek, then offered his free arm to the woman. Together, the three of them headed toward the community room at the back of the building, where they were enthusiastically greeted at the door by a woman who looked about ninety, with light blue hair and cat-eye glasses dotted with rhinestones. She wore a laminated pin that read, *Call me Paulette! And I'll call you... for a good time.*

"Are you kids ready to boink?" she asked, holding out a bucket filled with what looked like fat magic markers.

"I... guess so?" Ally laughed.

"Bingo boinkers," the woman explained, uncapping one and pressing the tip against the back of her hand. It left a bright blue dot about the size of a nickel—one of a dozen Ally could see. "You use them to mark your cards when they call your numbers."

"I think they're called dabbers," another woman— Lorraine, according to her name tag—said.

"Daubers, actually." Roscoe paid their entry fees, then helped himself to a green dauber from the bucket, along with a stack of bingo cards and name tag stickers from an adjacent table.

"You all can call them whatever you want," Paulette said. "I call them boinkers, because that's what they do." She pressed it to her hand again, making another dot. "Boink!"

"I bring my own. They have glitter," Mrs. Dunn said, sliding two purple ones from her back pocket. Then, handing one to Ally, she winked. "For luck."

"Roscoe LeGrand." Paulette peered at Ally from behind her glasses. "Are you going to introduce us to your girlfriend, or do you need a spanking?"

"Spanking!" The one called Lorraine clapped her hands. "I'll get the paddle!"

"Ladies, calm down." Roscoe held up his hands in surrender, offering Ally a lopsided, apologetic grin that basically melted the panties right off her. Why was he so adorable? So sweet? "This is Ally Heinz," he said. "Please don't scare her off—I'm trying to make a good impression here."

Ally's cheeks flamed, but she did her best not to show

it, smiling and leaning in for hugs and kisses from the ladies.

"Five minutes, people." A older man came out into the entryway, dressed in a powder blue suit and ridiculously wide orange tie that probably should've been donated to Goodwill in the seventies. He looped his arm around Paulette and pressed a kiss to her cheek, making the woman squeal.

"Roscoe and Ally," Paulette said, "allow me to introduce John. Pardon his manners—he has a thing for PDA."

John kissed her again. "As if you don't like it, you saucy broad."

Paulette laughed. "I never said I didn't like it."

God, they were the cutest.

"How long have you two been married?" Ally asked.

"Married? To *him*?" Paulette looked at the man and made a face like she'd sucked down a lemon, then cracked up laughing. "Oh, honey, no. My husband died years ago."

Mine too, she almost said, feeling an instant kinship with the woman. She wondered what had happened, whether they'd had a happy life together. Whether she'd had time to say goodbye. But instead of prying, Ally only said, "I'm sorry. You two just… You seem to have a connection."

"I should hope so," Paulette said, gently elbowing the man in the ribs. "John's my side piece."

"Oh." Ally's eyes widened as realization dawned. "*Oh!*"

Roscoe leaned in close, his warm breath tickling Ally's ear. "Don't ask. It's a whole *thing*."

Ignoring Roscoe, Paulette continued. "We were in the closet for awhile, only hooking up when that nosey know-it-all June Higgenbottom was away at her daughter's house. No prying eyes that way, if you get my drift. But you know what? Life's too short to worry about jealous rivals."

Ally pressed her lips together to hide her smile, but Paulette continued on, oblivious.

"June claims she had her eye on Johnny first, but that's a lie. She never showed a lick of interest until after she saw me dancing with him at the New Year's ball. I wore my lucky blue dress," she said, fluffing her hair, "which shows off my best assets."

"Here she goes," John said, rolling his eyes.

"It's true. Every time I wear it, I feel like a million smackeroos." She touched her shoulders and did a little shimmy. "Anyway, Johnny couldn't resist me."

"Still can't. She's the prettiest girl in the room." Then, in a lower tone, "Just wish she'd stop yammering once in a while, give those lips a rest."

"You didn't seem to mind these lips last night," she said, "when I—"

"Jesus, Mary, and Joseph," John said, gesturing at Roscoe and Ally. "These kids don't want to hear about all that. Trust me."

"Are you and Roscoe going steady?" Lorraine asked Ally.

Ally smiled, but Paulette, who seemed to find this line of questioning appalling, swatted Lorraine's arm. "Lorraine! Don't embarrass the poor girl." Then, lowering her voice to a whisper that pretty much everyone in the entryway could still hear, she told Ally, "I hope you're on the birth control pill, toots. Condoms can break, and the last thing you need is—"

"Thank you, Paulette, for your heartfelt concern." Roscoe grabbed Ally's elbow and steered her gently through the entryway with Mrs. Dunn, the tips of his ears turning bright red. "I think we'd better find some seats."

"Sit by us, Ally," Lorraine said. "Roscoe is distracting. He'll throw off your game."

Ally laughed. She couldn't argue with that kind of logic.

They settled in at a long table at the center of the room. Mrs. Dunn and John sat on either side of Roscoe, and Ally ended up across from them, bookended by Paulette and

Lorraine. Down at the other end of the table, two women sat together with their heads bent close, arranging a collection of troll dolls and other charms between them.

"This looks serious," Ally said.

"You'd better believe it," Paulette said. "Big money on the line here. Not to mention bragging rights." Her voice lowered to a harsh whisper as she jerked her head toward the women with the charms. "If you ask me, ol' June needs to be taken down a peg."

"Easy, Paulette," Roscoe warned. "You don't want Ally to think you're gossiping."

"Gossiping!" Paulette looked aghast. "I'm a vault, Roscoe LeGrand. A vault!"

"Except on Facebook," Roscoe teased, "where we're all fair game."

"Oh, that's different. Speaking of which..." She dug into the front of her blouse and pulled out a bright pink cell phone—Ally didn't even want to know where *that* had been stashed—and held it in front of her, leaning in close to Roscoe. "Say cheese, handsome."

"Cheese, handsome," Roscoe repeated.

With a few taps and swipes of her fingers, Paulette had taken the selfies and updated her profile pic. Ally was certain she would've snapped a few more shots, but a voice came over the loudspeaker, announcing the start of the game. At this, a hush fell over the room, the mood turning suddenly serious as all eyes dropped to the bingo cards on the tables.

All eyes except Ally's. And Roscoe's, which were decidedly fixed on hers.

She felt herself blushing again under his gaze, but she didn't look away. For her monumental show of courage, she was rewarded with a wink and smile, all for her.

"Good luck," Roscoe said.

Ally grinned. "You too, handsome."

"B four," the announcer called, and a ripple went through the room as everyone checked and boinked their cards. After that, the game moved at lightning speed, so fast Ally could barely keep up. She wasn't the only one—Roscoe abandoned his card about five minutes in, opting instead to help Mrs. Dunn.

It was hands down the sweetest, sexiest thing she'd ever witnessed.

Ally still couldn't believe the man was real.

And single.

And interested in *her*, a woman who'd spent so long inside her shell, she was practically a turtle. And not one of those cute baby turtles everyone coos over, but the old, slow-as-molasses, wrinkled ones. Despite all the podcasts and self-help books, most days she felt as if she'd been flipped onto her back by a rogue wave, waiting in the sand for someone to walk by and turn her over again.

What could he possibly see in me?

Beneath the table that separated them, Ally felt a nudge against her foot.

"You're asleep at the wheel," Roscoe said.

Ally blinked. "What?"

"B seven." Roscoe pointed at her card. "They just called it."

"What? Oh!" Ally boinked her card, closing out the last open spot on the top row. A surge of adrenaline flooded her chest, and she leapt out of her seat, suddenly breathless, laughter bubbling up from inside. "Bingo! *Bingo!*"

One of the facility volunteers came over to check her card, confirming the first win of the night and handing her an envelope with fifty dollars inside. Her entire table clapped and cheered—even June and her friend at the other end.

Roscoe grabbed Ally's hand and held up her arm as if she were a prize fighter. "First time here, ladies and gents, and she's mopping up the competition."

Mrs. Dunn beamed. "You must be her good luck charm, Roscoe."

"Karen, if I had a dollar every time I heard that, I wouldn't need to rely on bingo as my retirement strategy."

"Who needs a retirement strategy?" Winking at Ally, Paulette said, "Just marry rich. You know, honey, at your age you really have to start thinking with your wallet, not your—"

"Paulette," Roscoe said, "you are just full of insights tonight."

"And every night," she said proudly.

"No wonder John snapped you up when he did," Roscoe said.

At this, Paulette smiled, her eyes twinkling. Ally wondered what the woman was like when she was Ally's age. Probably full of fire, unafraid, just like she was now. And, Ally thought ruefully, she probably wasn't the type to just sit there letting her stomach tie up in knots while her brain kept serving up fantasies about kissing Roscoe LeGrand.

No, a woman like Paulette would just march right over there and make it happen.

Maybe I should be channeling Paulette instead of Savannah Hart...

The game continued on, but Ally was too distracted to mark her card now. Instead she watched Roscoe helping Mrs. Dunn, wondering if he had any clue just how damn charming he really was.

Oh, he knows exactly what he's doing, girl. Don't let that sweet smile fool you...

Ally swatted the thought away. She didn't need the warning; warnings were for people in danger, and she was perfectly safe. She'd already promised herself that this thing with Roscoe wasn't going very far, emotionally speaking. So what if she couldn't stop staring at his mouth, wondering what it would feel like to be pressed up against the wall while Roscoe shoved his hands through her hair and claimed her in a passionate kiss. She'd prepared herself for a possible kiss tonight, right? And so what if that kiss happened to lead to a little bit more...

A bolt of raw desire shot through her body, making her insides throb. Her thoughts ran away with her. All she could imagine now was Roscoe, unzipping the back of her dress, kissing his way down her body as he peeled off her clothes. Roscoe, unbuttoning his shirt and letting it drop to the floor as Ally reached for the button on his jeans and slid her hand down against the hot, smooth skin of his abs...

As if he could read her scandalous thoughts, Roscoe looked up at her again and caught her eye, his warm smile curving into something hot and dangerous.

I shouldn't like him so much. I shouldn't even be thinking *about letting this happen.*

Despite the alarm bells clanging in her head, Ally could not stop staring at his lips. Her body was sending her all the signals, all the signs that she wanted him— really, really wanted him. It was probably a bad idea, but at some point between the threesome joke and the bingo boinkers, she'd lost her ability to think rationally.

For the first time in years, the idea of being with another man—*really* being with him—filled her belly not with hot, sticky fear, but with anticipation.

Excitement.

Red-hot lust.

Roscoe tapped her foot with his again, only this time, he didn't stop there. He slid his foot between hers until their calves were touching. The small gesture felt shockingly intimate, and Ally's eyes darted around the table, certain everyone could tell what was going on just by the blush in her cheeks.

Everyone was still fixated on their cards, though. So Ally let her eyes flutter closed. In her little fantasy land, everyone around them disappeared, the table evaporated, and Ally climbed into his lap, straddling his muscular thighs, losing herself in the powerful grip of his big, strong hands on her ass as she rocked her hips against him...

She shifted in her chair, hoping to relieve some of the pressure pulsating between her thighs, but that slight movement rubbed her in *exactly* the right spot to make everything infinitely worse. It wasn't helping that the world's sexiest man was giving her fuck-me eyes across the table, heat emanating out through his jeans onto her bare leg like a beacon calling her away to some hot, delicious place. All she had to do was follow it, let him take her where her body wanted—no, *needed*—to go.

You are a grown woman. You have every right to feel these things, so let yourself. Let it happen. Just have fun…

It was crazy, it was out of character, and it was *definitely* out of her comfort zone, but Ally finally ceded control to her physical body. It felt like letting go of the rope in tug-of-war, and the instant she did, her entire body was swept up in a current of desire so strong she was certain everyone around her could feel it. She bit her lower lip and looked into Roscoe's eyes again, willing him to read her thoughts. Letting him right in.

Her eyes darted toward the exit, then back again.

Roscoe cocked an eyebrow, the mischievous glint in his eyes making her even more desperate for his touch. Ally nodded once. She was so far gone on him, so drunk on the entire fantasy, that she didn't even feel bad when Roscoe rose suddenly from his chair, making up rapid-fire excuses for why they needed to leave.

Ally got up next, babbling her hasty goodbyes and passing her remaining bingo cards to Lorraine. She was pretty sure she'd handed over most of her brain, too, because when Roscoe grabbed her hand and led her out of the community room, down an abandoned hallway, and into a pitch-black staff room at the end of the building, the only thought that popped into her mostly empty head was: *I hope to God he brought a condom.*

CHAPTER TEN

Feral.

It was the only word Roscoe could think of to describe the look in Ally's eyes tonight. He didn't know what the fuck was going on—with either of them—because she'd seemed skittish from the get-go, and he'd brought her out tonight with every intention of being a perfect gentleman. Bingo, a nice dinner out at his favorite Greek place, maybe somewhere for coffee after. He figured if he played his cards right, he'd get to kiss her. To taste those soft, pink lips. He would've considered that the perfect ending to the night.

But one look in her eyes across that bingo table, and Roscoe knew she wanted much more than a goodnight kiss. And Roscoe, for all his gentlemanly efforts, was powerless to resist the siren call of a beautiful woman.

"Are we allowed in here?" she asked, giggling like a kid as the door snicked shut behind them.

"Don't know," Roscoe said. The darkness was all-encompassing as he reached for her, grabbing her by the hips and pulling her close. "I didn't stop to ask."

He felt her hands on his chest, sliding up to hook around his neck. Her fingers tugged at the back of his hair, his dick going instantly hard. Stifling a growl, he pressed his nose to the top of her head, inhaling her sweet, clean scent. God, she smelled so fucking good. *Felt* so fucking good.

"Did we really just sneak into a staff room in a nursing home?"

"Yeah, we kinda did. You okay?" he asked. Her heart was pounding hard, drumming against his chest, mirroring his own frantic beat.

"Let's see... I got flowers, I won my first time at bingo, and I'm about to make out with a superhot guy in the dark." Ally laughed softly. "How could I not be okay?"

"Wait... We're about to make out?" He dragged his lips across her forehead, down her nose, and pressed a kiss to the corner of her mouth, so fucking close he could taste the sweet cinnamon on her breath. "I thought you hauled me in here to talk bingo strategy."

"Excuse you!" She smacked his chest. "*You* hauled *me* in here. I'm just along for the ride."

"What choice did I have? You were totally flirting with me at the bingo table."

"That's what you do in the presence of a superhot guy who brings you flowers."

"Hmm. You're bolder in the dark. I like it."

"It's the vampire thing, remember?" Laughter bubbled up from her chest again. God, he loved the sound of that. His mind was already spinning with all the possible ways he could make her laugh.

But he didn't know how long they had in this room before they got caught, and his lips could only handle one thing at a time. Right now, cracking jokes was not a top priority.

"I remember," he said. Slowly, he backed her up, doing his best to avoid the conference table and chairs at the center of the room, their outlines just visible in the darkness. When her shoulders tapped the back wall, she let out a tiny gasp. He brushed his thumb across her mouth, making her shiver.

"Ally?" he whispered, out of his mind with desire as he cupped her face in his hands and leaned in close.

"Yeah?"

Her breath was hot, ghosting over his lips. Beneath his touch, he felt another tremble roll through her body.

"You're shaking," he said, running his hands down her arms. Her skin prickled with goose bumps.

"Don't worry." She let out a nervous whisper-laugh. "It's the good kind of shaking."

Roscoe smiled at her, even though he knew she couldn't see him in the dark. Leaning in close, his lips brushed the shell of her ear, her silky hair tickling his nose.

"Ally," he whispered again. "Can I kiss you?"

CHAPTER ELEVEN

Ally could not remember a time in her life when any guy —not in high school, not college, not even Dan—had asked permission to kiss her. It was so damn sexy, she nearly melted into a puddle right there.

"Yes," she managed. Her voice was unsteady, her insides burning, her knees trembling, but she was certain she wanted that kiss, now more than ever.

Roscoe's lips brushed her cheek, soft and gentle as a feather. Despite the tentativeness in his kiss, electricity crackled between them, making the hairs on the back of her neck stand on end. He kissed her again, his lips ghosting over her jaw, her chin, the corner of her mouth, each movement winding her tighter inside, flooding her core with molten heat. The darkness heightened her other senses, magnifying the whisper of his lips on her skin, the sound of his breath as it mingled with hers, the coolness of the cement wall against her back. She felt him pull back, and her lips parted a mere second before he cupped her face in his hands and kissed her full on.

She sighed into his mouth as their lips met, warm and soft and perfect, and when her sigh turned into a moan, Roscoe deepened their kiss, tangling his hands into her hair and pulling her closer. He was so confident, so in control, Ally wanted nothing more than to let go. To let herself be carried away by this current, no matter where it might take her.

Reaching for his shirt, she trailed her fingers down the center, working her way through the buttons until she'd revealed his bare chest, her hands exploring every solid ridge and ripple her eyes couldn't see. His skin was smooth and hot to the touch, and when she dragged her nails lightly down his abs, she felt his muscles contract in pleasure.

Roscoe was strong and sure, but God, he made Ally feel like she was the one with all the power. Even her lightest touch had him groaning against her lips, silently begging for more as he worked his way down her neck.

"Roscoe," she whispered, breathless and hot as he teased her with his tongue. "That's... *God*."

He left a hot kiss on her collarbone, then moved on to her shoulder, gently nipping her skin as his hands slid around her waist and up her back, fingers seeking the zipper at the base of her neck.

"Okay?" he whispered.

"Not exactly," she teased. "I'm still dressed."

Laughing, Roscoe slowly unzipped her dress, his warm touch a stark contrast to the cool air-conditioned air on her newly exposed skin. She slipped her arms from the dress as Roscoe pushed it down to her waist, his strong, calloused thumbs brushing her bare nipples.

Ally was in divine agony—there was no other way to put it. His every touch, every caress left her wanting so much more.

Roscoe lowered his head and licked her nipple, then sucked the aching bud between his lips, his stubble scratching her breast as Ally trembled, barely trusting her ability to stand upright.

All of her attention was on her body. On the goose bumps rising on her skin, the white-hot pulse of desire between her thighs, the free-fall sensation in her belly as Roscoe teased and sucked, kissed and caressed. But somewhere in the back of her mind, a tiny voice was warning her to slow down. To take a breath. To put an end to this before she tumbled into something that could not be reversed.

That's your fear talking, girl! Savannah Hart's voice said. *Kick that nosey nelly to the curb and embrace your passion!*

"I'm embracing it!" she nearly shouted.

"Um..." Roscoe laughed, standing up to kiss her. Her nipples ached in the chilly air, longing again for his mouth even as he teased her with this palms. "Embracing what?"

Ally hadn't realized she'd said it out loud, but she wasn't about to let the opportunity go to waste.

"This." She reached for the button on his jeans, unfastening them and sliding her hand inside his boxers, seeking his hardness.

"For the record," Roscoe said, letting out a sigh of pure pleasure that made Ally smile, "I fully embrace... your embracing of... your... *God*, yes. That."

It was shocking, the feel of another man. Hot and hard for her. Thickening at her touch as Roscoe lowered his mouth to hers with another sigh, his hot breath tickling her lips.

Time slowed. Everything around her narrowed into this one tiny pinpoint of awareness:

I'm touching another man, stroking him...

A flame of guilt flickered inside, fracturing the intensity of the moment, and Ally drew back suddenly as if she'd been burned.

"Ally?" Roscoe whispered. "Are you okay?"

"I'm..." Ally sucked in a breath, let it out slow. She waited for the guilt to rise, to consume her until there was nothing left but tears and regret.

But the seconds ticked by, and none of those feelings came. The tiny flame inside sputtered out almost as quickly as it had arrived, and Ally sighed in relief. She was fine. Absolutely fine.

"I'm so sorry. I'm fine." She trailed her fingers down his chest again, reaching for the waistband of his boxers. "Where were we?"

Roscoe grabbed her hands, holding them still against his abs. "You sure you're okay? We can stop if you want to."

"I'm good. Just a little rusty," she admitted. "It's... been a while for me."

"Why didn't you say anything?" he asked gently, releasing a hand so he could brush the hair from her face. His thumb trailed along her jaw. "We don't have to—"

"I know," she said. "I want to. Really."

"Are you sure?"

"I'm—"

A noise at the door startled them both—someone was jiggling the handle.

"Shit," Roscoe whispered, laughing. "Raincheck?"

"Definitely."

After a quick kiss to seal the deal, they split apart, hastily reassembling their clothing. Ally couldn't find her shoes, and her hair was probably a dead giveaway, but at least she'd managed to get the dress back up before the lock gave way and the door opened, bathing the room in fluorescent light from the hallway.

"Oh," a woman's voice said. "I didn't realize this room was taken. Guess we should've made reservations."

Ally squinted at the silhouettes in the doorway, waiting for her eyes to adjust.

"Roscoe? Ally?" the woman laughed, and Ally finally recognized the couple. "Oh, my. This is awkward."

"Hi Paulette," she said brightly, forcing a smile. "John. Is the game over already?"

"Apparently for you two it isn't," Paulette said, staring pointedly at the bulge in Roscoe's pants. "What's going on in here?"

"We're just leaving," Ally said, right as Roscoe said, "Thought we saw a mouse."

"A *big* one," Ally added. "Huge."

John snorted back a laugh.

"What are you two up to?" Ally asked innocently, as if her swollen mouth and crazy almost-sex-hair and the situation in Roscoe's pants were an everyday occurrence here in the Wellshire Estates staff room.

"We were looking for a mouse too," Paulette said with a wink. "But I suppose we'll have to look else-where. Besides, I'm pretty sure June Higgenbottom saw us leaving, and you know how *she* is."

"Right," Roscoe said.

"Well, since it's obvious none of us are getting any tonight, would you two like to join us for a cocktail instead?" Paulette asked. "Southern Comfort Manhattans are my specialty."

"Oh, now you're just showing off," John said. "Metamucil cocktails are more your specialty."

"As awesome as that sounds," Roscoe said, "we'll have to pass."

Paulette gave them both another once-over, then smirked. "Okay, then. See you again soon, I hope?"

"Count on it," Roscoe said. Then, lowering his voice to a conspiratorial whisper, "And maybe we should keep this... mouse situation to ourselves, right? Wouldn't want June to catch wind of it."

"No, definitely not." Paulette smiled as she backed out of the doorway, then made a zipping motion across her lips. "I'm a vault, Roscoe LeGrand. You know that."

The moment she and John were out of earshot, Ally said, "So. How long before the entire population of Wellshire knows?"

"Hmm." Roscoe tapped a finger against his lips. "Staff or residential?"

"Both."

"Put it this way: Paulette's going to love holding court at breakfast tomorrow."

"At least she didn't ask to take a selfie." Ally flipped

on the overhead light and located her purse on one of the chairs.

"I'm just glad I'm maintaining my record as worst date ever." Roscoe opened the door, gesturing for Ally to head out ahead of him. "For a minute there, I thought you were actually starting to like me."

Ally laughed. "Who says I don't?"

"Let's recap." Roscoe put his arm around her, leading them both down the hall toward the exit. "I take you to bingo. Bring you to an old folks home to make out." Roscoe inhaled deeply. "It smells like Ben Gay in here. God, my off-ice game really sucks."

"Hey, I won fifty bucks! The night's not a total loss."

"You *are* kind of a bingo badass."

Ally grinned. "Right?"

"Well, they play every other Saturday, so any time you need a good boinking, give me a call."

Heat flooded Ally's face, but still she laughed. She hardly knew the man, but somehow being with Roscoe felt so easy, so natural. It sounded strange to think of it that way, but to Ally it seemed as though they'd been friends for years.

Out in the parking lot, Roscoe paused in front of the passenger door of his SUV, turning to offer her a surprisingly shy smile. "The best part about dating senior citizens on the side is that their night ends early enough for me to go on another date. It's like a two-fer."

"You are *such* a scoundrel!"

"There's actually a great little Greek place next door I was hoping to show you. *And* a bowling alley, if you're up for more games. Close enough to walk, even." Roscoe held out his hand, the hopeful sparkle in his eyes offering an invitation *and* a promise. "Unless you've got plans?"

This was her chance. She could make an excuse, feign exhaustion from the unexpected turn of events, from the unexpected onset of all those people, from the mortification of getting caught by Paulette and John, and all the gossip that was sure to follow. It would be easy enough to ask Roscoe to take her home, to wish him well, to put the night behind her and never look back.

She suspected Roscoe knew she'd do just that. The silence stretched on between them, the hope in his eyes slowly fading into a dull acceptance.

But instead of bowing out, Ally surprised them both.

"Well, I *was* going to head home, put on my slippers, and pour myself a Metamucil cocktail, but I suppose that can wait." Ally took Roscoe's outstretched hand. "You know, I've never actually tried Greek food."

Roscoe put his hand on his heart, mouth open in mock horror. "What kind of backwoods childhood did you have?"

"In our house, wheat bread was considered ethnic food."

"Oh, Ally. You're lucky you met me when you did."

She was beginning to agree with him.

"Brace yourself." With a glint in his eye that promised mischief, he pointed at her and said, "I'm about to pop your souvlaki cherry."

Ally laughed. The night had taken such an unexpected turn. It wasn't until after dinner and drinks, after dessert and coffee, after a marathon game of bumper bowling in which Roscoe still managed to throw mostly gutter balls and Ally got an earful on bowling shoe design from a self-professed bowling shoe connoisseur named Earl, that she felt those nervous butterflies skittering inside her once again.

"Roscoe..." she started, searching for the words. They were back at her house now, standing on the front porch to say their goodbyes, lulled by the melodic hum of the crickets and a sprinkler running next door, and Ally wasn't quite sure how to end the evening. Despite how much fun they'd had, she wanted to get this off her chest. To explain.

"What happened earlier," she tried again, looking up into his eyes. "I really am sorry."

"Wait... What happened earlier?" He snapped his fingers and smiled, resting a warm hand on her shoulder. "Right, I remember. I got to hang out with a gorgeous woman all night, make out with her in the staff room, eat my weight in souvlaki and rice pudding, and get my ass kicked in bumper bowling, which was a thing I didn't think possible before tonight."

Ally smiled. "Well, when you put it like that..."

"It *is* like that." Roscoe reached up to tuck a lock of hair behind her ear, his warm hand lingering on her neck. His eyes glittered, drawing her back in. If it wasn't for the fact that she had neighbors, she might just try to pick up where they left off earlier...

"And I can't wait to do it all again." Roscoe's declaration brought her back to the moment.

Ally couldn't hide her relief. "Really?"

"Really. I was thinking Thursday," he said. "After you get off work. Yes?"

"Are you asking me on another date?"

"I am. Are you accepting?"

"That depends. Will the ladies of Wellshire be joining us?" she teased. "Or Earl, fanboy of bowling shoes large and small, funky and fresh?"

Roscoe shook his head, trailing his thumb across her lips. "Next time I want you all to myself. No sharing."

Ally grinned. She was powerless to resist.

"Thursday sounds great." She glanced at her watch— it was well past midnight. Thank God Reggie was staying at Clarissa's tonight. "As long as you have me back at a respectable hour next time. Reggie will be home, and I don't want her getting suspicious."

"Sorry, beautiful. I'm not making any promises about

bringing you back at a respectable hour. In fact..."
Roscoe leaned in close, nipping her earlobe and kissing
the sensitive skin behind it. In a low growl that made her
knees weak, he said, "I don't plan on being very
respectable at *all*."

CHAPTER TWELVE

Roscoe was fucking *wired*.

He'd been on the ice since four in the morning, trying to burn off some of his nervous energy—no dice. At five-thirty he'd called Henny and the boys, dragging their asses out of bed for an unscheduled practice before Wednesday's clinic. Dick move, maybe, but screw it— they all needed the workout.

But even after an hour of on-ice sparring, Roscoe was still jacked up. Try as he might, he couldn't shift his focus onto the ice. He hadn't seen Ally since Saturday night at the Wellshire—four days felt like a fucking eternity—and now his mind was totally stuck on her, on that soft smile, on the way her short hair set off a long, gorgeous neck. It was shorter in the back, and darker there, and it came down in a V that had him dreaming about running his tongue down the little dip at the base of her neck. He wanted to taste her skin, to leave a trail of hot, wet kisses down her spine as his hands gripped her thighs. They'd come close the other night, and he hadn't been able to stop replaying it in his mind, fantasizing about the parts they hadn't quite gotten to before they were interrupted…

"You're practically vibrating," Henny said, yanking Roscoe back to the moment as he crashed into the players' box. "I haven't had coffee yet. Or morning sex, for that matter." He shook his head, scowling at Roscoe. "Remind me why we're friends again?"

"There's not enough coffee *or* sex in the world to deal with this bullshit." Kenton slumped onto the bench and pulled off his helmet, panting like a dog. "Not to mention this fucking hangover."

"Christ. It's Wednesday," Roscoe said. "Besides, you shouldn't be partying this close to the season open."

"And you shouldn't be this ugly," Kenton said, "but hey. Them's the breaks."

"Speaking of breaks, dickhole…" Roscoe punched him in the shoulder, but before Kenton could retaliate, a commotion in the tunnel caught their attention.

"Is it nap time in here, children, or can we actually play some hockey?" Walker Dunn asked as he and Eva emerged onto the rink. They were tan and glowing from their island-hopping adventure, but otherwise geared up for a day on the ice, not the beach.

Roscoe skated over to them, tackling Dunn in a big, sloppy, welcome-back hug.

"Whoa, okay, I missed you too." Dunn cracked up, slapping Roscoe on the back. "But I have a question." That damn smirk on his face told Roscoe everything he needed to know—of course he'd spoken with his mother, gotten the low-down on Roscoe's bingo game date. "Who the fuck is Ally Heinz, and why won't my mother shut up about her?"

"Yeah." Eva skated up close, gave him a quick peck on the cheek, followed by that death glare of hers. "I don't know whether we should be offended at being kept out of the loop, or happy that our sweet little Roscoe has finally found someone special."

"Found someone to seal his nuts in a jar, most likely," Kenton said. "Not a fate *I* would choose." Pretty fucking priceless considering all the quality time he seemed to be spending with Clarissa Finch. But Roscoe was too damn happy at the mention of Ally's name to argue. All he could do was nod and smile, keep the mystery alive as he counted down the hours until he'd see her again. Tomorrow night felt like an eternity away.

"Who is she, anyway?" Jarlsberg asked.

"No one you know," Roscoe said.

"Roscoe," Kuznetzov said, feigning shock. "Are you saying Jarlsberg does not know his own mother?"

Jarlsberg laughed. "Fuck off, Kooz."

"Alright, Dr. Feelgood," Dunn said to Roscoe. "Enough dodging. What's the story?"

"You want a story? Fine. Once upon a time, this over-tanned, piña-colada-sippin', beach bum motherfucker showed up at my rink. So I dragged his pampered little ass to center ice, gave him the biggest beat-down in history, and finally wiped that stupid smirk off his face." Roscoe grabbed a stick from the box and tossed it to Dunn, flashing a predatory grin. "And they lived happily ever after."

All that time on the beach had made Dunn soft, and Roscoe had no trouble kicking the man's ass from here to next Sunday, burning through some of his excess energy in the process. He'd also strong-armed him into helping out with the clinic, which was a bonus for Roscoe and the kids alike.

Unfortunately, the kids were not on their best behavior today—totally Clarissa's fault. It was only their third practice, but they'd spent most of the morning with photographers from the Buffalo News, dicking around with lighting and positions and God knows what else just to get a few usable shots. Then Clarissa dropped the mother of all bombs—one of the news affiliates wanted to set up a live shoot for next month and was looking for a few kids to be interviewed on camera. Once the kids heard about their shot to be on TV, getting them to concentrate on their speed drills and footwork was damn near impossible.

The only one of the bunch who held it together was Reggie. The girl was as determined as ever, no signs of slowing down. Every challenge Roscoe and the boys offered up, Reggie met head on, absolutely fearless. Roscoe had started calling on Reggie to demo the more advanced techniques, encouraging her to partner up and help out some of the weaker links in the chain.

To Roscoe's surprise, they actually listened to her. Even Nick Harper seemed enthralled, despite the fact that she was stealing a bit of his thunder.

"Forty-four is one to watch," Dunn said, nodding toward Reggie during one of Henny's intense passing drills. She was down by the net at the far side of the rink, chasing after a renegade pass from the Harper kid. "I can't believe how quick she is."

"You're telling me," Roscoe said, glancing at his stop watch. Damn—he hadn't seen anyone who could skate that fast in a long time—not even on his own team.

Without breaking her stride, she scooped up the puck, boomeranging back around the net and charging out toward center ice. A couple of kids chased after her, but Reggie left them in the dust.

"Bring it home, kiddo," Roscoe shouted. She picked

up the pace and shot toward Kooz at the other net, a blur in her blue-and-white jersey. Before he even knew what was happening, she took the shot.

And despite Kooz's best efforts, she fucking made it.

Roscoe couldn't hide his excitement.

She was *made* for this game.

"You see her go after the puck like that?" Roscoe asked the group. "That's how it's done, guys." Then, waving to the kids that had hung back, he called them out by number. "Six. Twenty-two. Eleven. Front and center. This next shot is all you."

With the help of his teammates and his star player, Roscoe encouraged the other kids through the next round of drills, making sure every last one of them got a few shots at the net.

"Nice work, guys." He clapped, beaming at all of his little prodigies in turn, already imagining the youth cup trophy they'd be winning later that summer. "Take ten to cool down and hydrate, then we'll regroup for a pep talk before I set you free."

Spent and happy, all of them scurried over to the players' box for their towels and water bottles except for one.

Reggie took off her helmet and shook out her long blonde hair. Her cheeks were red, her eyes bright blue in the harsh light of the rink.

"What's up, kiddo? You getting tired of running circles around these boys yet?"

Reggie laughed. "No. I just wanted to talk to you about something." Her smile disappeared, and Roscoe felt his gut tighten. Call it instinct, call it an omen, but he'd had enough of these conversations with his nephews to know that the look on her face did not bode well.

Please don't tell me you're quitting...

"Hey," he said gently. "You okay?"

"Don't take this the wrong way, but..." Reggie sighed, then scrunched up her face like she'd just gotten a whiff of the boys' locker room. "Are you and my mom, like, a thing now?"

Roscoe nearly fell on his ass, which was saying something, considering he'd been standing perfectly still. "I, uh... I'm..." He scratched his chin, unable to hold her gaze. "Is that what she told you?"

"Right," Reggie huffed. "I'm not stupid, you know."

"Yeah, I *do* know that, Reggie." If he wasn't so thrown off, he'd probably laugh. Seemed Reggie's fearlessness extended off the ice, too. "But what makes you think your mom and I have something going on?"

"The flowers, for one thing."

"Flowers?"

Reggie rolled her eyes. "Big romantic bouquet, front and center on the dining room table. Ring a bell?"

"Maybe one of her colleagues sent them."

"Please. She's been at that job for like, five minutes. The only other person she knows in this town is Aunt Clarissa, and I know they're not from her—she sends candy and wine and goody bags from her PR events."

"You have an Aunt Clarissa? Who works in PR?"

Reggie stared at him like he was at least ten steps behind. Which, admittedly, he was. "Uh, yeah? Clarissa Finch is my mother's best friend. She's the reason we moved out here, actually. I thought you guys worked together?"

Roscoe nodded. Reggie might've put the clues together, but it was obvious Ally hadn't mentioned their date to Clarissa—Clarissa would've called him in for a meeting at some ungodly hour, lectured him on his obligation to clean up the team's image, and forbade him from dating anyone, let alone her best friend.

He didn't know whether to be relived or concerned that Ally had apparently kept their night together under wraps.

"Sure," Roscoe said, forcing a smile. "I just didn't realize you guys were connected."

"And," Reggie went on, "Mom's been lying to me about her plans, too."

"That doesn't mean she's making those plans with me, Reg."

"But it's so obvious! After all her drama about not

letting me play, now she's suddenly interested in hockey, asking me all kind of questions about Roscoe LeGrand *this* and Roscoe LeGrand *that*. And you're standing here trying to play it off, but you *totally* like her."

He couldn't hide his grin. "She... She was asking questions about me?"

"Oh my God!" Reggie laughed, pointing at his face. "You are so busted."

"Shit." Roscoe sighed, still unable to erase his damn smile. "I mean, shoot."

"So what's the deal? Dating? Friends?" She lowered her voice like a co-conspirator. "Friends with ben—"

"Reggie. This is..." Roscoe scrubbed a hand over his mouth. He knew how to skate, knew how to play bingo, and he made a hell of a bruschetta, too. But when it came to navigating the complex dynamics of teen girls and their moms, he was *way* out of his element. "It's probably something you and your mom should talk about."

"Oh, no. I'm not saying a word to her yet. I'm saving this for ammo."

"Ammo?"

Reggie shrugged. "One day I'll want to go somewhere, like on a date or something, and my mom will be like, 'that's not appropriate for a girl your age,' because she's overprotective like that, right? But then I'll be all, 'what about the time you were making out with my hockey coach? How inappropriate was *that*?' And she'll realize her argument was flawed from the start, and she'll have no choice to let me do whatever I want." Reggie smiled the dazzling smile of a kid who thinks she's got it all figured out. "It's kind of perfect, actually."

Roscoe could only laugh. "You are one scary-ass kid. You know that, right?"

Reggie laughed too, pulling the helmet back on her head. Once she was all geared up again, she met his eyes, her gaze suddenly serious. "If you ever tell my mom this, I will totally deny it, but I think it's kind of cool. You and my mom, I mean."

Roscoe cocked an eyebrow. "*Kind* of cool?"

"Well, also kind of *gross*, but in a cool way."

Roscoe cracked up. He was pretty sure she'd meant it as a compliment, but just in case, he knocked on her helmet and said, "You've just earned yourself ten more laps, double-fours. Full gear. I want to see total puck control at all times."

"You got it." Reggie beamed at him, never breaking eye contact as she fastened her chin strap and skated backward toward the pile of pucks the others had abandoned at the net. Seconds later, she was off, scooting around the ice by herself like there was nowhere else she'd rather be.

Roscoe laughed at himself. Couldn't help it—he'd just gotten bitch-slapped by a fifteen-year-old girl.

SYLVIA PIERCE

Reaching for the phone in his pocket, he sent a quick text to his sister, Lena.

Just wanted to say hey, Leenie Beanie. Give that baby girl a big kiss from Uncle Roscoe.

He was about to check in with his parents, too, but before he could pull up their contact info, a hand clamped down over his shoulder from behind.

Fucking Dunn.

"Dude," Dunn said, "Your mystery woman is the kid's mother? That... can't be a good idea."

"I think it's a great fucking idea," Roscoe said, turning around to face him. "And also, none of your fucking business. Pardon my French."

"Oh, it's totally my business," Dunn said. "Just like you made it your business when I got together with Eva."

"And look how great that turned out for you?" Roscoe elbowed him in the ribs. He really was glad to have his best friend back. "What is it about us and beautiful women on ice?"

"Tell me about it." Dunn blew out a breath. "So, you and this woman—"

"Ally Heinz."

"Ally Heinz." Dunn nodded. "You guys just casual, or...?"

Roscoe thought about how she'd felt in his arms the other night, how she'd tasted when he kissed her. Didn't matter that they'd cooled things off quickly, or that their post-bingo date had progressed to a chintzy bowling alley instead of the bedroom. All it had taken was that first kiss, the hot press of her lips to his, her soft moan in his mouth like a promise, and Roscoe knew without question that when it came to Ally, "just casual" would never be part of the deal—not for him.

"*Or,*" Roscoe said firmly. "Definitely or."

CHAPTER THIRTEEN

No strings. No commitments. Nothing but easy, breezy fun.

And then it would be done, long before Ally ever had to confess her secret to Reggie or Clarissa.

Getting ready for Thursday's date, she felt the tiniest pinpricks of guilt in her belly, but there was no point in telling them the truth about Roscoe. Ally wasn't even sure what the truth was. That she liked him enough to temporarily swallow her dating fears and jump into this thing, knowing it would only go so far? That she'd run out on her lunch hour to buy a matching bra and panties made of something other than cotton? That she'd spent an extra half an hour in the shower, scrubbing and trimming and shaping like a professional landscaper for the proverbial "just in case" suddenly on the horizon?

I don't plan on being very respectable at all...

Roscoe's words echoed in her memory, sending a shiver down her spine as she checked out her reflection in the bedroom mirror. The new lingerie was gorgeous—pale pink satin with tiny black dots, trimmed in black lace, and it made her feel sexy as hell. Even if Roscoe never saw it, it didn't matter. She'd know she was wearing it, and she'd feel like—in the words of Paulette—a million smackeroos.

She hoped he *would* see it, though. Ally was pretty sure that she'd gotten all the major jitters out of the way last weekend after her penis-induced freakout at Wellshire. After so many years without seeing one—let alone touching .one—she'd forgotten how intimidating they could be. Kind of like the black bear she'd encountered one summer in the Rockies as a kid. Well, except that penises wouldn't trample your campsite in the middle of the night searching for the granola bars you'd forgotten to pack away even after your mom reminded you no less than five times. And also, penises didn't growl. As far as she knew. Perhaps she would test that theory later tonight...

Bottling up the remnants of her guilt, Ally put on her favorite coral-colored sundress and a pair of strappy turquoise sandals, grabbing a thin white shall in case it got chilly later. Other than advising her not to dress too fancy, her date had given no clues about what to expect tonight. Roscoe, she was quickly learning, thrived on surprises.

No one was more surprised than Ally. Not just at how easily she'd accepted his invitations, and not just at the rush of feelings he'd unleashed, the waves of giddiness, everything inside her buzzing and tingling whenever she thought of him.

No, those things didn't surprise her. What was most shocking to Ally was the fact that—despite the penis incident, which she was pretty sure was a one-time, getting-back-on-the-horse kind of thing—she wasn't afraid of being with him like this. Of having fun.

As long as she stuck to the plan.

In the days since she'd last seen Roscoe, once the delirious kiss-induced haze had cleared, Ally had figured it all out. She may not be the most experienced woman in the bedroom, but she did know this much: ongoing casual sex with a guy like Roscoe was not for her. They could spend time together, go on dates, make out, and fool around to their hearts' content, but once things progressed to actual sex, attachments and emotions would soon follow—at least on Ally's end. And her emotions were the very last thing that still belonged to her—the very last thing over which she had any control. She couldn't relinquish them, not even for a man whose electric touch left her body on fire, desperate for more.

Especially not for a man like that.

The solution was simple: once they had sex—tonight? Next week? In a month?—they'd part ways. Leave off on a high note before things got too serious and all the old worries rushed in, turning her into a puddle of nerves and fear and sending Roscoe packing anyway.

But what if he likes you? Like, really *likes you?*

Ally let out a dreamy sigh. Yes, they'd shared a connection that went beyond the physical—that much was obvious. But even if he did like her, it would all fade soon enough. The NHL regular season started in the fall, and there would be lots of training and prepping and traveling, and he wouldn't have time for Ally and all these cute little dates. Reggie would be back in school, and Ally would dive headlong into building her new career and their life here in Buffalo. No tears, no drama, no hard feelings.

No feelings at all, actually.

Savannah Hart might disagree on her approach, but for Ally, the plan was the only thing allowing her to move forward right now. Because no matter how badly she wanted to believe Savannah's mantras—*Being vulnerable is your biggest strength! Pursue your heart's desires with unapologetic ferocity!*—personal experience had taught her a hard lesson.

It was a whole lot easier to be brave and bold in the

face of adversity when you knew the adversity had a built-in expiration date.

"You brought lasagna? On a picnic?" Ally tucked her legs up underneath her dress and repositioned herself on their blanket, holding out her hands for the plate Roscoe had just served her. It was still hot, thanks to the insulated bag he'd packed it in, and weighed about twelve pounds.

Ally tried the first bite, moaning unapologetically. She felt like she'd died and gone to cheesy, meaty, saucy heaven.

That wasn't even counting the rest of the food he'd brought—bruschetta, olives, caprese salad with smoked mozzarella, wine so smooth and rich it felt like liquid silk on her tongue. He'd prepared a gourmet feast for her, and by the time she'd arrived and followed his directions to this secluded little grove in the middle of Chestnut Ridge park, he'd had it all laid out on a blanket, wine already opened, a bouquet of flowers in a vase in the grass, his broad smile making her heart stutter.

"Correction," he said now. "I *made* lasagna. And it's not just any picnic. It's a special occasion."

"Our second official date?"

"Well, that and the meteor shower." He nodded up toward the sky, and Ally stretched out her legs and tilted her head back. The sun still floated well above the horizon, the sky a peaceful shade of blue streaked with wispy clouds.

"It's not dark enough," she said.

"Doesn't mean it's not happening." He nudged her bare foot with his. "Nature works in mysterious ways, Ally Heinz, and rarely for our entertainment."

Ally laughed. "You are the eternal optimist."

"You're right." He tugged on a lock of her hair, tucking it behind her ear with a soft touch that left her aching for more. "There's only one thing that could kill the mood—you not liking my cooking. Total deal-breaker for me."

"No chance," Ally said, trying not to think too much about the deal-breaker comment. Deal-breakers were for long-term things. Serious things. Things that Ally didn't have the luxury of dreaming about.

Ally took another sip of wine, and they ate their main course in companionable silence, mostly on account of Ally going in for seconds and thirds while Roscoe watched with barely contained glee. Ally didn't need to tell him it was the best lasagna she'd ever tasted. She'd cleared her plate twice over, and by the end, she was pretty sure it was written all over her face. Literally.

"You've got a little..." He leaned in close, stroked the edge of her mouth with his thumb. "Sauce. Right here." He pressed a gentle kiss to the same spot, lingering long enough to make her heart rate skyrocket.

What was it about this man that had her stomach tying itself into a pretzel? Yes, he was an amazing kisser. Strong. Sexy. Confident, with just the right amount of vulnerability to keep him human. But her attraction to him was so much more than that. This close on the blanket, enveloped by his clean, masculine scent, staring into his boyishly charming hazel eyes, Ally was utterly captivated.

"Have I told you..." Roscoe whispered, his breath tickling her lips. Soft as powder, he trailed his hand up her calf, over her knee, stopping just inside the edge of the fabric, leaving a trail of fire in his wake. "...how much I fucking love this dress?"

Heat flickered in Ally's chest, her heart pounding so hard she could hear it in her breath. She nodded mutely, her lips refusing to obey her brain and form actual words. They were all alone out here, hemmed in by towering oaks and maple trees, their cars the only two in the tiny dirt lot beyond. There was nothing stopping them from picking up where they'd left off at Wellshire. Nothing stopping them from sliding out of their clothes, lying back on the blanket, and giving in to the fullest extent of their obvious mutual attraction.

Hadn't Ally been hoping for just that? Wasn't it the whole reason she'd taken extra care getting ready tonight? Bought the sexy lingerie, made the grand plan for her graceful, high-note exit?

Ally sighed. Now that the moment was here, she wanted to slow it down. Linger just a little longer in this peaceful, happy bubble where they could play and flirt and kiss and eat delicious Italian food and not worry about the goodbyes looming on the horizon.

Forcing herself to cool it, Ally pulled back and reached for the wine and glasses, filling them up and passing one to Roscoe. If he was thrown off by her actions, he didn't show it, his eyes just as mischievous as ever.

"So." Ally sipped her wine, gazed up at the sky. It was still too early to see any meteors, but the thought made her smile anyway. "Tell me your story, Roscoe LeGrand."

Roscoe laughed. "Which one?"

"I've got choices?"

"Always." He sipped the wine, then tipped his glass toward her with a wink. "But choose wisely, young Jedi, because I've only got four stories and I have to ration them out slowly."

"Since you put it that way," she said, "Hockey. Start there. Maybe you can help me understand why my kid likes it so much."

"What's not to love?" He finished his wine, then set down the glass, talking animatedly with his hands. "You're out there on the ice, right? And you know you're part of a team—something bigger than just you. Everyone's counting on you, and you're counting on them, and when you're playing with guys like Dunn and Henny, it's almost like you can read each other's minds. On a good night, we're absolutely in sync, and there's nothing like it. But it's also a mindfuck, because in that split-second moment before you make a pass, or wind up for that perfect shot, you *are* alone. Everything else just disappears. You're out there by yourself at the edge of the world, no sound, no other guys, no screaming fans. Your entire purpose is narrowed down to that one thing, that one tiny moment, and it all happens in a millisecond. That feeling... God, I wouldn't trade that for the world."

Ally nodded. The way he described hockey reminded her of painting, actually. It didn't happen like that every time, but she remembered times when creating something seemed to transport her to another world. Time stopped. Stress and sounds and other people vanished. For those few moments, there was only Ally and her brush and canvas, colors appearing before her eyes as if she were merely a messenger translating a vision inspired by something too large to comprehend.

She smiled at the unexpected memory, glad that Roscoe's story had unearthed it for her.

"When did you first start?" she asked.

"I think I was about four?" Roscoe said. "There was this huge pond down our block, and every winter it would freeze solid enough for the neighborhood kids to skate on it. My brothers all played, but they'd never let me go. Then one day my mother, who was particularly tired of my whining, told them they couldn't go out unless they let me tag along." Roscoe laughed. "I don't remember walking there, or putting on the skates or anything like that. I just remember the feeling of being out there, freezing my little balls off, trying to watch and learn, just so damn excited they were actually letting me play. Mom says I never took no for an answer again. My brothers outgrew it, but I never stopped skating. I can't even tell you how many times I ditched school just to be out on the ice."

"Is that why you barely passed?"

"That is one of many reasons, but yeah." Roscoe ran a hand through his hair, his eyes sparkling in the fading sun. "I love hockey, Al. It's my whole world."

"Really? I had no idea." Ally laughed, and Roscoe started telling her about his rookie days with the Tempest.

She loved hearing his stories, loved the way he lit up as he talked about his game. He was so full of joy and passion—not just about hockey, but with everything. The food, the wine, bingo and bowling, the way he touched her... God, everything about him was just bursting with life and vitality. Just being near him made her feel like a kid spinning around in the sun, twirling and laughing until she collapsed in a dizzy, delirious heap.

It was addicting.

Suddenly, she wanted to kiss him. She wanted to feel the press of his lips again, the hot slide of his tongue, the commanding touch of his hands on her thighs. Screw her worries and her failsafe plan—right now, the only thing Ally wanted was to be utterly claimed by this man.

There was a pause in the story. His tongue darted out to wet his lower lip, and Ally gasped.

Roscoe cocked his head. "You okay?"

Ally nodded, mute. *What had he been talking about?*

"I take it you're not impressed?"

"I'm... I..." Try as she might, Ally was lost. "I must've zoned out."

"Are you kidding me?" Roscoe laughed. "That was my best story. Seriously."

"Sorry." Ally held up her empty glass. "I think it's the wine."

"A glass and a half?" Roscoe smirked. "Maybe I'm just boring you into a coma. I told you to choose your stories wisely. Now I'll have to tell you the one about—"

"Roscoe?" Ally leaned forward, resting her palms on

his thigh as she lowered her gaze to his succulent mouth. Maybe it *was* the wine, or the sultry summer air, or the way Roscoe was staring at her like he'd never seen anyone so beautiful, but Ally was overcome with a feeling of boldness that bordered on reckless, and she did not want to let the opportunity pass. "Maybe you should just kiss me instead."

CHAPTER FOURTEEN

There was no build-up, no teasing jokes or slow, lingering kisses.

Roscoe claimed Ally's mouth in an instant, his hands tangling in her hair as they tumbled backward onto the blanket. He kissed her like a man possessed, and she welcomed it, losing herself in the commanding stroke of his tongue, the delicious scratch of his stubble against her chin.

They were side-by-side on the blanket, but Ally wanted more of him. All of him. She shifted onto her back and pulled him on top of her, opening her legs as he settled between them. He was hard, his cock bulging against his jeans, and Ally wondered how long he'd been in such a state. Desperate for more, she fumbled with his button and zipper, but she couldn't reach him. Roscoe groaned into her mouth, deepening their kiss as his hips rocked forward. The press of his strong body on top of hers left little room for maneuvering.

"Not yet," he whispered, reaching for her hands. In one strong motion, he pinned her wrists to the blanket behind her head, capturing her lower lip with his teeth, nipping and teasing as his other hand slid down to her waist. "Okay?" he asked.

Ally nodded. Everything he did was exquisite, and she wanted every part of it.

He sank onto her with his full weight, and her legs wrapped around his hips, pulling him closer. His hot, hard length throbbed against her clit, nothing but a few scraps of fabric holding back a torrent of desire.

She arched her hips, heat and pressure building between her thighs, the friction driving her wild. She'd never wanted to come so badly before, so desperately.

"Let me touch you." Roscoe's breath was hot and urgent in her mouth, a command she was more than happy to obey.

Gathering her dress into her hands, she bunched the fabric up around her waist, revealing her bare thighs and the pale pink triangle of her panties.

"Jesus," Roscoe whispered. Heat radiated from his touch as his fingers slid over her belly, her thighs, teasing the sensitive skin beneath the lace edge of her panties. If he didn't touch her soon—harder, faster, *more*—Ally would go mad with unrequited lust.

"Please," she whispered, grabbing his forearm, arching her hips to get closer to his elusive heat.

Roscoe grinned like a wolf, tracing a line across her abdomen from one hip bone to another. "Close your eyes."

The moment she shut out the world, he slid his hand down the front of her panties, fingers gliding over her clit, stroking her.

"How badly do you want to come," he asked, slowly sliding a finger inside her entrance, then dragging it out. It was just enough to tease her, to give her a taste of her wildest dreams.

Ally couldn't even form words. She moaned in response, writhing on top of the blanket, her skin buzzing, every nerve ending electrified.

She shouldn't want him so badly. Shouldn't be thinking about tearing off her panties, freeing him from his boxers, and begging him to slide inside her, hard and deep.

But oh my *God*, she *was* thinking about it. Imagining how good it would feel to have this man between her thighs. To lose herself in every stroke.

Her thoughts were exquisite, making her even wetter.

"Show me," he said, pressing another kiss to the corner of her mouth. He teased her entrance again, two fingers this time, sliding inside her as his thumb ghosted over her clit. "Show me how you like to be touched."

His voice was deep and low, demanding in a way that made her insides fizzy. Her eyes still shut tight, Ally's body took over, arching into his touch.

"That's it," he said, thrusting deeper. Faster. She met him stroke for stroke, riding his hand. "Don't stop."

"Kiss me," she begged.

His mouth was on hers in a flash, his kiss as possessive as his touch, his tongue sliding between her lips as he continued to stroke her with fevered intensity, heat building between her thighs, her core throbbing as he brought her closer to the edge of a place she hadn't been in longer than she cared to remember.

The fire in her body was all-consuming, swallowing her in its white-hot fury. Logic evaporated. Fear turned to smoke and ash. She was there. Right there, her legs trembling, her muscles tightening, and then...

Roscoe captured her final gasp with another kiss, swallowing the sounds of her release as the orgasm crashed through her body, warm waves lapping at her skin, sending tingles all the way down to her toes.

Ally wasn't sure how long she lay there, eyes closed, skin cooling as her breathing slowly returned to normal. But when she finally came back to her senses and opened her eyes, she found Roscoe staring down at her, the hunger in his eyes plain.

Ally lowered her gaze to his boxers, the bulge behind them barely contained. He had to be close. So close that any other guy would've been begging her to touch him, to stroke him, to suck. But Roscoe seemed happy to let Ally set the pace.

Maybe that was why she felt so comfortable with him. So open.

And maybe that was why Ally, once content to follow the lead in bed and most other areas of her life, felt the sudden and overwhelming urge to reach inside his boxers, wrap her fingers around his thick, perfect shaft, and take control.

There was no freaking out this time. No fear, no anxiety, no regrets as she tightened her grip and stroked him. God, he was perfect in every way.

With a wicked grin that made him moan, she said, "Now I want to know how *you* like it."

CHAPTER FIFTEEN

Somewhere between his second helping of lasagna and the hockey stories, Roscoe must've fallen asleep.

It was the only explanation—this was all a dream. Because as far as he knew, he hadn't done a single thing in his life to deserve the little slice of heaven that was Ally Heinz, still glowing from the orgasm he'd just given her, looking at him like she was about to grant every last one of his wishes.

"I like it just like this," he said, kissing her again. The hot press of her luscious lips made Roscoe dizzy enough —never mind her firm grip on his cock. Fucking *hell*, that felt good.

He kissed her jaw, her neck, his mouth hungry for the silky smoothness of her skin. The air around them was quickly cooling off, but Ally was warm and inviting, her skin glistening with a thin sheen of sweat.

Her touch drove him wild, but simultaneously made him jealous. He already missed the feel of her soft, wet flesh. He wanted to touch her again, too. Needed it.

He reached for her panties, sliding his hand down the front again, but she pulled back in a fit of giggles.

"Not fair," she said, grabbing his hand to stop its incessant wandering. "I already had my turn. Now it's yours. Close your eyes."

He did as she asked, but still grumbled.

"I don't care about fair," he said, feeling her pull away. "I just want to touch you again. Hear that sound you make when you—"

Roscoe's eyes flew open again. He couldn't help it; she'd put her mouth on him, sliding her tongue over the top of his cock as she sucked him between those luscious pink lips. He was done fighting, done joking, done doing anything other than letting his eyes drift closed and losing himself in the feel of her hot little mouth on his flesh.

With one hand flat against his abs, she gripped the base with her other hand, stroking him as she took him in deeper. Her silky hair fell forward and tickled his skin, and once again Roscoe wondered if this was all some crazy-ass dream.

She felt. So. Fucking. Amazing.

He slid a hand into her hair, cradling the back of her head, urging her to slow down. He was already so fucking close; holding back was a particularly exquisite bit of torture, but he wanted to make this moment last as long as possible.

"Fuck, Ally. That's... amazing. You're... I can't wait much longer..."

She moaned against his flesh, the vibrations of her voice making his balls tighten. Her lips, her tongue, her breath, her hands... All of it was conspiring to drive him mad with lust.

"Ally," he warned, opening his eyes to look at her. "I'm right there."

She looked up at him through her lashes, her gaze devilish. Roscoe tried to pull back, hoping to spare her, but she only sucked him in deeper, faster, her tongue pulsating against his skin...

Roscoe lost it, fisting her hair and thrusting into her mouth as he came in a white-hot rush. Ally moaned in response, sucking him until he finally stopped twitching, his body relaxing back against the blanket.

Slowly, she pulled away from him, her cheeks pink, her lips puffy. She sat up and reached behind him for the bottled waters he'd packed, passing one to Roscoe before downing her own in a few gulps.

When she finished, she lay back on the blanket next to him, staring up at the sky.

Roscoe propped himself up on his elbow, looking

down at her face. She was flush, her eyes sparkling and alive.

I did that. Put that look in her eyes. That color in her cheeks.

"Looking for those meteors?" he asked, stroking her cheek with his knuckles.

"I think I saw one." She met his eyes, her smile sweet and sincere. After a beat, she said, "Tell me what you're thinking."

"Two things. One, I don't want to wake up."

"Neither do I." Ally laughed, letting her eyes flutter closed. Roscoe resisted the urge to kiss her lashes. "So what's two?"

"Two," he said, resting a hand on her abdomen. Beneath his touch, beneath the fabric of her dress and panties, he'd spotted a bluebird inked into her skin, wings spread wide, just above the dark triangle of hair. "I so called it on the tattoos."

Ally let out a gentle sigh. "You found me out, Roscoe LeGrand."

"Are there more?"

"Wouldn't you like to know?" she teased.

Roscoe slid his hand below the hemline of her dress, inching the fabric up to reveal her creamy thighs. What he wouldn't give to press his face between them right now…

"You're not going to find them like that." She opened

her eyes and shot him a playful yet admonishing glare, then tugged the dress back down.

"Worth a shot." Roscoe shrugged. "Where's there's smoke, there's—"

"Not more tattoos."

"The bird is the only one?"

"The only one you're seeing tonight."

Fuck, she's so damn sexy.

"So you're saying there are more?"

"I'm neither confirming nor denying."

"If there *were* more, how many would there be?"

She rolled her eyes and laughed. "Fine. Six? No, seven. Wait! Eight. The bluebird was eight—I designed him right after I graduated college."

"Designed him yourself?"

Ally nodded. "Like I said, I used to paint and draw some. Nothing major. Just… little things like that."

"But not any more? Not even at work?" Roscoe asked. He knew she worked in marketing and design, but she hadn't told him much about the specifics. She didn't seem to like talking about it much.

"It's a corporate job," Ally said, "and I'm pretty much on the bottom rung of the ladder. When they do give me design work, it's mostly just fine-tuning someone else's work." She sat up again and reached for his water bottle, took another sip. "Actually, that's not entirely true. They did let me design the sign-up sheets for the office softball team. *With* clip art."

"Think you'll get back into it one day?"

Ally finished the water, then looked out across the park, smoothing her dress out over her knees. "Maybe when Reggie's older. For the foreseeable future, my priority is taking care of her. Giving her some stability. My art doesn't exactly fit into that scenario."

"Can I see the bluebird again?" he asked, scooting closer to her and putting an arm around her waist. "Please?"

Ally bit her lip, her cheeks turning pink. Roscoe was so fucking turned on he could barely think straight. Never in a million years did he think she'd actually show him again, but suddenly there she was, grabbing the hem of her dress and pulling it back, sliding it up above her hips as she rose up on to her knees. Inch by agonizing inch, she revealed the smooth skin of her thighs, and then her belly, freckled lightly from the sun. Roscoe pictured her lying out in her back yard on a beach towel, a tiny red bikini the only thing covering her perfect body.

"It's kind of faded now," she said, looking down at the tips of the wings peeking out above her panty line. "God, I haven't thought about it in forever."

"No?"

"Well, I see it, obviously. But it's just kind of there. Part of the background noise, you know?"

Roscoe shook his head, his fingers reaching across to trace the outline of the wings. "Nothing about you is background noise."

"It was always my favorite one," she admitted, lowering the dress and sitting back down on the blanket. "It used to remind me of freedom. Like, that feeling right after college when the world opens up and everything is still possible."

"Everything *is* still possible," he said. That's how it felt when he was with her. Like if she told him magic was real, he'd believe her without question.

It was strange. Despite their instant connection, and the obvious physical chemistry, he hardly knew her. And it's not like he'd been particularly unhappy with his lot in life—sure, maybe a little lonely sometimes, a little restless, just like anyone, he supposed. But those were just temporary moods. He always bounced back, always landed on his feet again.

But being with her this past week had made him feel like he'd been living his life in a haze, everything just slightly out of focus and out of reach. Then she'd come along and lit everything up, making him feel for the first time in his life like he'd been missing out on something the entire time.

Until now.

"Ally, you're—"

"Not everything," she said, her smile fading. "Sorry… What were you going to say?"

Roscoe sat up next to her and reached for her face, smoothing back that errant lock of her hair that never seemed to stay put behind her ear. Roscoe wanted to recapture that moment he'd felt a second ago, tell her just how… intense she'd made things. But she was drifting away into some other place, and Roscoe didn't want the night to turn dark and serious.

"Thanks for showing me the bird," he teased, nudging her with his knee. "Where did you say the others were?"

"Hmm. Maybe we should save those for the next date."

"Who says there's going to be another date?"

She gave a little shake of her shoulders, smoothing her hands down the front of her dress. "You want to see them, don't you?"

Roscoe unleashed a sexy growl. "You're so fucking hot."

He covered her mouth with his again, stealing her breath away with another kiss. But this time, she broke it off with a regretful sigh.

"If I could spend the whole night out here with you, I would," Ally said, glancing back up at the sky. The sun had dipped below the trees, leaving pink and orange streaks in the sky. It was probably close to eight, eight-thirty, and they still had a half-hour drive back to the city. "Alas, my coach is about to turn into a pumpkin."

Roscoe stared at her. "Sorry. I heard something about spending the night with me, and my mind sort of shut down. Could you, ah, repeat that part? About spending the night?"

Ally laughed, reaching for her purse and the phone inside. "Unfortunately I have an impatient teenager at home, and like all teenagers who think they're thirty-year-olds, she has a highly attuned bullshit detector." Ally angled her phone so he could see Reggie's text. *Where R U? X-Files starting in 20 min!*

"It's one of our new rituals," she explained. "X-Files on Netflix. I promised her I'd be back in time—she thinks I'm at a business dinner."

"Is that what you told her?"

Ally shrugged, slipping the phone back into her purse. "It seemed like the most believable story at the time. The other night, she spent the night with Clarissa, so I didn't—"

Ally's face paled, her eyes widening as she realized what she'd said.

Roscoe grinned. "Spoiler alert: Reggie told me about your connection with my PR manager."

Ally cringed. "I was wondering when that would happen. I'm sorry—I haven't said anything to her about this. I just didn't want to make things difficult for you guys at work."

At this, Roscoe laughed. "You kidding me? Clarissa thrives on making things difficult. Especially when it comes to me."

Ally narrowed her eyes, giving him a playful nudge. "I'm sure you had nothing to do with that, right? The picture of innocence?"

"Ever since I met you, anyway." Roscoe grabbed her hand, pressing a kiss to her fingers. "Speaking of Clarissa's scheming ways... Did Reggie tell you about the photo shoot yesterday?"

"Yes, and the interview thing next month. Apparently being a hockey goddess isn't enough for my kid. Now she wants to be a media darling, too." Ally laughed. "I didn't see that coming, but I guess this whole hockey thing is pushing her out of her shell."

"You okay with that?"

Ally thought about it a moment, then nodded. "She's happy, you know? That's all I want for her—all I've ever wanted—as hard as it is for me to push her out of the nest."

"Can't be easy letting her grow up." Roscoe thought again of his nieces and nephews. Regrettably, he hadn't been around in person for a lot of the antics, but his siblings told him the stories. "I've watched my brothers go through it, and now my sister's next in line. She'll be an amazing mom—I know it. But I get the sense teenaged girls are a special kind of hell."

"It has its moments," Ally admitted. "But I wouldn't trade it for the world. Unless she gets hooked in the spotlight and turns into the next Kardashian. Then I might rethink things."

"Why don't you come to the shoot?" he asked. "Some of the other parents will be there, and I'm sure Clarissa would be happy to see you. You can see your best friend at work. She's quite… intense."

"Hmm. Are you going to kiss me in front of her?" Ally slid her arms around his neck, turning her face up to look into his eyes. Batting her lashes, she said, "I won't be used as a pawn in your power games, Roscoe LeGrand."

"Wouldn't dream of it," he whispered, brushing a kiss across her lips.

They packed up the leftovers and trash, folded up the blanket, and headed out to the parking lot. While Roscoe loaded the stuff back into his SUV, Ally leaned against her car, shooting off a quick text to Reggie.

"I don't want her to worry," Ally said, looking up at Roscoe as he closed his trunk and crossed over to her car. "Knowing my kid, if I'm late for X-files, she'll start calling all the restaurants in town, looking for my imaginary business dinner."

Roscoe laughed. "I'm, uh... I'm pretty sure Reggie knows about us, Al."

"No. No way. I haven't said a word, and I've been super careful with calls and texts."

Roscoe leveled her with a glare. "This is Reggie we're talking about, right? Spunky as hell, does what she wants, highly attuned bullshit detector?"

Ally's face paled again, her eyes filling with worry as the pieces clicked into place. "Oh, God."

"You worry too much." Roscoe told her about the conversation, leaving out some of the specifics Reggie wanted to keep between them. "I really think she's okay with the idea of... us."

"Us? Roscoe..." Ally watched him for a moment, but her gaze was unreadable. She seemed to be searching for the right words—maybe the ones to let him down easy.

Fuck.

"I just meant... I..." he trailed off, afraid he'd already ruined his chances. "Is this not... what you want?"

"That's not it at all. Reggie hasn't seen me with... I mean, I haven't really been serious with anyone since... since her father, and I don't want her to be confused."

Roscoe nodded, giving her the space to continue, but she didn't. He was beginning to understand that caution was just part of the deal with Ally Heinz, and if he wanted to pursue this thing—to see where it might lead them—he had to accept that about her.

But he needed to know one thing, and he needed to know it right now, before he got any more tangled up in her life. Any more attached to this gorgeous, amazing, incredible woman who already—in a matter of days—had the power to bruise his heart.

"Is Reggie's father still… involved? With you, I mean. I get that he's her dad, but are you—"

"No." Ally looked up at him again, her eyes full of fire, full of pain. "It's not like that. Not at all."

Again, she clammed up, leaving Roscoe to fill in the blanks for himself. He felt like a dick for pushing, but he had his issues, too. Specifically, the one where he'd discovered his ex had been cheating on him with *her* ex for the last six months of their relationship. By the time he figured it out, he'd already bought the ring.

He opened his mouth to explain, but then thought better of it. Ally didn't need to hear that story. Not now.

Roscoe had believed Ally when she'd said her ex was no longer involved, but it was clear from the pain in her eyes that whatever had happened with him, she'd been deeply wounded. It stood to reason that Reggie hadn't escaped unscathed, either.

He felt a new surge of affection for them both, instinctively wanting to protect them. To keep them from re-experiencing whatever trauma they'd already endured. And that meant letting it go for now, letting Ally share things at her own pace.

And if she never felt comfortable sharing, Roscoe would have to accept that, too.

"She's your daughter, Ally," Roscoe said gently, reaching up to cup her face. "I'll support you however you want to play this. We can tell her together, or you can talk to her on your own, but I don't think we can keep sneaking around. She's already onto us, and lying to her is just going to damage her trust in you. Discretion is one thing, but I don't like the idea of starting a relationship with lies."

"Relationship?" Ally's eyes widened again. If the dating comment shocked her, the R-word apparently terrified her.

He dropped his hand, shoved it into his pocket. None of his words were coming out right all of a sudden.

"Ally," he finally said, "I don't know what's going on here, but I'm getting some serious mixed signals from you. No one's talking about a marriage proposal here, okay? I thought we were having a good time. That's all."

"You're right," she said, forcing a smile. "Roscoe... God, I don't know how to say this. I'm just... I love spending time with you. This whole thing has been amazing. We hardly know each other, yet I already feel like we've been friends forever."

"Same," he said, some of the tension dissipating.

"But I have to be honest with you," she said. "I'm not

really in the best place right now as far as relationships go." Her cheeks colored, but she pressed on. "I'm not implying that's what this is. And I'm not saying we should even have the 'what's next' conversation. I just feel like I need to be honest with you about this. I'm still dealing with my… with the past. And I just made a major life change, moving us across the country and starting a brand new job in a town where I hardly know a soul."

Roscoe smiled gently. "When you put it like that, the deck seems a little stacked."

"Exactly." She blew out a breath and hiked her purse up on her shoulder. "I'm having a lot of fun with you right now, and I'd love to… I don't know. Have more? But I can't make any promises beyond that. So if that's what you need from me, it's probably best if we go our separate ways."

Roscoe considered her words. Appreciated them, as much as he'd wished things were different. Honesty was always the best policy, whether it was his coaches critiquing his game, his Chief Executive Ball Buster reporting on their image issues, or a beautiful woman letting him know exactly where she stood.

"I hear you," he said. "And I'm good with all of that. But there are a few promises I *do* need."

Ally cocked an eyebrow, and Roscoe stepped closer, wrapping his arms around her again, burying his face in her neck. He took a deep breath, inhaling her lemony-sweet scent, then pulled back to meet her eyes.

"Can you promise me that you'll tell me if and when you're not into something—physical or otherwise? Even if you think it will hurt me?"

"Yes," she said softly.

"Can you promise you'll never keep me around out of pity?"

"Yes."

"Can you promise you'll tell me the moment you decide this isn't working for you?"

Ally nodded. "I can do that."

"Then we don't have a problem, Ally. I like you. I like spending time with you. I want to get to know you—Reggie too, whenever you're comfortable with that. I'm in this however you want it to be, no pressure. And no pressure on your end, but just so you know, I'm not the kind of guy who juggles multiple women. Not even casually."

Ally nodded, but her face was totally neutral. He waited for her to reciprocate, to reassure him that she was a one-man kind of woman, too, but it seemed she'd run out of promises for the night.

This woman is going to keep me on my toes.

He kissed her again, then stepped back as she got into her car and started it up. They'd agreed that Roscoe would follow her home to make sure she got there safe, but wouldn't come up to the house, just in case Reggie was watching.

Ally lowered the window, leaning out to offer him one last dazzling smile. Despite the seriousness of their conversation, he still couldn't believe how amazing their night had gone. How perfect she'd felt writhing beneath his touch, moaning into his mouth. And she fucking loved his cooking.

God, he was already addicted to her.

"You're lucky you've got a daughter to get home to," he said, crouching down so they were at eye level. "And that you already have your seatbelt on and the engine running. Makes it a hell of a lot harder for me to drag you back out to that field and pick up where we left off."

Roscoe kissed her again, wishing like hell he could convince her to stay a little longer, but knowing he wouldn't try. She'd shown him a glimpse of her wild side tonight, and he'd liked it. Probably more than he wanted to admit. But despite her eagerness, her playfulness, Roscoe sensed those old wounds were going to be an issue—maybe a bigger one than Ally herself even realized.

He didn't know the story about her ex. Didn't need to, really. But he knew enough to tread carefully. Hell, he'd had his own heart smashed once. Didn't want anyone opening up those old wounds, and he certainly wasn't going to do that to Ally.

So for now, he'd do what he did best: light and fun. Casual and breezy. No strings, no complications, no broken hearts.

"Here's my promise to you," he warned. Pressing a final kiss to her temple, he said, "I *will* see the rest of those tattoos."

CHAPTER SIXTEEN

From their seats above the rink, Ally and Clarissa watched in awe as Reggie and another kid demonstrated passing techniques for the camera crew down on the ice, their slick moves culminating in a slapshot that had Ally on her feet so fast, she nearly spilled her mocha. Reggie zipped around the ice in a heart-attack-inducing blur, but she was so flawless, so in control that Ally didn't have time to be nervous.

After making another impressive shot, Reggie skated over to the sidelines to answer a few questions for the reporter. Ally couldn't hear what she was saying, but the kid was beaming.

"She's amazing," Ally said. "I wish I had that kind of courage on the ice."

Clarissa, who'd had a front row seat to Ally's one and only skating disaster in college, smirked. "If you want lessons, I'm sure Eva Bradshaw would be more than happy—"

"Don't even joke about that. Pretty sure that fall scarred me for life."

"Yet you lived to tell the tale."

Ally returned her attention to Reggie. "God, she's such a natural out there."

"Surprising no one." Clarissa said, swiping through her iPad. Ally wasn't sure how all the technical stuff worked, but Clarissa was getting a direct feed from the cameras on the ice, and she'd spent most of the morning shouting orders down to the lighting crew. Sparing Ally a quick glance, she said, "I'm telling you, Al. I've caught a few of the practices, and these kids are really good. But Reggie? She was born for this sport."

"Now you sound like Roscoe." Ally laughed and settled back into her seat. "He's always saying stuff like that."

In the silence that followed, Ally realized how that must've sounded. "I mean," she added quickly, "he *did* say that a few times, back when I was first considering whether or not to let her play. I have no idea what he *always* says. I mean, it's not like I hang out in the locker room like a stalker or anything, but... Well, according to Reggie, he's been very... supportive." Ally took a a big gulp of her mocha, scalding her tongue in the process.

When she lowered her cup, Clarissa leveled her with

a piercing stare. "What's going on between you and Mr. LeGrand, exactly?"

"What? Nothing." Ally looked back out across the ice, watching Reggie skate back into the group with Henny and some of the other kids. "Why would you ask me that?"

"Would you like a list? Because I have one." Clarissa started counting off on her fingers. "One—when I got here for the shoot, you two seemed awful cozy down there."

"We were just going over the details. I wanted to know what to expect from all this, make sure Reggie was prepared for it. She's never been in the spotlight before, and I—"

"Two—you guys keep making swoony faces at each other whenever you think I'm not looking."

"No we don't. And swoony? Is that even a word?"

"It's totally a word, and you're totally doing it."

Ally scoffed. "I'm watching Reggie. It's not my fault her coach is always right there. I mean, that's kind of his job, Clarissa."

"Yes, he's always right there, all the way down by the net at the complete opposite end of the rink from where Reggie's hanging out. And three—"

"You exaggerator! That's—"

"*Three*," Clarissa said with a sly grin, "and perhaps most telling… When you say his name, your whole face starts glowing. I'm not kidding, Al. You're, like, radioactive for this guy."

"Now you're just imagining things."

"Really?" Clarissa narrowed her eyes, lowering her gaze to Ally's neck. "Am I imagining that hickey?"

"What? I don't—" Ally's fingers flew to her throat, probing all of the spots where Roscoe's lips had been last night. Jaw, neck, collarbone… God, just thinking about Roscoe's commanding, insatiable mouth on her body made Ally tremble inside. But even after nearly three weeks of secret dates and stolen kisses, there were still a few places Roscoe's lips hadn't tasted, and thinking about *those* places had the potential to work Ally into a full-on frenzy.

So she plastered on a smile and forced her thoughts back to Clarissa, who was now rolling her eyes at Ally and shaking her head.

"Girl," Clarissa said. "You totally walked into that trap. Hang on." She glanced at her iPad again, then stood up and made a series of complicated hand signals to someone on the ice. "They need to stay together down there. They're too spread out."

"You set a trap for me?" Ally laughed. "What kind of best friend are you?"

"The kind that's going to be sent into an early grave by these overgrown apes." She waved down to the ice again. "Dunn! Get your group closer to the net. We need more action shots. Goalie too." Without missing a beat, she turned back to Ally and said, "And the kind who knows you're hiding something, and you hate keeping secrets, and this one is so juicy it's probably killing you. So do us both a favor fess up."

Ally pressed her lips together, biting back another smile. Thank God Clarissa had started connecting the dots. She'd hated keeping this from her best friend.

"We're kind of seeing each other," Ally confessed. "A little bit."

"I knew it! Oh my God!"

"I wanted to tell you sooner," Ally said, "but I didn't want you to get all weird about it. Roscoe said you guys have kind of a difficult relationship. We both thought we should hold off on saying anything. Plus it's really new and I don't even know what it is or what I'm even doing half the time and I was scared to say it out loud and I just..." Ally sighed. "Why are you looking at me like that?"

Clarissa blinked, probably trying to process Ally's neurosis, which was no easy feat. "So he knew about our friendship, but I didn't know about your... whatever-ship?"

"*That's* what you're focusing on here?"

"I'm pretty sure that's a fireable best friend offense, Al."

"No, it isn't. Besides, I didn't tell him anything. Reggie mentioned it."

"Oh, that little traitor!"

"She didn't mean it, Clar. She didn't even know this was... a thing." *A whole thing...* A laugh bubbled up inside as Ally thought about Paulette and John at Wellshire. At this rate, Ally would land a starring role on that soap opera. "She's suspicious, but neither of us have confirmed or denied. I'm hoping she just drops it."

"Sure, just like she dropped the hockey thing. And the black paint thing, which she's never going to give up on—she told me all about her plan to convince you to say yes."

"You're right. I can't say no to her." Ally smiled. She was beginning to think that maybe it wasn't such a bad thing after all, letting Reggie make more of her own choices. "Anyway, I was planning to tell you. And Reggie, too, when the time is right. I just... I wanted to wait until it was a little more serious."

"How serious is it?"

"I'm not sure." Ally shrugged. "We've been on some dates."

"How many?"

"A few."

"Define 'a few.'"

"Like, eight dates," Ally said, trying to count. "Nine?

I mean, the first one doesn't even count. That was just... hockey business."

"Hockey business. Really." Clarissa pushed her glasses on top of her head, the iPad and the scene below all but forgotten. "I can't believe I actually have to press you for this information, but have you two—"

"No, we haven't." Ally rolled her eyes.

"Then what have you been doing on these eight or nine dates?"

"Well, let's see... We've played bingo with old people, gone on a wine tour, seen a few movies, taken one of those historic homes tours downtown. There's been a lot of Greek food, and Italian, and a couple walks in the park. Bowling twice." Ally's head spun just thinking about all the time they'd spent together these past few weeks; she could barely keep track of all the cute ways Roscoe continued to surprise her. "Oh, and he likes picnics—can you believe it? At sunset! During a meteor shower, which we couldn't even see because it wasn't dark enough, but he said that didn't mean it wasn't happening."

"Are you kidding me?"

"Nope. He even cooked the food himself. Some fancy lasagna thing that he wrapped in this special insulated bag to keep it hot."

Clarissa snorted. "God, I really want to vomit for saying this about LeGrand, but that's fucking *romantic*."

"Right? He's so cute, Clar. And thoughtful and patient. I'm completely insane most of the time, and he just... rolls with it. And like Savannah Hart says, you can't hide out at home under the blankets waiting for your Hogwarts letter. You need go out there and make your own kickass magic."

"That's what she says?"

"Well I'm paraphrasing, but yes! And you've said it too! How many times have you told me to dip my toe in the dating pool again?"

"Yes, with normal guys. Like IT professionals or accountants or, I don't know..." She held up her Starbucks cup. "Coffee house baristas. *Not* hockey stars."

"That is so elitist! Or, like, the opposite of elitist. Either way, totally messed up."

"It's called smart thinking, Al. I know these guys are sexy, and charming, and rich—shoot. Hang on." Something on her screen captured her attention, and she stood up again. "Marco!" she shouted. "Get another spotlight on center ice. There's a weird glare coming in on camera two." Then, back to Ally, "You can't let yourself get caught up in all that."

"I don't care about his money," Ally said.

"I'm not saying that. It's just... They seem like the whole package, right? But if something seems too good to be true, it usually is." Clarissa sat back down and flipped her iPad closed, which meant things were about to get real. "These guys know all the right things to say, all the ways to wine and dine women, all the exact perfect ways to smile and sparkle and make us feel like we're the only woman on the planet. Why, because they truly care? *Bzzzz*. Wrong answer. It's practice. Tons and tons of practice." She gestured down to the ice, where Roscoe, Dunn, and Henny were demonstrating more passing drills. "It's in their blood."

"So what? You've... practiced. More than a few times, if I recall. If I hadn't met Dan so young, I would've been practicing for the last twenty years, too." She thought of Roscoe again, the way he held her in his arms, the way his kisses seemed to devour her and protect her all at once. Her face flushed, but that was nothing compared to the fire crackling inside. Just like Savannah had said, Ally was more than ready to make her own magic. "In fact, I'm kind of looking forward to practicing again. When it comes to that strong, capable, hot-as-hell man down there, I'm planning to practice every day, five times a day, until I'm absolutely *perfect* at it."

Clarissa's mouth hung open, her eyes dancing with amusement. "Are we talking about dating, or—"

"Sex, Clarissa! I'm talking about sex! S-E-X! And there's nothing wrong with a woman who stands in her power and claims her own personal truth. And right now my personal truth is that I want hot, crazy, fierce, warrior-goddess sex with number fifty-six of the Buffalo Tempest, and I'm not going to apologize for it!"

"Preach, sister," one of the hockey moms sitting behind them said, and a some others laughed, unleashing a few good-natured catcalls. "You and me both!"

It was at that precise moment Ally realized just how loudly she'd been proclaiming that personal truth of hers, and she immediately clamped her mouth shut and snuggled down in her chair, wondering if it was possible to spontaneously combust in an ice arena.

Clarissa was trying so hard not to laugh, her lips were turning white. When she finally composed herself, her eyes turned serious once again.

"Ally," she said softly, "I'm telling you this for your own good, okay? You are not the only woman who feels that way about Mr. LeGrand or half the other single guys on the team. You need proof? Come to the games this season and see just how many women are lined up for them."

"So you're saying I can't compete with that?"

"Give me a break. You're amazing in every way, even if you do sound like a walking, talking, self-help book." Clarissa sighed, offering a warm, genuine smile. "I just don't want you to get hurt. And getting attached to a professional athlete is just... They're on the road all the time, different cities, parties, money... There's a lot to deal with. Lots of temptations. It goes to their heads. And if you ever got caught in the crossfire of something like that, it would destroy you. *He* would destroy you."

Ally thought about bingo night at Wellshire, the way Roscoe had helped everyone with their bingo cards, how they all adored him for reasons that had nothing to do with his status as an athlete and everything to do with his kind, compassionate nature. She thought about the way he insisted on opening the car door for her, and how he brought her flowers—not big showy bouquets, but normal grocery store flowers wrapped in cellophane, the kind that said hey, I was just running an errand when I saw these and thought of you. And she thought of the way he looked at her every time they saw each other after a few days had passed—like *he* was the lucky one.

"Roscoe seems pretty down to earth," Ally said. "He's just a man, Clar. Not a stereotype. Quit being so judgy."

"Roscoe? You're calling him Roscoe now? I don't even call him that, and I've been working with the team for months."

"You didn't go down on him in a field, though, that's the thing." The confession was out before Ally could stop herself. At least this time she wasn't announcing it to the whole arena.

"Allison Jennifer Heinz!" Clarissa shout-whispered. "You went down on him in a field?"

"Among other things." Ally sipped her mocha again, her tone much more casual than she actually felt. Heat bubbled up inside her as she remembered that night and every one after, a simmer quickly cranked up to boil. "He's so sweet. And he kisses like it's an Olympic level competition. And don't even get me started on the abs. My God, Clar." Ally shuddered. She literally shuddered, remembering how it had felt to run her hands over his abs, up his bare chest. She couldn't even bring herself to tell Clarissa about the other parts of his body she'd explored. He was so incredible it almost made her weep, but some things you just kept private, no matter how badly you wanted to share.

"You are a filthy, filthy woman." Clarissa let out a dreamy sigh. "And I am so jealous."

"You spend practically every day with a team of world class hockey hotties. Seems to me you'd have your pick."

Clarissa stared out across the ice, focusing her attention on a group of guys practicing in front of the net. Ally hadn't met them yet, but she thought Reggie had told her they were the defensive players.

"Clar? You with me?"

Clarissa suddenly waved a hand in front of her face, as if the very idea of hooking up with a hockey player was something to be shooed away. "That would be completely unprofessional."

"But also kind of fun." Ally grinned.

"I'm too busy for fun. *Especially* fun with hockey hotties." Clarissa huffed. "And Reggie? What are you going to tell her?"

Ally shrugged. "She insists she already knows. Keeps telling me I should just fess up, because she's mature enough to handle her—wait, let me get this quote right —"uptight, annoying, yet superhot mother going out on dates like an actual human instead of hiding out with ice cream and Netflix like a creepy lady-hermit."

"Oh, she has your number all right."

"Maybe." Ally gazed out across the rink again. Reggie and the kid she'd partnered up with earlier were showing some of the other kids a few moves, patiently repeating them in slow motion as the others tried to follow suit.

"So." Ally nudged Clarissa's knee with her own. "If Reggie's mature enough to handle it, how about my best friend? You okay with me going on a few more dates, maybe getting in some… practice time?"

Clarissa sighed and met Ally's gaze. Her eyes were shiny with emotion, and despite her earlier jokes, Ally felt her own eyes water in response.

"I don't want to see you get hurt, Ally." Clarissa reached for her hand, gave her a small squeeze. "Things are still so… so fresh. You know?"

The familiar lump lodged in Ally's throat, but she

swallowed it down. She didn't need Clarissa to remind her how fresh things were. It's not like she could go a whole day without thinking about everything she'd lost, without feeling that sharp stab of pain in her gut when she woke up in the morning and absently reached over to touch him on the other side of her bed, only to find it cold and remember all over again that he'd died.

Except... Hadn't she done just that? Gone a whole day—maybe longer—without that crushing pain?

Of course Dan was never far from her thoughts—there were a thousand little things every day that reminded her of him: Reggie had his eyes. Dan had picked out their couch, which Ally had secretly hated from day one but never had the heart to tell him. She thought of him whenever she couldn't reach something without standing on a chair, or when Reggie brought up a funny memory, or when she'd noticed the Hawaiian pizza on the Pasquale's menu and wondered whether he'd give it the thumbs-up.

But, she realized suddenly, when she tried to remember the last time she'd woken up to that awful, endless ache, she couldn't.

Ally rubbed her chest, blinking back fresh tears.

"Does he know about Dan?" Clarissa asked softly.

Ally shook her head. "It's not the kind of thing that comes up in casual conversation. Oh, hey, thanks for dinner, by the way, my husband's dead. Total freak accident. It was so messed up they didn't even bother with a lawsuit—just offered me a ton of money and a really nice floral wreath at the funeral. Can you pass the pepper?"

Clarissa was silent. When Ally looked up, she noticed Clarissa's cheeks were shiny with tears.

Ally sighed. In all her suffering over Dan's death, it was easy to forget that Clarissa had lost a friend, too. They'd all met in college, and the three of them had been extremely close. Years before his death, Clarissa had already started trying to convince Dan and Ally to move to Buffalo. Dan had always joked that he couldn't move to a city whose hockey team hadn't won a Cup in five years.

She wondered what he'd say now about her and Reggie living here. About Reggie playing for the Tempest youth team. About Ally dating the captain.

A smile tugged at her lips. The Tempest had finally won the Cup. She was pretty sure Dan would have liked that much, at least.

Resting her head on Clarissa's shoulder, Ally blew out a soft breath. "I'm sorry, Clar. I know it's hard for you, too. But I really feel like I'm ready to move on. Not to forget Dan, not to rush into something and avoid dealing with my grief. But to start looking forward instead of behind me. Does that make sense?"

"If that's how you feel, don't you think you should tell him about Dan? Talk about it a little bit?"

"I don't need to talk about it." Ally sat up again, wiping her eyes with her sleeve. "I've been *living* it for three years. Roscoe doesn't know anything about that part of my life, and I like it that way. He's the first person in three years to look at me with something other than pity."

Clarissa lowered her eyes, and Ally rushed to explain.

"I'm not talking about you. You're my best friend, Clar. You've been there for me through all of it. For Reggie, too. We never would've survived without you."

"You don't have to say that."

"But it's true. Things are different now. At least, they're starting to be."

"Ally, you're right. I *am* your best friend. I *know* you, way deep down. So don't try to put a gloss over all this and tell me everything's okay."

"It's not. Good lord, I promise it's not." Ally laughed, wiping a stray tear from her cheek. "But this thing with Roscoe? *This* is okay. Good, even. Really good."

Clarissa held her gaze a moment, then looked back out onto the rink. "But are you having fun, too? Like real, actual fun?"

"So much." And she was—Roscoe made her laugh, made her swoon. But what she didn't tell Clarissa was that since she'd started dating Roscoe, Ally felt herself expanding, opening up to life and love and passion in ways she'd never before experienced, not even with Dan. She adored her husband—he'd been kind and loving, an incredible father, and he took care of Ally and Reggie as though it had been his life's dream to do just that.

But holy hell, Roscoe was unlocking something inside her she hadn't even known existed. Something that had her—okay, maybe not *jumping* out of bed, but at least getting out of it with a smile on her face, looking forward to the day ahead.

And they hadn't even slept together yet.

"I just want this one thing," Ally continued. "One thing that's all mine, new and shiny, no old ghosts getting in the way."

Clarissa returned her smile, but her eyes were full of unwavering concern. "That's the thing about ghosts, though. Eventually, they *do* get in the way. And you don't always get to decide how and when they show up to ruin the party."

"I knew it! I so knew it!" Fresh from the locker room, Reggie clomped into the seating area with a bag of gear, a triumphant grin on her face. "You *are* dating my hockey coach."

"Reggie, what are you—"

"Jordan Pulaski, right winger? His mom was sitting

by you guys and she totally heard you talking about Roscoe! She said she even saw him kissing you when they first got here and you guys were near the box and didn't know they could see you. And then she told Jordan, and he told Nick, and Nick told me. Busted!"

"Who is Jordan Pulaski's—oh." Ally glanced behind her. The hockey moms who were sitting there during Ally's warrior goddess sex rant were noticeably absent now. "You shouldn't listen to gossip."

Next to her, Clarissa snorted into her fist. Ally elbowed her in the ribs.

"Well," Reggie said, grinning like she'd just figured out the physics of time travel, "since you're dating the coach, I was hoping you'd be okay with me maybe going out on Saturday with my... Well, he's kind of my partner on the ice. Roscoe paired us up to work with the other kids since we're kind of at the same level."

"Wait. Going out? Out where? Who is this boy?"

Reggie shrugged like it was no big deal, even though this was obviously a very big deal. To Ally, anyway. "Nick Harper," she said breezily. "He's really good, mom. And super nice. And it's mostly hockey business anyway."

At this, Clarissa let out a full-blown snort.

"Hockey business?" Ally asked. Panic rose in her throat.

"Just dinner and a movie with a few other guys from

the team and their girlfriends. And I can totally walk from our house, so you don't even have to worry about me getting in a car with a bunch of kids, and I would definitely be back by curfew."

"You've got this all figured out, huh?" Ally asked.

"Just… A bunch of them were talking about getting together, and I thought it sounded fun. We never really get to hang out outside of practice."

Ally considered it. There was a local movie theater a few blocks away from the house, and lots of little restaurants and cafes nearby. It wasn't an entirely ridiculous request.

"Please, Mom? I won't even be the only girl there. There's like, ten of us altogether."

Ally nodded. Maybe she felt guilty about lying to her daughter for so long about Roscoe. Maybe it was just Roscoe's big-hearted influence on her. Or maybe she was starting to shed some of her fear, just a little bit.

Either way, Ally suddenly found herself smiling. "Alright, Reg. I guess that would be okay."

"Really?"

"Yes, really." Ally laughed. "But he needs to meet you up at the house first so I can meet him properly—not in his hockey uniform. Do we have a deal?"

"Deal!" Reggie practically through herself at Ally, wrapping her into a tight hug. "Thank you thank you thank you, you are the *best* mom ever!"

"I'll remember you said so the next time I ask you to clean up your room or do the dishes." Ally dug her keys out of her purse and handed them over. "Go put your stuff in the car. I'll take you home on my way back to the office."

"Cool! Bye Aunt Clarissa!" She hugged Clarissa, hefted her bag over her shoulder, and scooted out toward the exit.

As soon as Reggie was gone, Clarissa said, "Who are you, and what have you done with Ally?"

"Stop. I'm not that bad."

Clarissa huffed. "You're really okay with this?"

"Not... exactly." Ally wrapped her hands around her mocha, unable to hide her devious smile as she scanned the ice for another glimpse of her man. "But don't worry. I have a plan."

CHAPTER SEVENTEEN

"Of all the things we've done to help a teammate get some ass," Henny said, "this is definitely the craziest."

Roscoe clamped a hand around the back of Henny's neck. "This has nothing to do with getting ass. Say it with me, just so we're clear."

"This has nothing to do with getting ass," Henny parroted.

From his other side, Dunn chimed in. "But if our boy doesn't get some after this—"

"Seriously?" Roscoe smacked them both. "We're almost at the door. Pull yourselves together."

The two of them were laughing their balls off, but Roscoe was nervous as hell. Why the fuck had he brought them along? Ally had asked him for a little moral support with this whole Reggie and Nick thing, and Roscoe had every intention of handling it on his own. But then he'd made the mistake of telling the guys that Nick had asked Reggie out, and of course they pounced.

Roscoe never should've opened his big dumb mouth.

Hindsight, man. What a waste.

Roscoe jammed his finger into the bell, shooting a final glare at his boys. Seconds later, Ally opened the door, clearly shocked to find three of the Tempest's starting lineup standing on her front porch.

"I brought backup," Roscoe said, running a hand through his hair. "Guess I should've called first."

"No, it's totally fine!" Ally beamed, and Roscoe blew out a breath. God, she was beautiful. God, he wanted to knock the guys off the porch, scoop Ally up in his arms, and carry her right inside to her bedroom...

"I'm Kyle Henderson," Henny said, shattering Roscoe's fantasy. "Henny. And this is Walker Dunn."

The guys, whose huge frames took up the entire space of the porch, held out their hands to shake.

"Oh, I met your mother, Walker," Ally said warmly.

Dunn smiled at her. "I heard all about it. She keeps asking when you'll come around again."

"Tell her I have to stock up on boinkers first," Ally said.

At this, Henny snorted. The grown-ass man actually snorted. Roscoe shot him another glare that he hoped conveyed his most intimate thoughts—namely: *I'm going to murder you in your sleep and make it look like an accident.*

"Ally?" a woman's voice called out. "Is that LeGrand?"

Roscoe cocked his head. He knew that voice. His balls knew that voice. Like Pavlov's fucking dog, they shrunk on command.

"Clarissa's here?" he asked.

"She insisted. Reggie's first date and all." Ally wrinkled her nose, opening the door wider and gesturing the men inside, where Clarissa stepped into the foyer with a glass of wine in hand.

"LeGrand, Dunn, and Henderson," she said. "The three amigos. Fancy meeting you here."

"More like *weird*," Reggie said, stepping into the entryway behind Clarissa. She blinked up at the three beasts at her front door, her eyes going from curious to concerned in a flash. "Oh, no! Did we have something on the calendar today? I didn't... I'm so sorry. I could get my skates, and—shoot, I should text Nick. I don't think he—"

"No, it's nothing like that," Roscoe said, offering a smile. He'd hoped Ally might tell her that he'd be coming by, but apparently she'd wanted the element of surprise. Poor kid had no idea what she was in for. "Though I appreciate your dedication to the game."

Reggie nodded. Her hair, which was normally shoved

under her helmet or matted to her head from a hard practice, was slicked back in a high ponytail that curled at the ends. One eye was all done up with pink eyeshadow and black eyeliner that made her look about twenty years old, and she had some kind of torture device in her hand that Roscoe thought had something to do with eyelashes. Or maybe it was a curling iron? Or possibly a can opener. What the fuck did he know?

"So… What *are* you guys doing here?" Reggie asked.

All three men answered at once.

Roscoe: "We were in the neighborhood—"

Dunn: "Your mom—"

Henny: "Harper needs his ass whooped."

"You're… You guys are joking, right?" Reggie's eyes widened. In a blur, she spun around to face Ally, threatening to erupt. "Tell me you didn't hire my hockey coaches to go all good-cop, bad-cop on Nick. Because if you did, oh my God, you are such a traitor, and I'm never speaking to you again."

"Honey, it's not a big deal." Ally's tone was calm and gentle, but Roscoe could've sworn she was biting back a smile. After all her worrying about Reggie on the ice, and all Reggie's stubborn-headed ways, Roscoe got the feeling Ally was enjoying this little power play. "They're here to see you kids off tonight, just like Aunt Clarissa."

Reggie rolled her eyes. "Right. Because *that's* normal."

"Would you rather cancel your plans?" Ally asked, her tone suddenly cool. Roscoe was relieved he wasn't on the receiving end of that iciness—damn, his woman could probably give Clarissa a run for her ball-busting money. "I'm sure Nick could find another girl to ask to the movies. Maybe someone older than fifteen, or someone who doesn't have a mother and an aunt and a coach who all care about her and want to be sure she's ready for the responsibility and privilege of dating."

"*Two* coaches who care," Dunn piped up.

Henny grinned. "And one who's just looking for a reason to give Harper a hard time."

"This is so unfair," Reggie grumbled, but the kid was clearly out of her element here.

Shooting a final death glare at Ally, Reggie stomped up the stairs to finish getting ready, and Ally invited Roscoe and crew to settle into the living room while she got drinks. Clarissa had already staked out a prime position in the armchair.

"So this is a group thing, then?" Roscoe asked, taking up one end of an L-shaped sofa. Dunn and Henny filled out the rest.

Clarissa laughed. "You're the one who brought the calvary."

"I didn't bring you, though," he said.

"I'm just here to make sure you boys stay out of trouble." Clarissa made a swirling motion with her finger, pointing at each of them in turn. "When you three get together off the ice, bad things happen. Very bad things."

Fucking Clarissa. Roscoe figured Ally had finally confessed their relationship to Clarissa that day at practice—he'd seen them sitting together during the media dog-and-pony show. He could only imagine what she'd told Ally about him—about his past indiscretions, his reasons for getting involved in the youth clinic in the first place. Then again, Ally hadn't given him the boot yet, so that had to count for something.

Still. *Fucking Clarissa.*

"I'm sure we all feel a lot safer now that the fun police are here," Roscoe said.

"Fun police?" Clarissa laughed, but it wasn't a happy one. "After the year you've had, you're lucky Gallagher hired a PR firm and not a parole officer."

Roscoe gritted his teeth, biting back a retort. She may have been the Ball Buster in Chief to Roscoe and the boys, but she was also Ally's best friend, which meant there had to be *something* good in that shriveled-up heart of hers.

"God, I need a new job," Henny said, blowing out a breath. "No offense, but this is all starting to feel like a big fat circle-jerk."

"Maybe you need different friends?" Clarissa suggested.

"Speaking of circle-jerks," Roscoe said, shooting a pointed glare at Clarissa, "anyone seen Kenton today?"

Clarissa lowered her eyes and shifted in her seat, but didn't say a word.

Finally found the magic words to shut her the hell up. Score!

"I'm sorry to drag you guys into this." Ally emerged from the kitchen with a few beers and a tray of chips and salsa. "This is just something I'd always assumed her dad would do, you know? Suss out the boys, make sure their intentions were honorable."

"Oh, they're never honorable," Henny said, reaching for a beer and twisting off the cap. "You gotta know that going in."

Roscoe elbowed him. "Not all of us are mouth-breathing meatheads."

Clarissa snorted.

"Yeah we are," Henny said. "Especially at that age."

"Gotta go with Hen on this one," Dunn said. "As far as teenaged girls are concerned, there's no such thing as a nice guy."

Ally slumped into a chair next to Roscoe's side of the couch, her eyebrows pinched together tightly. She looked like she was about to be sick.

"Don't listen to them," Roscoe said. Instinctively he reached for her knee, but then remembered Tweedle Dee and Tweedle Dumb on the couch next to him, and knew they'd make a big deal out of it. So he gave her an awkward shoulder punch instead. "Just leave it to us, Al. We'll set the boy straight."

Ally nodded stiffly, reaching for a chip from the tray she'd set on the coffee table. She tried to laugh at Dunn and Henny's jokes, tried to chat with Clarissa, tried to smile when Roscoe caught her eye, but she was nervous as hell. She'd been nibbling on the same chip for ten straight minutes when the doorbell finally rang.

Ally looked like she'd just seen a ghost.

"I got it." Roscoe rose from the couch. "You guys sit tight."

He headed into the foyer just as Reggie bolted down the stairs.

"Easy there, freight train." Roscoe stopped her in her tracks two steps before the bottom. She was almost eye-level there, and he could see she'd put on the rest of her makeup, added a little more eyeliner. She was trying to look so grown up, but to Roscoe, she still seemed so young, so innocent.

He felt a little kick to his heart that went beyond the feelings of a concerned coach looking out for one of his players. In their time together on the ice, he'd really come to care for Reggie, both as a player and as Ally's daughter. He wanted her to be okay. To not let anything bad happen to her.

"Um, Roscoe?" she asked, standing on her tiptoes to see past him. "Can I get the door?"

"No." Resting his giant hands on her shoulders, Roscoe looked her square in the eyes. "Don't rush this, forty-four. Let sixty-one sweat it out."

She folded her arms across her chest. "Isn't that kind of rude?"

"Not in this situation. You don't want him to think you're too excited to see him."

"But I *am* excited," she said, bouncing on her toes. "Nick is, like, basically amazing. Not only is he awesome at hockey, but he's really funny. And sweet. And I really, really like him. Okay?" She beamed, despite the fact that Roscoe was blocking her way. God, she looked happy.

Harper, if you hurt her...

"Nick doesn't need to know you feel that way," Roscoe said. "Let him wonder a bit. Trust me on that."

"You guys are being weird."

"Humor us. We're old and our hearts are frail."

Reggie rolled her eyes. Unlike her mother's eyes, Reggie's were bright blue, but the gesture was almost identical. "So, do I look okay? Is this too casual? I can't trust Mom to give me an honest opinion. If she had her way, I'd be wearing a turtleneck and baggy pants."

Roscoe smiled. She had on jeans and some kind of tight sparkly shirt with flowers and sequins on it. Roscoe had no idea how teenagers dressed for dates these days, but one thing was certain: "You need a sweater, kiddo."

"Oh, great. You're channeling Mom." Reggie sighed. "It's summer."

"Sure, but once the sun goes down—"

"It will be ten o'clock, and I'll be home already. My curfew is nine-thirty."

The doorbell rang again. Reggie looked like she was about to explode.

"Just a sec," Roscoe called out toward the door. Then, to Reggie, he said, "What did I say about humoring a few old guys? Go upstairs and get a sweater. Double-check your hair or something."

"Why?" Her hands flew to her hair. "Is it bad?"

"No, that's not... Look. Just give me a few minutes to talk to Nick. Can you do that for me?"

Reggie sighed. "Can you promise not to go too hard on him? To be nice and not super weird or embarrassing?"

"I think I can manage that," he said.

"Fine." Reggie huffed, but she was smiling as she turned around and bounded back up the stairs.

Roscoe watched her go, her ponytail swishing across her shoulders, and that thing in his heart jerked again. She reminded him of his sister, Lena, back when she'd endured the same kind of first-date torture they were subjecting Reggie to now. Reggie reminded him of his nephews, too—of how much love he had for them, how every new addition to his ever-growing family had filled his heart nearly to bursting, only for another kid to come along and make it grow even larger, even fuller. Roscoe had never known how boundless the human capacity for love was until his siblings had started blessing him with nephews and nieces.

And then he'd met Ally and Reggie, and his heart had expanded even more.

He could only imagine what it would be like to have his own children one day.

Before Roscoe could go too far down the road to his imaginary happily ever after, the bell rang again.

Squaring his shoulders, Roscoe stepped down the stairs and reached for the front door. He wrenched it open to find a very surprised, very confused, and slightly startled boy staring up at him with wide eyes and a gaping mouth.

"Um… Roscoe?" Nick asked.

"Nick Harper." Roscoe grinned, folding his arms across his chest. "We need to talk."

CHAPTER EIGHTEEN

"Are you okay?" Clarissa asked, pressing a hand to Ally's abdomen. "Or are your ovaries melting?"

Ally laughed and swatted her hands away, but Clarissa had totally called it.

The two of them had escaped into the kitchen under the guise of refilling their wine glasses, and now they huddled near the archway, spying on the scene unfolding in the family room. Poor Nick had looked like the proverbial deer in headlights when Roscoe had first brought him inside, but thirty seconds into the so-called "straight talk," Walker and Henny discovered the Xbox One.

Ally had worried Reggie would be upset when she came downstairs and found her coaches monopolizing her date in an intense game of *NHL 17*, but—true to her hockey-loving roots—the kid inserted herself right in the middle of it all, grabbing a controller and shouting at the screen like the rest of them.

That had been an hour ago.

"So much for the good-cop, bad-cop routine, huh?" Ally laughed, noticing with a sense of pride that the kids were currently kicking ass against the guys.

Clarissa only smirked. "And so much for pretending this thing with Roscoe is even *remotely* casual, because girl, if you could see the sappy look in your eyes right now…"

Ally gave her another playful swat. "As if you're so immune to the charms of sexy hockey players. Give me a break. You just like giving them a hard time."

Clarissa shrugged and sipped her wine, ducking Ally's gaze in a way that felt almost evasive. It was odd, but before Ally could press her on it, Clarissa was looking up at her again. "Okay, I fully admit that Roscoe and I have an antagonistic relationship, and maybe I've been a little harder on him than necessary, which I have a tendency to do when I feel intimidated."

Ally pressed a hand to her chest. "Wait. Are you actually admitting a character flaw?"

"Don't be ridiculous. I'm just saying that maybe Roscoe… isn't exactly horrible."

"Isn't exactly horrible?" Ally cracked up. "Is this you gushing?"

"I'm just saying that I wouldn't blame you if you

wanted to have his babies." She gestured with her glass toward the family room. "That is pretty much the most adorable thing I've seen all month. If I had a camera crew here right now I would totally—*wait*." Her face lit up with that look she got whenever one of her genius media ideas struck. She set down her glass and reached for her phone.

"Oh no you don't." Ally laughed, snatching away Clarissa's phone and tucking it into her back pocket. "Not everything has to be turned into a media opportunity."

"No, but as far as opportunities go, this is a pretty damn good one." Clarissa sighed, reclaiming her wine and gazing back out into the family room. "Three strong, sexy NHL guys playing video games with the kids from their clinic. *Hockey* video games besides! God, this stuff practically writes itself."

"Let's just enjoy all this ovary-melting goodness while it lasts—no cameras for once."

"I'll remember that when you try to take pictures of the kids before they leave on their date."

Ally gasped. "What date? They're not going anywhere—they're having a blast. That's why this is so brilliant. Even better than Roscoe and the boys trying to put the fear of God into Nick. He can't do anything stupid if they don't even leave the house, right?"

Clarissa put her arm around Ally. "Poor, sweet Allison Heinz. So innocent. So hopeful. So dumb."

"Hey!"

"As soon as this game ends, the kids are going to hightail it out of here, because no matter how much fun they're having right now, it would be *way* more fun without any adults around. And you—"

"But they're having fun!"

"And *you*," Clarissa continued, "are going to give them your blessing and let them go, because dating is all part of growing up and experimenting and figuring out what you want and becoming a decent, compassionate, loving person instead of a bitter, awkward, shut-in who's highlight of the week is when the UPS guy comes to the door with the new vibrator she ordered. Cheers!"

Clarissa clinked her glass to Ally's and winked.

"Excuse you." Ally frowned. "That is *not* the highlight of my week. For your information, I don't even own a vibrator."

"I was talking about *my* week. And what? We need to fix that." Then, gazing out at Roscoe again, "Or maybe he'll take care of that for you."

"Here's to hoping."

"Wake up, ref!" Reggie shouted at the screen. "That was totally high-sticking!"

Walker laughed. "Sorry, kiddo. Ref didn't call it, it never happened."

"You guys cheat like—oh my God!" Reggie was incredulous. "Did you just score?"

"Not sure," Walker said in mock innocence. "Is that what that flashing light means?"

"I'm gonna need more snacks to deal with this level of cheatery." Reggie laughed, reaching into the bowl on the coffee table for a handful of chips.

"Don't worry, forty-four," Roscoe said. "Grandpa Dunn over here is getting close to retirement. Soon you'll be skating circles around his old decrepit ass."

"I already do," Nick said.

The kids cracked up.

Everyone was having such a great time—especially Reggie. Ally couldn't remember the last time she seemed so… joyful. That was the word for it. Not just happy like she'd been on the ice that first day of the clinic, but truly content, shining from the inside out. Despite the fact that three celebrity NHL players were crowded onto the couch in their family room, and her first date had been totally hijacked, and her mother and aunt were sipping wine and spying on them from the kitchen, the whole thing felt so normal. So nice.

And Roscoe? God, he was good with Reggie. So patient and kind and funny and sweet and just… perfect.

When he turned his head and caught Ally staring, he winked and smiled, and Ally felt her cheeks warm.

"Look at you guys!" Clarissa laughed softly. "You've got him wrapped around your little finger."

Ally waved away her words and headed back to the fridge in search of some more snacks, but Clarissa would not let it go.

"And," she went on, "I suspect you're quite snugly wrapped around his."

Ally handed her two avocados and a red onion, then continued rooting around for some queso she'd bought the other day. "What if I am?"

"As much as it pains me to say this," Clarissa said with a sigh, "Roscoe *is* super sweet with you and Reg."

"And not horrible, as we've already established."

"He obviously cares about you both."

"Eat it, punks!" Henny shouted from the living room, his declaration followed by whoops and cheers from Walker and Roscoe. The kids groaned in unison.

"We were robbed," Nick said.

"Nah," Walker said. "You just got your butts whipped because you're two young punks who don't understand the finer points of the game."

"No way," Reggie said. "We totally let you win on account of your decrepit frail hearts."

Ally laughed. Queso in hand, she closed the fridge and turned her attention back to her friend, raising her voice to be heard over the commotion of the game. "I care about him, too, Clar. So what do you have to say about that?"

"I'm only going to say one thing," Clarissa said.

"When have you ever only said one thing?" Ally asked, pointing at the pantry. "Grab the other bag of tortilla chips for me. Third shelf down."

Clarissa got the chips and a big bowl to dump them in. "Hey, I've kept my mouth at least partially shut on occasion."

"Which occasion?"

"I don't recall at the moment, but if you let me check my phone, I'm sure it's in my calendar somewhere."

"I'm sure it is." Grinning, Ally reached up into the cupboards above the dishwasher for a couple of bowls, glad she'd unpacked most of the kitchen stuff. She poured out some queso into one, then got to work cutting an avocado. "You might as well spit it out. Don't keep me in suspense." When Ally looked up again, she was surprised to find that the playful glint in Clarissa's eyes had turned a little more serious.

"I'm worried that this little crush of yours is going to get you in serious trouble, Ally," Clarissa said. Then her smile returned. "But if he truly makes you happy, and he continues to be... not horrible... I'm totally on board with it. I mean that." Clarissa shook her head, but she was still smiling. "Who knows? Maybe he'll even get out on skates one of these days."

"Ha! Don't hold your breath."

"Noted." Grabbing her purse off the counter and her phone from Ally's pocket, Clarissa shot another faux-warning glance at Ally. "Just behave yourself. Okay?"

"Whatever *that* means." Ally rolled her eyes and laughed. "You taking off?"

"Yeah, I need to head back to the office. I've got a… a thing." Clarissa checked her phone, then leaned in for hug. Lips close to Ally's ear, she said, "Call me later. I want all the details. Otherwise I'm sending the UPS guy over."

"What details?" Roscoe asked. Both women jumped at the sound of his voice, deep and gravelly and much closer than Ally realized.

"Roscoe!" She fumbled one of the avocados, sending it rolling across the kitchen floor to his feet. "I thought… Aren't you playing with the kids?"

"Game over," he said, bending down to scoop up the avocado. "Your kid and her boyfriend got iced."

"No time for a rematch?" Ally asked.

"Nah. They need to head out or they'll miss their movie."

"Bye, Mom!" Reggie zoomed by the archway, practically dragging Nick out by the hand. "Be back by curfew!"

All the old nerves and worries came rushing back. Clarissa was right—they were still planning to go out after all. What if they got into an accident on the walk over? What if Reggie choked at the restaurant—did Nick know first aid? What if he tried to take advantage of her, or did something to embarrass her in front of the other kids?

And who were these other kids? Nick seemed nice, but how could Ally be sure the others wouldn't mistreat her?

What if Reggie was growing up faster than Ally could handle it?

No. She couldn't go through with this.

Ally opened her mouth to stop them, but Roscoe was already on it.

"Just a minute there, Mr. Harper," he said, stopping both kids in their tracks. Reggie pressed her lips together, probably to keep herself from saying something smart-assy, but Nick got that same deer-in-headlights look again.

"Where are you taking her for dinner?" Roscoe asked.

Nick shrugged. "Um… Applebees?"

"Umapplebees?" Roscoe said. "Never heard of it." He pulled out his wallet, handed Nick a few bills. "Class it up, Harper."

"I can't take your—"

"You can, and you will," Roscoe said. "Consider it an investment."

"Is that, like, legal?"

Roscoe chuckled softly. "As long as I'm not signing you to the Tempest roster, I don't think you need to worry about it. Dinner's on me tonight, okay?"

"You think I have a chance to get on the roster?" Nick's face lit up like a Christmas tree, and so did Reggie's, and immediately Ally relaxed.

Nick really was a good kid—Ally could tell just by the way he looked at Reggie, how respectful he'd been even with the coaches who'd clearly ambushed him today. And here in the kitchen, standing amongst the big, brooding hockey players, both kids looked even younger than they were. Even more innocent.

Ally sighed, trying to hold on to her daughter's light. To that big beautiful smile, stretched from ear to ear. *Let Reggie have this day…*

Henny jumped in. "You need to finish school first, and work your ass off on the ice for the next several years. But it's not out of the realm of possibility."

"Assuming you treat Reggie right," Roscoe added. "I don't think I need to elaborate on what I mean, do I?"

Nick nodded, meeting Roscoe's intent gaze. "No, sir."

"Are we clear?" Roscoe asked. "Because I don't care if you are one of my best players, Harper. Anything goes sideways tonight, and you won't have to worry about planning any more dates. The only thing you'll be getting frisky with is the bench."

"Mom!" Reggie gasped.

Ally only smiled. "Anything goes sideways tonight," she said, "and Roscoe and the bench will be the least of Nick's problems. Clear?"

"Yes, sir," Nick said. "Um. Sirs. And ma'am," he added, smiling nervously at Ally. "Nothing will go sideways—I promise. We're going to dinner with a few other kids from the team, then the movie starts at six forty-five. I know we said we'd come home straight after, but there's an ice cream place next to the theater, and I'd love to take her there before we come back, if that's okay with... everybody?" He looked around at the adults in the room, his eyes pleading and nervous and cute.

"Please, Mom?" Reggie asked softly, bouncing on her toes. Ally could not remember the last time the kid bounced so much in a single day.

Ally pressed her lips together and closed her eyes, hearing the familiar battle in her head—do I let her do this, or do I put my foot down and keep her safe in her bubble? It wasn't the hockey debate this time, but it may as well have been. It all came down to the same question: *Am I ready to let her grow up? To let her have a normal life, even after everything we've been through?*

But this time, the answering voice was loud and clear.

You are. Especially *after everything you've been through. She deserves this happiness. She needs it.*

Yes, Ally realized. It was one thing to shut herself in, to avoid risks, to shield her own heart from attachments.

But she couldn't do that to Reggie. Her daughter deserved to be happy, to grow up loved and supported in everything she chose to do. Letting her go on her first date with Nick may be a small thing, but it was an important one, something Ally could give her without a fight. Without all the usual ultimatums and anxieties and arguments she typically heaped on her poor daughter.

Ally opened her eyes and smiled at the kids, tugging on one of Reggie's curls. She was growing up so fast... But as much as Ally wished she could hit the pause button, she knew she couldn't stop time. All she could do was help Reggie make the most of it.

Blinking back tears, Ally said, "That's fine by me, Nick. Just have her home by nine-thirty, quarter to ten. Sound good?"

Nick beamed. "Absolutely, Mrs. Heinz."

Reggie was still smiling. She tugged Nick's hand again and turned to go, but then turned back just before they reached the door. "Thanks, Mom," she whispered, pulling Ally into a quick hug. "Love you." Then, to Clarissa, "Bye, Aunt Clar. See you soon!"

Clarissa waved. "Have fun, kids."

With the kids heading out, the guys followed behind, waving goodbyes to Ally and Clarissa and stealing a few more chips for the road. Ally pretended not to notice the teasing smirks they shot in Roscoe's direction on their way out.

Roscoe was still holding the runaway avocado, and now he set it on the counter, leaning so close to Ally she could smell his familiar, intoxicating scent. Immediately her heart rate kicked up.

"So," he said, his eyes bouncing between Ally and Clarissa. "What were these details you two were talking about?"

Ally swallowed hard. She'd hoped he'd forgotten. "Clarissa was just asking about… bingo. I was telling her how I won that time at Wellshire."

Roscoe smirked. *Damn it*, he was so freaking adorable. And so not buying this. "Bingo details, huh?"

"It's a pretty detail-oriented game, Mr. LeGrand," Clarissa said dryly. "Lots of things to keep track of. *Balls* and such."

Oh my God, I'm going to murder her!

"Too bad you can't stick around, huh Clarissa," Ally said.

"What?"

"You have to go. You have that thing."

"Right, that thing." Her eyes widened. "Oh! I *do* have a thing. You two have fun doing your… thing. Whatever that thing may be." Then, with a final smile and a sing-song lilt in her voice, "As long as it doesn't end up on YouTube!"

Ally was definitely going to murder her. Ally would end up in jail, and poor Reggie would be completely parentless and forever traumatized, but Ally could not let this mortal embarrassment go unpunished.

But Clarissa was safe for the moment—Ally had much bigger problems.

Starting with the fact that for the next four hours, she'd be all alone in the house with Roscoe "my dimple will melt your panties and your ovaries in a single bound" LeGrand, who was currently looking at her like he wanted to devour her.

And after weeks of kissing and touching and coming close but not quite all the way, Ally was more than ready to let him do it.

CHAPTER NINETEEN

"Learn something new every day." Roscoe grabbed Ally's hands and backed her up against the kitchen counter, enjoying the new blush darkening her cheeks. "You've got a crush on me."

"What?" she said. Her perfect breasts brushed against his chest, rising and falling with her breath. "I think you misheard."

"Doubt it." Roscoe slid a hand behind her, palming her ass. His fingers toyed with the frayed denim of her cutoff shorts, grazing the skin beneath the curve of her ass. Damn, she was so soft. "Oh, I get it. I'm totally crushable."

"Full of yourself, maybe. But crushable?" She wrinkled her nose and laughed, awkward as hell, and Roscoe was a damn goner.

Everything got real quiet after that, no sounds but the

soft ticking of the bird clock on the wall and Ally's steady breathing. She was still grinning, her eyes catching the late afternoon sunlight that filtered in through the kitchen windows.

"What are you thinking?" she finally whispered.

"You're so beautiful it hurts." Then, because the lump in his throat choked off anything else he might've said, he kissed her.

Ally melted against him, her arms looping around his neck as their bodies came together, warm in the summer heat. The taste of her sweet mouth drove him wild; he'd never get enough of it. Of her.

"Is she coming back?" he whispered, barely breaking their kiss.

"Clarissa? No. And the kids won't be back for hours. And I've got no plans, just in case you were wondering."

"Good." Roscoe grinned. "So let me tell you what I'd like to do."

Ally shivered, breath catching as he ran his thumb along her jaw, his fingers sliding into her hair. He didn't trust his voice not to betray everything he was feeling inside. So he leaned in close, his lips against her ear as her hair tickled his nose, and whispered everything on his mind.

"I'd like to run my fingers over every inch of your body," he said, "starting with your shoulders and working my way down to your breasts. I'd like to take your nipples into my mouth, one at a time, and suck on them until you beg me to stop. I'd like to slide my hand between your thighs and find out just how wet you are for me. And after that, I'd *really* like to lay you out on the bed and fuck you with my mouth until you're hot and drunk and dizzy from the pure pleasure of it."

He waited a beat, gave her a minute to catch her breath. Then he undid the top button of her blouse, skimming his fingers over her collarbone. "But first I need to take off your clothes."

Ally nodded, breath ghosting over her lips, her eyes dazed and dreamy as Roscoe stroked her skin.

"It's been a long time since…" she began, fighting off another shiver, "…since I've done anything for… for the pure… whatever…"

Roscoe let out a low chuckle at her sudden inability to speak. "Pleasure isn't a dirty word, gorgeous. Not unless you want it to be."

Ally closed her eyes and moaned at his touch, a desperate, needy sound that made his dick throb. "I want it to be," she whispered, her nipples pebbling beneath the thin fabric of the blouse. "Please."

"Well, since you asked *so* nicely…" Roscoe unfastened her remaining buttons to reveal the lacy black edge of her bra. The soft, full mounds of her breasts peeked out over the top, an invitation Roscoe would *not* refuse. He leaned forward, brushing his nose across the lace and her silky-soft skin, inhaling the sweet lemon-sugar scent that was all Ally.

She moaned again, sending another pulse of heat to his dick. His tongue darted out from between his lips, tasting her soft flesh.

"Sorry," he said, "but this shirt has to go." He slid his hands beneath the hem and lifted it over her head, tossed it onto the kitchen table behind them. He palmed her breasts through the lacy bra, her nipples poking against the fabric, stiffening further at his touch. Unclasping the bra and letting it drop to the floor, he took the weight of her breasts in his hands, savoring the sensation and warmth.

Leaning down to taste her again, Roscoe captured one stiff peak in his mouth, rolling the other between his fingers until Ally was panting and weak.

But she wasn't begging him to stop. Just the opposite.

"More," she said, arching her back and pressing her breast against his mouth. "Harder."

He obeyed, flicking her nipple with his tongue, then sucking it into his mouth, grazing her lightly with his teeth. His cock throbbed inside his jeans, aching with need, but it wasn't about Roscoe right now. This was all for her. His woman.

Dropping to his knees, he unfastened and unzipped her shorts, sliding them down her hips and pressing his face to the damp silk of her panties. Heat radiated from between her thighs, her scent enveloping him as he bit and tongued the fabric, teasing her. Ally fisted his hair, tugging him closer as he slid the panties down to her feet, leaving her exposed and vulnerable and so, so sexy.

Jesus, he wanted to bury his tongue inside her. Worship her flesh until she couldn't remember anything but his lips on her sweet pussy.

"Roscoe..." His name was a whisper on her lips, floating out like a feather as she leaned back against the counter. He kissed her thigh. Her hip bone. Her belly. Slowly, he worked his way up her body until he was standing again, taking her face in his hands.

"You take my breath away," he said, his gaze lingering.

Ally smiled, a little shy, then turned slowly, letting him see her fully, showing off the remaining tattoos Roscoe had only glimpsed in pieces before now—a wing here, a flower petal there, a heart and swirl over there. But now he took it all in, the tapestry of her life painted on the canvas of her skin, and it was just as gorgeous and alive as she was.

Delicate flowering vines crept up the left side of her body, starting at her hip and climbing the curve of her waist close to her back, then curving back along the outer edge of her ribcage, slinking up the side of her luscious breast. Two interlocking crescent moons graced the back of her thigh. The bottom of her shoulder blade bore a stylized heart pierced with three swords, the tips blooming not with blood, but flower petals that fell into a garden of tangled vines. Beneath that was a poem:

> Reclaim your wild woman self,
> for she calls to you
> in every beat of your heart.

"Did you write this?" he asked, tracing the words with his fingers.

Ally nodded, turning around to meet his gaze again. "When I was twenty. I had it tattooed on my body so I would never, ever forget." She gave him a sad smile. "Maybe I should've had it tattooed on the front, where I could see it."

Sunlight still streamed in through the window behind her, lighting her up again, and somewhere in the distance a group of neighborhood kids screeched and laughed, probably running through a lawn sprinkler, and Roscoe couldn't remember a moment in his life that had felt so singularly perfect.

Roscoe took her face in his hands, searching. Was she scared? Embarrassed? Hopeful? He didn't want to mess this up. Didn't want to pressure her.

"Ally?" he whispered.

"I'm here," she whispered back. She was trembling

now, her eyes shining with sudden emotion, raw and vulnerable. But her smile was warm and inviting.

"For the record, you're the wildest, most passionate woman I've ever met."

This got a laugh. "Maybe you need to get out more."

"I was thinking I need to stay in more. Preferably with you." He kissed her, soft and sweet. "But before we take this any farther, I need to know you're okay with this."

She looked up at him again with those beautiful brown eyes, and Roscoe swore his heart stopped. How had this even happened? One minute he was wrangling a bunch of kids on the ice, trying to figure out how to get back into his coach's good graces, and the next she came charging into his life. No matter what she said next, no matter what happened or didn't happen today, nothing would ever be the same for him.

He was falling in love with her. That's all there was to it.

"I told you it's been a while for me," she said. "Being with a man."

Roscoe nodded.

"You were worth the wait," she whispered, pulling him close. "But Roscoe?"

"Yes, beautiful?"

"I don't think I can wait much longer."

Roscoe laughed, wrapping his arms around her and

lifting her onto the countertop. Her legs wound around his hips, and he kissed her again, hot and hard and intense. He felt her go boneless, melting into his embrace.

He was losing control; he felt it spiral out from inside him and slip away, knowing there wasn't a damn thing he could do about it. Ally was all that mattered now. The silk of her hair brushing against his cheeks, the whisper of her breath as she panted and sighed. Wet heat emanated from between her thighs and warmed his belly, making his cock throb. She leaned forward and reached for the button on his jeans, then the zipper, nimble fingers sliding down to glide over his shaft.

Fuck, she always felt so good. Her touch, her kiss, all of it had the power to completely undo him. If he let his dick call the shots, he'd already be balls deep inside her, both of them halfway to oblivion, but no way was he letting that happen. Fast and easy? Not with Ally. It was *never* that way with Ally. He'd waited too long for this moment—a white-hot fantasy that had started after their first meeting on the ice, finally made real. Here. Now. They had the house to themselves. All the fucking time in the world.

And he intended to use that time *very* wisely.

Reaching for her hand, he pulled away from her touch, ignoring the angry protests of his dick, hard and hot and more than ready to rock.

"Not yet," he said, silencing her protests with another kiss. Her moan rumbled through his mouth, and he deepened their kiss, sweeping his tongue across hers, losing himself. Pulling back to look her in the eye, he grabbed her delicate wrists in one big hand, pinning her hands behind her. With his free hand, he traced the shape of her lips, her chin, her throat. The frantic beat of her pulse throbbed just below the skin.

Ba-dom, ba-dom, ba-dom…

He'd caged her in, no escape from his powerful grip, no getting past his muscled chest. Anyone who walked in on the situation would've thought he had the upper hand, but Roscoe knew the real deal.

He was utterly powerless. This woman owned him.

Completely.

She stared up at him with those beautiful honey-brown eyes, open and vulnerable, and he knew right then what she was offering him. What a gift it really was.

"You can trust me," he whispered, needing her to know it.

Ally bit her lip, nodded once.

"This only goes as far as you want it to. Any time you want to back off, we back off. If you feel even the slightest bit—"

"I know, Roscoe."

"Scared or—"

"Roscoe." She cut him off with a gentle kiss. When she pulled away, fire sparked to life in her eyes, and Roscoe felt the heat of that gaze all the way down to his damn toes.

"I want this," she said. "You. All of you. I'm ready."

Lowering her hand, Ally reached for him again, the sensation of her touch unleashing a fresh torrent of desire.

Roscoe groaned, eyes rolling skyward as he fell deeper under her spell. He was playing a dangerous game, letting her have her way, giving in to her touch, but now that she was stroking him, slow and tight in her soft, warm hand, he couldn't pull away. Not this time. Heat coiled in his belly, his balls tingling, and Christ he had to kiss her again, to taste her, to devour her lush, wet mouth.

He pulled away from her touch right before he came, forcing himself to count backward from ten, talk himself back off the ledge.

Still locked in a passionate kiss, he lifted her into his arms, her legs tight around his hips as he carried her upstairs to the bedroom.

He'd never been inside the room before, but he wasn't here for a tour. He set her down on the edge of the perfectly made bed, then pulled a few condoms from his pocket and set them on the night table.

Ally grinned. "Presumptuous, aren't we?"

Roscoe laughed. "I've been carrying them on every date since you mauled me at the old folk's home."

"What? You were the mauler in that scenario. I was just an innocent—"

Her words trailed off as Roscoe stripped off his clothes. It was the first time she'd seen him completely naked, too, and he liked the way her gaze trailed down his body, the way her mouth parted when he fisted himself, the way her eyes darkened with lust.

"Come," she whispered, inching backward on the bed, and that was all it took. He couldn't even pretend to resist, to deny the effect she had on him.

Roscoe dropped onto his knees in front of her, gripping her thighs and gently urging them apart.

"Ever since I met you, all I could think about was touching you," he said. "Tasting you. God, Ally. You drive me crazy. Everything about you drives me absolutely fucking crazy."

"I tried to warn you. I'm all over the map, Roscoe."

"That's not what I meant."

"But I'm—"

"Beautiful." He kissed her thigh, savoring the sweet-and-salty taste of her skin. "Amazing." Another kiss, this one lingering a little longer, a little closer to her center. "Powerful."

They'd been dating for weeks, and though she'd already put her mouth on him in ways he'd be dreaming about well into his nineties, this was the first she'd let him see her like this, the first she'd let him taste her bare flesh.

He pressed a kiss to clit, savoring the moment.

Ally moaned softly, sliding her fingers into his hair and pulling him closer. Her touch was like none he'd ever felt, so sensual, so deliberate, he'd never tire of it. She touched him like she was tasting him through her fingertips, hungry and greedy, sucking up every little bit he had to offer.

And he was glad to give it to her.

No more savoring, no more lingering. He needed her like a drug. He licked her wet heat, losing his mind at the way her body shuddered beneath him. Her taste was intense and heady and every time he pulled back, his mouth watered, desperate for more of her. He kissed her again, gently sucking her clit between his lips, flicking it with his tongue until her thighs trembled. He pulled back, blowing a hot breath across her bare flesh, holding her down on the bed while he drove her wild with his mouth.

"Roscoe," she moaned, her head lolling back on the bed, back arched like a cat as her hips rocked against his face. "Don't tease me. I… I can't… Please!"

At this, he grabbed her ass and pulled her close, burying his tongue deep inside her, urging her with every thrust to just let go. Let go of her inhibitions, let go of her fear, let go of everything bad or scary in her life. He wanted her to take whatever she wanted from him, whatever she needed, whatever she'd been dreaming about since their very first kiss. He wanted to fuck her senseless with his mouth, to make her feel so fucking good she'd never allow another man's face between her thighs.

He wanted to find that passionate, uninhibited, untamed wild woman inside and make her fucking *scream*.

So that's exactly what he did.

CHAPTER TWENTY

Ally stared at the ceiling, the room spinning around her as she slowly came back to her senses. The ceiling fan was on overdrive, its chain clicking ceaselessly against the glass lamp, but despite its best efforts the air was still thick and hot and heavy, and a sheen of sweat coated her skin. Normally she didn't like the heat, but now it felt sultry and seductive, laced with something secret and forbidden she'd denied herself for far too long.

Her body was still trembling from the insane orgasm Roscoe had just given her with his mouth, but she wasn't even close to finished. She wanted him on top of her. Needed him there, hot and slick and hard, finally fulfilling the promise inherent in his every touch, every kiss since the very first.

For so long she'd promised herself that this would be it, their final epic act together before they went their separate ways. But all of her carefully laid plans and protections seemed so ridiculous now, unnecessary and impossible to uphold. She was falling for him, hard and fast. No matter what happened next, she could no more turn her back on this than Reggie could turn her back on hockey.

Roscoe was still on his knees, the hot mist of his breath warming her thigh. Hands threaded in his hair, Ally tugged gently, urging him to begin the long and sensuous ascent of her body. And that's exactly what it felt like—an explorer mapping her curves and dips with his mouth, claiming the territory of her body one kiss, one inch, one whisper at a time. By the time he reached her mouth, she was wet and throbbing again, so desperate for the hot thrust of him that she almost begged him.

Roscoe was just as eager, and they moved to the center of the bed, his cock pressed against her belly, hard and hot, all for her. She'd had him in her hands before, in her mouth, sliding between her lips as her tongue teased and stroked and tasted. She'd felt him through the fabric of his jeans, grinding against her as they'd rolled around at the park. But she'd never had him inside her, and the anticipation of what was coming unleashed a rush of energy that electrified her nerves and sent her into a full-bodied shiver.

Roscoe shifted until the thick ridge of his cock

pressed against her clit. At her involuntary gasp, he kissed her neck and said, "Okay?"

"More than okay," she whispered, nipping at his earlobe. "Just... Give me a second. Just like this." It had been so long since Ally had felt the full, delicious weight of a naked man against her body, she wasn't ready for it to end. She felt small and protected, nestled snugly beneath this strong, kind man who could make her laugh as easily as he could drive her wild. She wanted to savor everything about this moment, this feeling, to store it up and save it for her loneliest nights, those agonizing stretches of darkness where only the shadows kept her company.

Because right now, with Roscoe in her bed, skin slicked with sweat and heat and desire, both of them panting and wild, Ally felt the sun blazing inside her, chasing away those old shadows that had kept her hiding and scared for so long.

He reached up to brush his thumb across her lips, unleashing another shiver, then pressed his mouth to hers. The kiss was exquisite, and Ally moaned his name, arching her body to get closer.

Roscoe grabbed the condom from the night stand and tore open the wrapper, rolling it on and teasing her entrance with the tip of his cock. Ally cried out in pleasure, her muscles wound tight, everything inside her simmering. She couldn't wait another moment.

She wanted him inside her, filling up all the spaces that had gone empty for so long. *Too* long.

Parting her thighs, she rolled her hips and dug her nails into his back, and Roscoe plunged into her, strong and perfect and full.

I've done it. Made love to another man.

Hot guilt raced suddenly down her spine, settling like a rock in her gut. Her thighs clamped involuntarily, and Ally felt her throat tighten, tears threatening to spill.

It's not cheating. He's gone, Ally. He's gone.

Ally closed her eyes and took a deep, shuddering breath. She hadn't felt this way with Roscoe that first night in the park, his fingers slipping inside her, touching her until she moaned with pleasure. She hadn't felt this way when she'd taken him into her mouth, not on that night nor all the nights since. She hadn't felt this way moments ago, his face between her thighs.

But this? This was everything. The most physically intimate moment a man and a woman could share. And for the first time in her entire life, she was sharing with a man who wasn't Dan.

Ally opened her eyes, meeting Roscoe's gaze. His eyes were dark with lust, but also full of the genuine concern she'd come to know from him.

"Okay?" he asked again, his whispers a caress on her lips.

She nodded, not trusting her voice. Her body was

trembling, her thighs clenching, her stomach tumbling, but Ally knew in her heart she *wanted* this. Needed it. Needed him to take her away from all of the pain, all of the ghosts, the endless ache inside her.

No, she realized with a start. That was her fallback line, the one she'd told herself in her mind all the times she'd thought about this moment. Now that it had arrived, she knew deep down that her need had nothing to do with the past and everything to do with right now. With Roscoe. With the way she felt in his arms, safe and protected and cherished.

Roscoe brushed a kiss across her lips. "You sure?"

Ally smiled. In the wake of his tenderness, the prickly feeling inside subsided, cresting and falling away again like a wave. She waited a beat, then another, but it was gone.

"Yes," she whispered, reaching up to cup his face.

I've never been so sure of anything in my entire life. She opened her mouth again to tell him just that, but those felt like big words, huge words, too heavy and important to say out loud just yet. So she leaned forward and kissed him, hungry and eager, sealing away the words for another day and telling him in every other way she knew how: *yes, I absolutely want this.*

Roscoe's perfect cock thickened inside her, growing even harder as her body relaxed to accommodate him fully, her hips urging him into a new rhythm, slow and deliberate, then faster, deeper, harder and faster still, each stroke urging her closer to the edge until finally her thighs clenched and her body gripped him tighter and Roscoe came with a roar, shuddered against her body until she let go too, all at once, losing herself in their shared release until everything in her began to spin in the most delicious way, faster than the fan over their heads.

"I have a confession," Ally announced. She'd been drifting in and out of sleep, wrapped up in Roscoe's embrace as he traced slow circles on her back, and she had no idea how much time had passed. It wasn't dark yet, which meant they still had a while before the kids returned from their date, and Ally had no plans to move from the bed until she absolutely had to.

Roscoe nuzzled her neck, his hair tickling her chin. "You want to do that again?"

"No. I mean, yes, of course. But that's not it." She sighed into his hair, inhaling the scent of his shampoo. It was better that he wasn't looking into her eyes. "When we first started hanging out, and it was clear we'd eventually... You know. Get physical and—"

"Oh, you mean when you mauled me in an old folks' home?"

"Hey! We've been over this. *You* mauled *me*."

"Fine. Let's just call it a mutual mauling."

"A mutual mauling. Right." Ally laughed, but her smile faded and she closed her eyes, snuggling tighter against him. "I told myself that as soon as we finished doing this, we'd have to end things."

"Finished what? Sex?" Roscoe pulled back and reached for her chin, tilting her head so she had no choice but to open her eyes and meet his gaze. His eyes were guarded, all traces of humor suddenly gone. "Are you saying this is it?"

"No! No, nothing like that." Her cheeks heated in embarrassment, but somehow Ally knew Roscoe would understand. "It sounds ridiculous now, but I just… I was scared. I thought it would be better to go out with a bang before things got too complicated. End on a high note, you know?"

"Ally." Roscoe shook his head. "Why did you think we'd end at all?"

"You're an NHL player. You've got training and media stuff and traveling and games, all the attention that goes along with that. And I'm just…" She broke their gaze and lowered her eyes, unsure how to complete the thought.

"Just what?"

"Just plain old—"

"Stop. Look at me, Ally."

Ally sighed, finally meeting his eyes again. The earlier confusion was gone, replaced with fierce determination.

"The only acceptable answer to that question," he said, "is that you're just the most amazing woman I've ever met. Your attention is the only attention I care about." He tightened his hold on her, sighing against her skin. "As far as I'm concerned, no one else exists. Not for me. Do you understand what I'm saying?"

Ally's heart hammered against her chest. She had a pretty good idea.

"Yes," she whispered. "I'm... I'm saying the same thing."

She was overcome again with that same feeling she'd had that first time with him in the restaurant—the night they'd come to refer to as their first non-date—when he'd held her hand beneath the table and brought her back from the darkness of her thoughts. Now, just as then, she felt safe with him. Calm. Content.

And this time, there was no fear lingering on the doorstep, waiting to rush in and burst that perfect bubble. No anxieties and what-ifs and worst case scenarios.

This time, there was only Roscoe, warm and naked and alive, holding her close.

A feeling of pure joy bubbled up inside her, spilling out in a laugh.

"Okay," Roscoe said, returning the smile. "Now that we've got that out of the way."

He rolled on top of her again, settling between her thighs. He was hard and ready for more, and a rush of desire flooded Ally's core.

"What are you doing, Roscoe LeGrand?" she teased, already parting her thighs to accommodate him.

"I figure if you're kicking me out as soon as we finish having sex, there's only one option." Roscoe reached for another condom, grinning like an idiot. "We're not going to finish."

CHAPTER TWENTY-ONE

"Why didn't you tell me we were going to Wellshire? I didn't bring my boinkers!" Ally looped her arm through Roscoe's as they headed across the parking lot toward the entrance.

They'd been dating for more than a month, spending almost every free moment together, yet Roscoe's insatiable appetite for surprises showed no signs of slowing down.

"We're not here to play bingo," he said. "And it's for a good cause, so you can't say no."

"But how do I know if I'm prepared?"

"Ally. I'm not taking you up Mount Everest. You don't need gear or a permit for this date. Only a smock, which I'm told will be provided for us upon entry."

"A smock?" Ally glanced down at her pale green

blouse and gauzy white skirt. "Am I dressed appropriately for this?"

"You..." Roscoe pulled her against his chest, sweeping the hair back off her face and pressing a sweet kiss to her lips. "...are absolutely stunning, as always. But..."

"Didn't your mother teach you not to follow a compliment with a but?"

"She would agree with me on this *but*, which is to say that you are a total pain in *my* butt. But you're also adorable and sexy and highly talented in ways that I'll never mention in front of my mother or anyone else's, so I've decided to keep you around for now." He flashed that dimpled grin that never failed to disarm her, and opened the door to the building. "Now let's go—they're waiting for us."

They headed inside and down to the community room, where they were immediately greeted with cheers by the ladies of Wellshire, who'd grown attached to Ally these past few weeks. She and Roscoe had been back for bingo and card games twice since their first date, both times joined by Walker and his fiancée, Eva. Ally was growing pretty attached to them, too—Eva had even hired Reggie to babysit her daughter Grace last weekend.

It was still so unreal. Ally had arrived in Buffalo two months ago, putting on a brave face and going through the motions, trying to set up their house and get into the groove at work, keep things moving forward for Reggie's sake. She hadn't imagined how quickly new friends would come into their lives. How much she'd enjoy the company of other people again.

How much she'd come to care for a man whose touch, whose kiss, whose charming smile had the power to make her feel light and happy.

It wasn't that long ago when Ally had assumed those feelings were forever out of reach for her, tucked away on a shelf like so many distant memories, dusty and forgotten.

She blinked away tears of gratitude, taking in the sight before her.

The community room had been utterly transformed. Tables that usually held bingo cards and boinkers were now covered with plastic tablecloths, each of them set with tabletop easels and white canvases. Over every chair, the promised smocks hung in waiting. The stage that typically held the bingo machine was now set up with two large easels, one holding a blank canvas, the other a finished painting.

Overhead, a huge banner proclaimed:

Candy's Canvases: Paint Your Heart Out!

"We're painting?" Ally unlinked her arm from Roscoe's, turning slowly to take in the full scene. The room was already packed with people, most of them clustered around the bar, others finding their places at the table and putting on their smocks.

Roscoe nodded, gently cupping her chin. "I know you said art doesn't have a place in your life right now—and maybe you're right, as far as your career goes. But I thought you might enjoy a little trip down memory lane." Then, leaning in close and lowering his voice, "If canvas doesn't work for you, we can always go home and paint you a new tattoo. I've already got a spot in mind."

"I'm sure you do." Ally smacked him on the chest. The butterflies were dancing around inside her stomach again, happy and excited. She couldn't remember the last time she did anything even remotely artistic, but suddenly her fingers were itching to hold a paintbrush again, her mind already envisioning the colors swirling onto the canvas. "I can't believe you brought me to paint night!"

"Did I overstep?"

"Are you kidding me?" She looped her arms around his neck and grinned, big and bright, standing up on her tiptoes for a kiss. She lingered there, enjoying the softness of his lips, the feel of his strong hands as they curled around her waist.

"It's perfect," she said, finally pulling back. How the hell had she gotten so lucky? "*You're* perfect."

"I'll remember you said that." He pressed another

kiss to her lips and groaned softly, the smooth vibration sending a ripple of desire down her spine. As much as she wanted to paint, another minute of his seductive touch and Ally would drag him back to the staff room for a *different* kind of trip down memory lane…

"Since you two are busy getting busy," Paulette proclaimed loudly, "Lorraine and I will go get drinks."

Ally laughed, reluctantly breaking from Roscoe's embrace.

"To be continued," he promised with a wink, then led them to a table at the center of the room where Walker, Eva, and Mrs. Dunn were already seated.

Mrs. Dunn had her smock on backward, but other than that, she seemed to be doing well. Last time they'd come for bingo, she didn't seem to remember meeting Ally, but now she greeted her by name, her smile mirroring Ally's own.

Ally grabbed a spot across from them, letting Roscoe settle in next to Mrs. Dunn. She liked it better than sitting next to him—that way, she could look up and see that smile any time she wanted to.

"This was such a great idea," Mrs. Dunn said. "Painting is even more fun than boinking."

Roscoe choked back a laugh. "I'm not so sure I—"

"Lock it down, brother." Walker shot him a warning glare. "That's my mom you're talking to, remember?"

"Please." Mrs. Dunn swatted his arm. "You think I

can't appreciate a good sex pun?"

"*Mom.*"

"Where do you think you and your brothers came from—the baby tree?" She shook her head, a sly grin spreading across her face. "Before he turned into an asshole, your father and I used to—"

"Alrighty then!" Walker put his arm around his mother, pulling her into a hug. "As much as I'd love to follow this conversation right down the rabbit hole, I'm pretty sure I just died inside, so maybe we could wrap this thing up."

Under his breath, Roscoe grumbled, "That's what *she* said…"

"Ally?" Walker glanced at her across the table, his eyes pleading. "Help me out here. Tell Mr. Loverboy to keep his sex puns to himself."

"Ally," Roscoe said, "Tell Mr. Tightwad that sex puns are the gift that keeps on giving."

"Speaking of giving…" Walker held up a menacing fist. "Guess what I'm giving you in about five seconds?"

"No way," Roscoe said. "My girlfriend will leap across the table and kick your ass."

Ally cracked up. Before she could respond, her phone buzzed—Clarissa, letting her know that she and Reggie were heading to the movies, and that Reggie wanted to stay the night.

No problem, Ally replied. *Have fun!*

You know we will! You okay? What does Mr. Ovary-melter have on the agenda tonight? ;-)

Ever since that day with the kids at Ally's house a couple of weeks back, Clarissa had been warming up to Roscoe. More specifically, to the idea of Roscoe and Ally as a couple. She'd even eased up on him at work, complimenting him on how smoothly the clinic was running, asking for his input on some of her media ideas.

Ally smiled. They'd come a long way since June.

Raising the bar, as usual, Ally texted back now.

Lorraine and Paulette returned with the wine, joined now by John, all of them thrilled at the opportunity to paint. Now that they were all assembled, Ally stepped back and snapped a quick picture of the group, then sent it over to Clarissa. If anyone would understand how much something like this meant to Ally, it was her best friend.

Before she could check on Clarissa's response, the event organizer made an announcement that it was time to get started. Dropping the phone back into her purse, Ally donned her smock.

Roscoe, who looked adorable in his, pushed the sleeves of his dark blue Henley up to his elbows, revealing his muscled forearms. "Ready?" he asked Ally, his eyes glittering.

"You have no idea." Ally sipped her wine, then turned her full attention to the perky red-head on stage.

"I think we're all in for some fun tonight," the woman said. Her smile was infectious. "Am I right?"

"As long as the bar doesn't run out of Chardonnay," Lorraine shouted. Their table erupted in cheers.

"I see we've got our usual rowdy bunch in the house," the woman up front said with a grin. "Just try to keep the paintings PG tonight, okay Lorraine?"

"No promises." Nodding toward Roscoe and Walker, she said, "I'm feeling particularly inspired by the company tonight."

Everyone laughed at that.

The woman continued. "For those of you who don't know me—"

"And for those of us who don't remember!" Mrs. Dunn called out. Walker frowned at her, but she and her friends laughed.

"Yes, for you, too," the woman said. "I'm Candy from Candy's Canvases, and I'm your tour guide for tonight's artistic adventure." She was easily the most chipper woman Ally had ever encountered. "Now, last time this was all for fun, right? But the lovely staff here at Wellshire informed me that you've all decided to auction off tonight's creations to raise money for Alzheimer's and cancer research."

More cheers and clapping. Ally beamed—it was such a cool idea. The surprise date was turning more incredible by the minute.

Leave it to Roscoe, Mr. Ovary-melter indeed.

"If you've never worked with acrylics before," Candy continued, "don't worry! We'll go through this step by step, and by the time we're done, you'll feel like the next Georgia O'Keefe. Sound good?"

"I'd rather feel like the next Beyoncé, if you don't mind," Paulette shouted.

"You and me both, sister." Candy laughed. "Okay. First we need to gather our paints." She gestured to the finished painting on her easel. "I'm going to tell you the colors I used to achieve this look right here, but remember, you're free to choose other colors. Don't limit yourselves! This is your adventure. Embrace your inner artist! Or, as my girl Samantha Hart says, 'Make your own magic!'"

Ally lit up inside. Could this night get any better? Not only was she painting, and doing it for a cause close to her heart, but the artist in charge was a *You Glow, Girl!* fan. It felt like fate, and she looked at Roscoe and smiled. *Thank you,* she mouthed.

Thank me later, he mouthed back. *Naked.*

Ally grabbed the plastic palette beneath her easel, then followed the others to a table set up with big plastic bottles of paint. As they moved down the line, Candy told them how many pumps they'd need from each color.

Paulette was ahead of Ally, loading up on black and

white paint.

"No color? Ally asked.

"I'm having an existential crisis," Paulette said. "All the color is gone from my soul."

"That… sounds serious," Ally said.

"My doctor put me on heart pills. Says I have to limit my physical activity for a few months."

A flicker of fear touched Ally's chest. "I'm so sorry to hear that, Paulette."

"Not as sorry as John. We just discovered a new staff room," she said with a sigh. "With a door lock."

"Well." Ally bit back a smile. As long as Paulette was still cracking jokes about her so-called side piece, Ally knew she'd be just fine. "I'm sure you'll be back to your old self again soon."

"From your lips to God's ears, toots. In the mean time, I got him a copy of *Fifty Shades of Grey.* Should hold him over until my ticker's back in working order."

"I hope so." Ally didn't want to ask whether she'd meant the book or the movie.

Once everyone had settled back in at their tables, Candy got started, leading them through the base coat and the basic shapes that would—for some of them, anyway—become a vase of highly stylized calla lilies.

"Oh, hell," Paulette said suddenly, narrowing her eyes at John's canvas. "Your flowers look like vaginas."

"Flowers? I thought we were painting vaginas!" John

glanced down at his palette. "Damn. I'm gonna need more paint."

"What you need are better drugs," she said, setting down her palette and brush. She went to stand behind Roscoe, checking out his progress. "What's going on over here?"

Ally offered him a sympathetic smile. Poor guy was staring at his canvas as though he were willing it to combust.

"I really suck at this," he said.

John pointed at Roscoe's canvas. "His look like vaginas, too."

"John!" Paulette rolled her eyes.

"What? I'm only calling it like I see it."

"You're calling it like a pervert."

John winked and pointed his brush at her. "You say that like it's a bad thing."

"Last time I checked," Walker said, stepping back and squinting at Roscoe's painting, "Vaginas don't have teeth Dude. What are you *doing*?"

"What? Those are dew drops."

"It's your technique." Paulette reached for his hand, furrowing her brow. "You've gotta dab, not smear."

"I *am* dabbing."

"No, you're attacking." Glancing up at Ally, she said, "I hope he's not this brutish in the bedroom. Unless you like that sort of thing, which is none of my business, but

I'm a safe space if you ever want to chat about it. Preferably in detail."

Ally laughed. "I'll keep that in mind. Thank you, Paulette."

Roscoe glanced up and met Ally's eyes, his own full of mischief as Paulette wrapped her hand around his.

"Light strokes," Paulette said, guiding his hand over the canvas. "Like this."

"That's too much paint, Paulette," Lorraine offered, but Roscoe was barely paying attention. His gaze was fixed on Ally, the dimple flashing in his cheek.

"You two are bordering on disgusting," Walker said to Roscoe.

Eva smacked him. "Oh, like we aren't?"

"We're a little more subtle," he said.

Roscoe laughed. "Says the man who proposed at the end of a playoffs game in front of millions of fans, and then proceeded to dry hump his new fiancée on the ice?"

"To be fair," Ally chimed in, "it *was* pretty romantic."

"You saw it?" Roscoe asked.

"Reggie and I watched a video." She smiled at Walker and Eva. "Though I might have to do a rewatch. I don't remember any dry-humping."

"That's because there wasn't any," Walker said. "Just your boy and his wishful thinking." Walker shook his head, then pointed his brush at Ally. "You'd better hope he pops the question in private."

Ally felt her whole body heat up, her cheeks blushing. *Pops the question?*

Her eyes darted over to Roscoe, but thankfully Paulette had recaptured his attention, guiding him through the rest of his masterpiece.

Ally had already finished her painting. It looked a lot like the one on the stage, with just a few color variations. It was okay—some might even call it nice. But now that she was warmed up, Ally wanted to try something different.

She asked for another blank canvas, then headed back to the paint table, loading up her palette with all different colors. Before tonight, it'd been more than a decade since she'd done anything other than doodle on a piece of paper, but her body was buzzing with renewed creativity, a renewed sense of inspiration sparking up inside.

Back at the table, she let her brush wander across the canvas, painting a background of deep midnight that faded to lavender at the top of the canvas. She wasn't even sure what she had in mind, only that she'd be taking full advantage of Candy's "don't limit yourselves!" advice.

Suddenly, the colors she had weren't enough. She needed more. Different. She started mixing new shades —sunny marigold first, then a deep emerald green, a turquoise swirled with indigo, four different shades of lavender. Images took shape on her canvas, materializing from the tip of her brush. No longer constrained by flowers in the vase, Ally's muse took flight, racing across the canvas. With every stroke, her heart expanded, filling her with a joy so unexpected it brought tears to her eyes.

Yet, as surprised as she felt, all of this was also familiar.

It was as if she'd just walked into the house of a very dear friend she hadn't seen in decades, one she knew so intimately, so completely, it was as if no time had passed at all.

Ally dimly heard Candy explaining her shading techniques, but soon Ally was in her own world, swirling and mixing, dotting and stroking, adding layers and life to her painting as if an entire story was rushing out of her heart, dancing out from her fingertips onto the canvas. Ally was no longer just painting a picture—she was revealing it, slowly coaxing the secrets of her heart to life. Instead of flowers in a vase, her new canvas held a lush garden, a carpet of pale pink peonies, a glittering blue river flowing into infinity. When she ran out of room, she grabbed another blank canvas from an unoccupied easel and let the tangle of grapevine spill over, blossoming into another garden, midnight, its blooms and leaves tinged silvery blue by the full moon that hung in the night sky. Instead of a river, this time she painted a lake, clear and still. There on the shore a woman appeared, nude and utterly unselfconscious as she knelt before the water, scooping it into her hands.

Ally swore she could feel the cool water in her own hands, could taste the sweet purity of it on her lips as she added the finishing touches. Her heart banged inside her chest, her blood zipping through her veins, her entire body alive and on fire.

She couldn't even remember the last time she'd felt this way, this—God, there was only one word for it. Alive.

Her midnight gardens complete, Ally stepped backward, slowly getting her bearings. Still perched on the stage, Candy was explaining the difference between highlights and mid-tones as the rest of the crowd tried to follow along, some working diligently on their canvases, others working diligently on their wine. Ally felt as if she'd just come out of a trance, and when she looked across the table, she found Roscoe watching her intently, his own painting efforts abandoned, his eyes full of something that looked a lot like wonder.

Extricating himself from his smock, he rounded the edge of the table and came to stand before Ally.

"Everything okay?" she asked with a smile, setting down her bush and palette.

"I'm in love with you," he whispered. Then, without a second thought for the packed community room, Roscoe took her face in his hands and kissed her.

CHAPTER TWENTY-TWO

Ally didn't remember packing up her paintings for the auction, or saying goodbye to their friends, or anything about the drive home. One minute Roscoe was kissing her senseless in the middle of the art room while all the Wellshire residents cheered and whistled, and then they were stumbling into her house through the front door, frantically shedding their clothes. Surely they must have come up for air during the drive over, but in that moment it seemed to Ally as if they'd been kissing for hours, the rest of the world put on pause just for them.

All that existed for her now was that kiss, the sweet press of his mouth, the heat of his breath as it intermingled with hers. Her heart hammered wildly, but this wasn't the old familiar beat of Ally's anxiety. This was new, louder, even more frantic, yet beautiful and strong —a beat belonging to this man alone.

I'm in love with you.

The words echoed in her memory, filling her with warmth and happiness as Roscoe lifted Ally into his arms and carried her up to the bedroom without a word.

Gently he laid her on the bed and stripped off the rest of her clothes, his eyes roving over her naked body, drinking her in like he always did. Only this time, he seemed to be seeing her through new eyes.

"You take my breath away," he whispered.

Ally felt herself blush, but she didn't look away. Not for an instant. She ran her paint-flecked hands through his hair, marveling once again that this beautiful, compassionate, amazing man had come into her life.

Had fallen in love with her.

Closing her eyes, she sank into the delicious pleasure of his kiss on her neck, the swirl of his tongue behind her ear, the heat of his breath warming her skin as he traveled down her chest, her belly, between her thighs.

Her legs parted easily, welcoming his hot mouth against her flesh. She was so close to the edge, so close to shattering into a million pieces, but she wouldn't. Not yet.

She pulled back, arcing her body away from his dangerously seductive mouth. "I don't want to come without you."

A low, sexy growl rumbled in Roscoe's chest, and then he was on top of her, his mouth closing over hers, capturing her kiss as his muscled body pinned her to the bed. She tasted herself on his lips, his tongue, and it made her even more wet for him, more desperate for the feel of his smooth, thick cock between her thighs.

But Roscoe liked to take his time with Ally, to draw out her pleasure until she could barely stand it, and no amount of begging or writhing would change his mind.

God, she loved that about him.

He moaned into her mouth, allowing her to savor his kiss for only a moment longer before pulling away, slowly dragging his tongue down her neck, into the hollow of her throat. He kissed her collarbone, then closed his mouth over her nipple, sucking her until she ached with need. Her core throbbed, everything in her pulsating and hot.

"Please don't tease me," she whispered, even though she knew it wouldn't do any good. Roscoe was a master at the fine art of teasing.

"You teased me all night," he said, sliding his hand down between her thighs. His thumb circled her clit, slow and torturous. Ally closed her eyes and whispered his name, but he was relentless, fingers brushing her entrance. "Watching you paint," he said, dipping briefly inside her, then pulling out. "You were so fucking wild tonight. Beautiful. All I could think about was taking you home, spreading you out on the bed like this. Touching you. Tasting you."

Ally shook her head, raking her nails down his back and grabbing his ass. She arched her hips, trying to entice him closer. "I want you inside me. I can't wait."

"Not yet, beautiful." Roscoe stroked her again, his thumb still teasing her clit, making her whole body shudder. "Close your eyes."

Ally surrendered, her eyes fluttering closed as she gave herself over to his command. Roscoe sucked her nipple again, teasing her with his teeth, his tongue. She was dancing on the precipice of her release, everything in her winding tight, her core throbbing as Roscoe touched and teased and…

"Roscoe!" Ally gasped, her eyes opening wide as he finally slid inside her, so deep and perfect it nearly stopped her heart. Her body was screaming out for the pure, blissful release waiting for her just on the other side, but she held back, forcing herself to relax, to deny it, to hit rewind and make this last as long as possible. They had the whole night together, and Ally intended to enjoy every intense, seductive, red-hot moment.

Roscoe rolled his hips, filling her once more completely before pulling back out, driving her wild, inch by agonizing inch.

Without warning he grabbed her hips and flipped her onto her stomach, then slid back into her entrance from behind, slow at first, then faster, harder. Ally pushed up onto her hands and knees and tilted her hips, taking him in deeper, pushing backward against his thrusts, her whole body begging for more.

God, she wanted it so badly—the deep ache she was already beginning to feel in her thighs, the constant reminder that would bring her right back to this moment every time she tried to sit down tomorrow. As if he could read her body's every desire, Roscoe gripped her hips and dug his fingers into her flesh. He owned her. Possessed her so completely, Ally nearly forgot her own name.

She'd never been so excited, so wet, so close to spontaneous combustion in her entire life.

"More," she breathed, barely able to get the word out.

Roscoe growled behind her, then ran his hand up her back, his fingers sliding into her hair, grabbing a fist full. She pushed against the headboard again, backing into him, still wanting more.

Roscoe leaned forward, sliding his hand around her front, down between her sweat-damp thighs.

"Tell me," he whispered, his breath hot in her ear as he ghosted over her clit. "Tell me how to make you—"

"Roscoe!" Ally gasped. It was too late—she couldn't hold back another second. Her thighs trembled as her body tightened around him, the flames in her lower belly exploding in a raging inferno as he plunged inside. Roscoe let out a final, raspy growl and grabbed her hips again, shuddering against her flesh as he rode out his own release. After what felt like an eternity, they collapsed together onto the bed with a final shared gasp of pure pleasure.

Cocooned by his strong, heavy body, Ally closed her eyes, inhaling his scent, memorizing the way it made her feel. Roscoe pressed a kiss to her bare shoulder, then reached for her hand, giving it a squeeze so gentle and reassuring it brought tears to her eyes.

He was in love with her. Roscoe LeGrand was in love with her.

"Roscoe," Ally breathed, but her voice was gone. Her words were gone. She wasn't even sure whether her heart was still beating, her lungs still breathing, her blood still singing in her veins. All she had left was the taste of his kiss and the memory of his fevered touch still coursing through her body.

Ally smiled. Right now, that was all she needed.

Two hours and another marathon session later, spent and dizzy and light as a butterfly, Ally collapsed onto the bed and stretched out on her stomach, her hands sliding beneath the cool pillow. Roscoe lay next to her, tracing the tattoos on her back with a light touch. Ally drifted in and out, barely conscious of anything but the delicious ache between her thighs, every muscle in her body crying out with delicious exhaustion.

She had no idea how much time had passed when she heard Roscoe talking to her. They'd gone so long without words, it took her brain a minute to translate.

"Should I set an alarm for tomorrow?" Roscoe was asking. His voice was low and smooth in the darkness. "So you don't miss work?"

"Mmm. Aren't we playing hooky from real life?"

Roscoe pressed a kiss to the back of her neck, making her shiver. "This is our real life."

Ally let out a sigh of pure contentment. It didn't seem possible that this was her real life. She almost didn't want to open her eyes, afraid he'd vanish like so many of the best dreams.

But the promise of seeing his face again was too tempting. Slowly, her eyes fluttered open.

Roscoe was watching her intently, and when she looked up at him, he grinned.

"What are you smiling at?" she teased.

"I'm sleeping over." He sounded like a kid bragging to his friends about how he'd gotten the best Christmas present. "Right here. In your bed. With you."

"Yes, and we've got the whole place to ourselves until morning. I don't want to speak for you, but I don't plan on getting out of this bed except for emergencies."

"We're so on the same page, it's not even funny."

They sat up together, leaning against the headboard for support. Roscoe laced his fingers through hers.

"I had a great time tonight," she said softly.

"Me too." Roscoe kissed her shoulder. "Ally, when you said you could draw and paint, I had no idea you could do... *that*."

"Honestly, neither did I." Ally smiled, remembering the way she'd felt in front of the canvas—like her entire body wanted to break out in song. "Guess I've evolved from my dead bird phase."

"That's an understatement." Roscoe shook his head. "You're amazing, Ally. You made something that could hang in a damn museum. And that was just paint night at the Wellshire community room. Why did you stop painting in the first place?"

Ally shrugged and rested her head on his shoulder. "I made other choices. Let it go."

"But you're an artist," he said. It wasn't a question, and the certainty in his voice left no room for argument.

"Wow." Ally laughed. "No one has called me the a-word since college."

Roscoe grabbed her chin, tilting her face toward his. "No one has seen what I saw tonight. What I see every time I look into those big brown eyes. There's so much inside you, Ally. So much love and fire and passion and just... everything."

Ally's heart thumped hard in her chest. She hadn't

thought about her creative dreams since before Reggie was born. But suddenly she found herself inviting some of those dreams back in.

It was a dangerous thing, letting yourself dream. Samantha Hart might not think so, but Ally knew how fragile a dream could be. How devastating when things didn't work out.

"I don't know jack about painting, okay?" Roscoe continued. "But I know what it feels like to want something that badly. To get a taste of something and just know down in your bones that it's exactly where you're supposed to be. I saw it in you tonight, Ally. As soon as you started on that canvas, it's like you were just… transported. Possessed. And if you've got something that big inside your heart, you need to find a way to get it out."

She hadn't thought about it like that, but now that Roscoe had said it, Ally didn't think she could have worded it any better.

She did have things inside her, things clamoring for expression. Pain and joy and creation and love and death and life and everything in between. Life had done its best to crush her, and in many ways it had succeeded. Dan's death had left a gaping hole in her chest—no one would ever deny that. But now Ally wondered whether there was another hole inside her, too—one she'd put there herself long ago.

She was an artist once. A free spirit who poured her

creative passions out onto canvas or paper or wood or any medium she could get her hands on.

Dan had fallen in love with her then, with her art that had been so much a part of who she was. But over the years, their lives had taken a different path. Not bad, just different. He'd chosen to go into management, and she'd chosen to stay home with Reggie.

She didn't regret those choices—never had. It was what she'd truly wanted at the time, and raising Reggie had given her life unexpected meaning and purpose and challenges she never could have predicted. She wouldn't trade any of that—not for the world.

But just as her life had taken a new path after she'd fallen in love and married Dan, so had her life taken another path after his death. She hadn't chosen that path —she'd been shoved onto it, crashing down on her hands and knees. But that didn't mean she had to keep lying there in dirt, waiting for something—or someone— to come along and save her. Maybe it was time to stand up and dust herself off.

Maybe it was time to start exploring her passions again. Isn't that what Reggie was doing? Bravely stepping out onto the ice every week, working her heart out for Roscoe and their team, coming home from practice exhausted and happy? Doing what she loved, no matter what the risks and the pain?

Tears welled in her eyes, but Ally was smiling, her

heart filling up with something she hadn't felt in years: inspiration.

"What's so funny?" Roscoe asked. Ally was full-on laughing now, the idea taking root and blossoming into a full-blown garden in her heart, just like the paintings she'd done at Wellshire tonight.

When she spoke again, she was practically giddy. "I think I'm going to start painting again. Not just at Wellshire. But seriously."

She bolted out of bed, not even bothering to cover herself. Her mind was too busy thinking about the possibilities. The house had a decent sized den off the living room—she could easily turn that into a studio. There was plenty of natural light, windows for ventilation, and lots of shelving for her supplies.

Ally couldn't believe this was happening. Her art was a thing she'd locked in a box so long ago, she honestly thought she'd lost the key.

Until tonight.

Until Roscoe.

Yes, he'd taken her painting tonight, putting her in front of a canvas for the first time in more than fifteen years. But more than that, he'd inspired her. Encouraged her. Made her feel safe and whole and unafraid again.

Roscoe LeGrand had made her believe in the impossible.

And Ally had fallen madly, insanely, impossibly in love with him.

She opened her mouth to tell him just that, but as soon as the L-word formed on her tongue, she froze. Her lips went numb, her mouth dry. Behind her ribs, her heart skittered and skipped, making her feel light-headed. With every erratic beat a new fear pulsed, warnings echoing against her skull.

Love never lasts.

You can't have it all.

You are going to lose him, just like you lost Dan.

All the levity she'd felt, all the elation about her art and Roscoe and their bright, beautiful future vanished in an instant, and in rushed the darkness, sucking her under a wave of pure terror.

The walls were closing in, the air leaking out of the room, the lights dimming to black.

Her eyes darted toward the door, then back to Roscoe, who was looking up at her like she'd hung the damn moon.

"Ally," he breathed.

Ally forced a smile she didn't feel, then cut her eyes back to the door.

She had to get out of there. Right now.

CHAPTER TWENTY-THREE

Roscoe had never seen anything so beautiful in his life.

Ally stood naked before him, her skin glowing in the moonlight, lips swollen from kissing. There were flecks of blue and green paint in her wild hair, a violet smudge on her chin, and whether it made sense or not, Roscoe saw his entire future reflected in her eyes. Hockey games. Trips to Maine with his family. All the art shows he was sure she'd book. Reggie's graduation. They'd be together through it all.

It was crazy. *He* was crazy. But that's how he felt. Deep in his heart he knew there would be no backing off now. No giving her space, no waiting patiently to see where this thing led. When it came to Ally Heinz, he was in.

All in.

Roscoe took a breath. Then another. He was so

fucking in love with her it made his chest hurt. He had to touch her again. Kiss her. Claim her completely.

"Ally," he breathed.

She smiled again, but this time it didn't reach her eyes.

Something had changed.

"I, um…" She looked at the door again, then reached for the silk bathrobe hanging from a hook on the back of it. "I…"

"I don't think so." Roscoe leaned forward and snatched away the robe, shoving it behind his back. "You," he said, patting the spot on the bed next to him, still warm from her body. "Bed. Now."

She smiled again, but it was way off. She looked a little pale, too.

"Hey," he said. "What's going on? You look—"

"Thirsty." She smiled again, a little softer this time. "And starving. You must be, too."

Roscoe opened his mouth to protest, but his stomach growled, giving him away.

"Tell you what," she said. "You stay here and keep the bed warm, and I'll go down and fix us something to eat."

"Let me." He rose from the bed, but she waved him away.

"Roscoe, I'm fine. Seriously. Just don't get too excited —I'm not the gourmet chef in this operation."

"No, but you *are* naked." Roscoe grinned, taking in the full view of her sexy curves, her tattoos. "Whatever you make will automatically taste better."

She finally laughed, and Roscoe relaxed. She just needed a little refueling, that's all.

While Ally raided the fridge, Roscoe ducked into the shower for a quick rinse, hoping whatever snack she came up with would be fast and easy. He may be the foodie of the pair, but when it came to choosing between snacks and his woman, there was no competition.

Especially when that woman was naked.

Roscoe showered in record time, shut off the water, then reached for the stack of clean towels he'd spotted on the vanity counter. But Ally had left a half-open purse there too, and his big-ass hands managed to knock her stuff right into the sink.

Not bothering to fully dry himself, he wrapped the towel around his waist and stepped out of the shower, hoping he hadn't ruined anything from her bag. Wallet, checkbook, and phone looked okay, along with a couple of tubes of lipstick and a lotion.

Underneath all that, a small picture frame lay face-down in the sink.

Shit. He gingerly picked it up and turned it over, hoping like hell he hadn't cracked the glass.

Nope. But what he saw instead damn near stopped his heart.

A note, tucked into the corner outside the glass, smudged a bit from the water in the sink, but still legible.

Can't wait for tomorrow, Allycat. —Love, D

And the photo behind it, kicking him right in the gut.

Ally, tangled up in the arms of another man. It was a casual shot, but they were dressed in formal wear, maybe for a wedding or party. Probably dancing, stopping just long enough to smile for the photographer. The dude was looking at the camera, but Ally… Hell. She only had eyes for him. Her entire face lit up, that smile stretching from here to California.

Roscoe wondered if Reggie had taken the photo. Or Clarissa. Or maybe someone else in Ally's orbit, some other part of her life he didn't know because she hadn't let him in.

A stab of betrayal shot through his heart, kickstarting it once again.

Roscoe leaned back against the counter, the only thing holding him up. His heart thudded against his ribs like a damn wild animal, his head spinning. He could've dealt with anything—*anything* Ally could've possibly thrown at him.

But not this.

It was his worst nightmare come to life, a replay on the darkest, most painful time in his life. He tried to resist the toxic pull of the past, but he was helpless in its grip, memories flashing through his mind like a slideshow... Walking into his house after a grueling week in California, wanting nothing more than to surprise the woman he loved... Finding another man's shoes by the door... Holding out hope that it was her brother, her father, their elderly neighbor... Following the sounds of her laughter to his bedroom...

Lock it down, asshole. Ally isn't your ex. There's an explanation.

Dragging himself back into the bedroom, he wanted desperately to believe it—that there was some perfectly logical reason for Ally to carry around a framed photo like this. And the note... Hell, there weren't too many ways to interpret that.

He slumped onto the bed in his towel, still gripping the frame in his hand.

Ally finally returned from the kitchen carrying a big tray stacked with shit. She'd put on a long T-shirt, but her hair was still rumpled and wild, her cheeks pink.

I did that. Put those sexy as hell knots in her hair. That blush on her cheeks. Not *him.* Not *this dude in the picture. Look at her—she couldn't fake something like that.*

Right?

Setting the tray on top of her dresser, Ally said, "We've got your standard cheese and cracker spread, some hummus and veggies, strawberries from the... Okay, you know what? I have to tell you something."

When she finally turned to look at him, she was

smiling again. Her real smile—the one that lit her up from the inside and made him feel like the luckiest damn bastard in the world. Whatever was bugging her before seemed to have vanished. She looked so peaceful now, so beautiful, Roscoe almost didn't want to ruin it. Because once he said something, once he showed her this picture and demanded answers, what they had together would change. No matter what the explanation, Roscoe knew that things could never go back to the way they were even fifteen minutes ago—innocent and perfect. Unmarred by his doubts, however quickly they might pass.

But things *had* changed. Roscoe could no more erase that picture from his mind than he could erase this man from Ally's past. Or present.

As for the future? Fuck, it hurt too much to think about that.

"Ally," he whispered. His throat was tight with emotion, his gut churning.

Roscoe watched her eyes fill with concern, watched her smile fade, watched her gaze lower to his hands. Watched as recognition dawned, draining the color from her face.

His fingers gripped the frame so hard they were turning white.

Things were *not* looking good.

"Where... where did you get that?" she asked.

But Roscoe only had one word for her, soft and quiet, the stone-cold calm in his voice belying the storm of emotions swirling inside.

"Explain," he whispered.

And please don't let this be what I think it is.

CHAPTER TWENTY-FOUR

Ally couldn't breathe.

She'd just spent the last fifteen minutes down in the kitchen trying to channel Samantha Hart, digging deep for some of that fierce warrior goddess courage, and she'd finally done it. Not much—her heart still felt too vulnerable and soft—but enough to admit the depth of her feelings for Roscoe. She'd fallen in love with him too, and no matter how scared she was, she needed to tell him.

Roscoe was supposed to tell her not to worry. He was supposed to take her into his strong, protective embrace, kiss her forehead, promise her that they could be truly happy together. That nothing bad would happen to them.

She wasn't supposed to find him sitting on her bed,

clutching that photo, looking at her like she was a total stranger.

Ally blinked back tears, trying to catch her breath. She didn't know what was worse—seeing Dan's picture —the one that had gotten her through more than a few dark nights—crushed in Roscoe's hands, or seeing the look of utter despair that picture had put in Roscoe's eyes.

"Dan," she breathed. It was an answer. A confession. A plea, all at once.

The room spun, her world collapsing all over again as the details of Dan's death slammed into her from all sides. The last time she'd seen him smile. His final words to her as he'd rushed out the door for work that morning. The phone call from his boss. The sad, helpless look on Dan's assistant's face as Ally exited her car. The ambulance and police. The feeling of utter despair as she was forced to take Reggie out of school and tell her the horrible news…

"Ally?" Roscoe said now, yanking her back to the present. She had never seen so much fury in his eyes, a terrifying mix of anger and hurt. "I'm only going to ask one time. Who. The hell. Is Dan?"

"That's… Reggie's dad. My… He was my husband." The words came out, but Ally didn't know who was speaking them. She was floating out of her body, there but not there, watching the scene unfold as if it were a movie.

None of this was her real life—was it? Ally wasn't the one trying to put things back together after that brutal loss. She wasn't the one who'd fallen in love with Roscoe so hard and fast it left her dizzy, only to lose it all in a single moment. She wasn't the one who'd left her man sitting on the bed in nothing but a damp towel, staring up at her like she'd just smashed his heart.

And the photo? Who was its owner?

Still floating in some other place, Ally watched her hand reach for it now, some latent instinct to keep the photo intact, but Roscoe only held on tighter.

It felt like a punishment. She'd let her guard down too soon, let Roscoe right into her heart. And inevitably, in the process of making room for something new and amazing and utterly unexpected, she'd pushed Dan out.

"You told me the two of you weren't involved," Roscoe said, tossing the picture onto the bed. The anger had vanished, his tone turning cold and empty, yanking Ally right back into the moment.

You are going to lose him. Maybe you already have.

In an instant, she saw the whole of their relationship flash backward through her mind, one amazing memory at a time. Making love tonight... Painting at the Wellshire... Video games with Reggie and Nick... Picnics and parks and bingo and a thousand flirty texts and calls... Making out in the staff room... Their accidental non-date... Right up to that first time she'd ever seen him, strong and confident on the ice, his sexy dimple threatening to break down every one of her walls.

Roscoe had been patient with her all this time, and she'd betrayed him. Not in the way he thought, maybe, but a betrayal nevertheless. Because she'd let him believe that she was whole and unbroken, a woman who could love him the way he deserved to be loved.

Looking into his eyes now, Ally knew he was going to walk away from it all unless she could give him a reason to stay.

She took a shuddering breath, hoping it would give her strength, keep her calm, but still the words wouldn't come. Not the big ones, the ones that would explain it all. Those words didn't exist. Not now, not in the midst of her sadness and guilt and fear and confusion.

The old familiar darkness seeped into her heart like smoke.

All she could manage for now was a simple answer to his statement.

"We're *not* involved, Roscoe. Not anymore. He's—"

"You're carrying his picture around." Roscoe rose from the bed, letting his towel fall to the floor as he hunted for his clothes. "And who knows what else you've got in that bag. In this room. His clothes? Toothbrush? More pictures? Videos?"

He pinned her with his eyes, and Ally nodded. Yes, she had all of those things. And more. All taped up in boxes stacked in her closet. She hadn't been able to get rid of his possessions—not when he died, and not even when they'd moved.

Again, she wanted to tell him this. To sit him down, take a deep breath, and let it all out. Open the closet, the boxes, her fucking heart. Tell him the whole truth and make him understand.

But Ally was mute, her whole body trembling, panic squeezing her lungs. Her tongue was fat and useless as the anxiety attack took hold.

Roscoe made a sound like a laugh, then stepped into his jeans. "That's all I needed to know."

She'd never seen him so rattled. In their short time together, he'd become her rock in so many ways—allaying her fears about the dangers of letting Reggie play hockey. Surprising her with flowers and fun dates and making her laugh, never pressuring her or making her feel like she wasn't enough, never pushing her to talk about her past. He'd always seemed so content to let her set the pace, so ready to reassure her when she was having a hard time.

Now he was the one falling apart, and Ally just stood there letting it happen.

Powerless as the panic seized her body.

"Roscoe," she whispered, her ears ringing. "Please slow down. Please... I'll tell you everything, I just..." She sucked in a breath, desperate to slow her racing heart, to fill her lungs, to *breathe*. "I need a minute... I need some air and—"

"You know, I almost proposed to someone once."

Ally gasped, his words like an arrow momentarily piercing through the haze of her anxiety, but she still couldn't speak in complete sentences. She didn't want to know his history yet. She needed to tell him about Dan. "Roscoe, wait—"

"*Almost*," he repeated. "Had the ring and everything, had it all planned out. Then one night, I came home a day early from a week on the road, and you know what I found in my very own bed? My just-about-fiancée fucking her not-quite-ex. Turns out she'd been fucking him for half our relationship. So you can see why I might be a little sensitive here."

Ally sucked in another breath, shock and jealousy warring within, knowing she had no right to those feelings. No right to his pain. "This isn't like that."

"You're not giving me much to—"

"I love you," she said softly, meeting his gaze again. Then, with more conviction, "I'm in love with you."

Roscoe's eyes widened a fraction, but before Ally could even find the strength to say it again, to reassure him, to run to him and kiss him and give him every reason he needed, his walls went right back up again.

"No," he snapped, grabbing his shirt from the floor and yanking it over his head. "Don't do that. You don't get to throw that at me in the middle of an argument."

"Sorry," she said automatically. God, her timing sucked. She reached for one of the waters she'd brought in, twisting the cap and trying to gulp some down. Her hand was shaking so badly, most of it spilled.

"Sorry?" Roscoe let out a dry laugh. "For what? Telling me you're in love with me? Or this?" He grabbed the picture from the bed, held it up in front of her face.

Roscoe's fingers. Dan's smile. Ally's pain.

Her past collided with her present again, another explosion, the fallout tearing her apart inside. All of this was her fault. Not just because she hadn't told him about Dan, but because she'd tried to convince herself she could handle a relationship, that she was well enough to move on from Dan's death, that she could keep her own secrets and tell Roscoe about them in her own time, no harm done.

Instead, she'd ignored her instincts and let things go too far, too fast, too… everything.

But that's who Roscoe was. Ally had seen that spark in him right from the start.

She had it once, too. That spark. That desire to see and taste and experience everything, no matter what the risk. But after her husband's death, Ally's spark had fizzled out. Since then she'd hoarded her feelings like a miser, too afraid to share. To live. To love.

Roscoe was the complete opposite. He lived—and loved—with a passion bordering on recklessness. Reggie was like that too—with hockey, certainly. And one day, she would be reckless with Nick Harper, or some other boy she decided was worth her entire heart, because Reggie was an all-in kind of girl.

As much sleep as Ally had lost worrying about Reggie, deep down she envied her daughter. Ally had her podcasts and borrowed self-help mantras, but Roscoe and Reggie? They were the real deal. Brave and courageous, authentic in every way.

Looking into Roscoe's haunted eyes now, she wondered if she could do it. Live out loud. Be brave.

"There are things I haven't told you," she said, taking a steadying breath, then blowing it out slow. If she could just slow this whole thing down, clear her head, maybe she could get the words out. "Things about my past. My marriage. But I swear to you, Roscoe, it's not what you think. Dan is… He's…"

Ally faltered again, her throat burning with unshed tears. She wanted to scream with frustration. It was as if the dreaded d-word triggered her body's inner security system, shutting her down every time she got close to talking about it. It was just like this in the aftermath of the accident—the panic attacks, the tears. It was the reason she'd turned to books and podcasts instead of therapy after the accident; for Ally, it was a lot easier to hear about someone else's tragedy than talk about her own.

"Dan is *what*, Ally?"

"He's... He's..."

Roscoe sighed, his shoulders sagging as Ally watched the last of his trust flickering out like a candle. "It doesn't add up. You never talk about him, but you're still..." Roscoe looked at the picture again, shaking his head. "I'm an idiot. A fucking idiot. I really should've known better than to think this could be any different. That it was real."

Tears gathered in her eyes, but Ally couldn't blame him for thinking that way. She owed him an explanation, and she wanted to give it to him—more now than ever before. But she needed air and space, silence, time to open her heart and invite Roscoe into the darkest, deepest parts of her past. And Roscoe needed an immediate explanation, a short answer to a long and complicated situation.

The ghosts had finally crashed her party, just like Clarissa had warned.

It all seemed so unfair. So goddamn unfair that she'd been given a second chance at love—that this amazing, incredible, loving man had come into her life—but that it had happened at the wrong time. Another year, maybe two? That would've been perfect. But she was a hot mess, just like she'd told Clarissa after the first time she'd met Roscoe, and no amount of laughter and fun dates and sweet, sinful kisses would fix that.

A surge of anger rose suddenly inside, nearly sending her to her knees. But instead of crumpling, she embraced it, clung to it like a life raft. Anger was good. Anger filled up the holes inside, kept her heart pumping when all she wanted to do was curl into a ball and die.

"So I'm cheating on you, right?" she snapped, all the rage she'd repressed after Dan's accident bubbling up from within. "Like your ex? That's the only possible explanation?"

"No. Just the most logical one."

"You know what? *I'm* the idiot who should've known better." It'd never been so clear to Ally than in this moment just how much she hadn't dealt with, how much she'd swallowed down just to be able to get out of bed every morning, just to keep feeding herself and taking care of Reggie and paying their bills and not falling completely apart. She was barely functional for that entire first year, barely hanging on, but somehow she found a way to put that grief and anger and rage on a shelf, seal it in a box, and stay alive. Days turned into weeks, into months. And now, after three years, it was finally catching up with her, burning so hot inside she was sure she'd turn to ash before the night was over.

"It was selfish of me to drag you into my messed-up life," she said. "I wasn't ready for a relationship when we met, and I'm obviously not ready now."

"Really? Which is it, Ally?" Roscoe shoved a hand through his hair, his eyes blazing with new heat. "Because you say you're not ready, but then you're worried about what you're dragging me into. Is this about me, or you?"

"Both of us. I don't want anyone to get hurt." Ally realized how stupid that sounded even before the words were all out, but she pressed on anyway. "I just think we got into this a little too quickly, let things happen too fast, and all of a sudden—"

"Are you talking about the sex? Because I told you a dozen times we could turn down the heat. Newsflash, Ally. That's not what I'm here for."

Ally swallowed hard. *Sex. Heat.* The words sent her blood racing, memories of their time together crashing through her body. Despite her roiling emotions, her core throbbed with desire, still primed and aching for his touch. His kiss. His everything.

"No," she said now, desperate to hold on to her anger, even as she felt it leaking away. "It's not the sex. I'm... God, I don't know, Roscoe. I'm just... I'm scared, okay? Scared shitless."

"What are you afraid of?" Roscoe demanded.

That I'll share my secrets, show you my personal demons, and you'll never look at me the same way. That the fire in your eyes when you make love to me will turn to pity. That you'll treat me like I'm weak and broken, too fragile to handle so much passion and love. That I'll lose you, one way or another...

But Ally couldn't say those things out loud, so she settled on, "You? This? Everything!"

"Bullshit. You want to know what I think?" Roscoe asked. "All that stuff in the beginning about Reggie and hockey, not wanting her to play. I don't think you were worried about her. I think you were worried about yourself."

"That makes no sense."

"It's the same thing with us. You're not afraid of me. Of us. You're afraid of you. Afraid that you'll lose control."

"It's not—"

"Someone in your life—or something—took away your control, and you've been fighting like hell to get it back ever since." Roscoe stepped forward, closing the gap between them. He slid his fingers under her chin, tilting her head up until their eyes met, looking at her with a mix of frustration and desire. Water dripped from his hair onto his shirt, and all Ally wanted to do was slide her hands into his wet, silky hair, pull his mouth to hers, and kiss him until their pain evaporated...

"Let me tell you something about control, Ally," Roscoe said, his breath warm on her lips. "It's a fucking lie. Something we say to convince ourselves it's okay to get out of bed every day, because the truth is just too fucking dangerous to contemplate."

He held her gaze for another moment, staring at her so intensely it made her tremble.

But then he closed his eyes, let out a long sigh, and released her.

Roscoe turned away, picking up his wallet and keys from the nightstand.

"Are you... Are you *leaving*, leaving?" she asked, heart hammering behind her ribs as she waited for his answer.

"Ally, I just..." He sighed, finally turning around to look at her again. There was no glint there, no laughter, no love, no fire, no frustration. He'd shut down completely, all the emotions that were once so easy to read replaced suddenly with a shield of pure ice. "I need some space. Okay?"

Maybe she could've talked him into staying. Into giving her a little more time to compose herself, to find all the words to make this story make sense. He looked at her as though he wanted her to do just that.

But in the end, she couldn't. Because in the end, she

really was weak and scared and broken, and no amount of borrowed podcast pseudo-wisdom could cover that up.

"I'm sorry," she whispered.

"Yeah," Roscoe said, his stone-cold gaze a total mismatch for the raw pain in his voice. "Me, too."

And then he was gone.

CHAPTER TWENTY-FIVE

In the age-old history of bad days, this one definitely put the shit icing on the crap cake.

"Sixty-one!" Roscoe blew his whistle, stopping the kids mid-practice. "You falling asleep out there?"

"I'm doing the best job I can," Nick Harper shouted back. He looked exhausted, and for about half a second, Roscoe felt bad for him. It was a rare practice without any media hoopla, and he'd been running the kids hard for an hour, pushing them right up to their limits.

Still. The youth tournament was less than three weeks away, and no matter how hard they worked, Roscoe couldn't get consistent results. Reggie and Nick were strong and solid, and a handful of others were close seconds, but the majority of the kids lagged way behind. At this rate, they'd be going home with a pocket full of jack shit—well, unless he counted the nosediving public opinion polls sure to follow a loss, not to mention another black mark on Roscoe's record. He needed this win. The whole team did.

"Your job," he said to Harper now, "is to get that puck into the net. You're missing every shot. Hence, you're not doing your job. And if you're not doing yours, I can't do mine."

Roscoe shoved a hand through his hair and blew out a breath. He was being a total prick—again. Pretty much his standard operating procedure lately, and he was starting to hate himself for it.

"Alright," he said to the group. "Take five to hydrate. Then I want the forwards on center ice with me. Kenton, Jarlsberg, Kooz—collect your starters and run 'em through defensive drills until they can stop pucks with their eyes closed."

"What about us, Mr. Sunshine?" Dunn skated up to Roscoe and cut his blades, showering him in shaved ice. "Christ, you look like old balls on a soggy cracker."

Roscoe wiped his face on his sleeve. "You can go fuck yourself."

"Eh." Dunn shrugged. "Not as fun when there's only one."

"Tell me about it."

"Ouch." Dunn at least had the decency to look surprised. "What the hell happened? You two were pretty damn cozy last weekend at Wellshire."

"Don't remind me." It twisted his gut to think about how happy he and Ally had been that night. How quickly it'd gone to shit.

"Hey," Dunn said. "What's going on?"

Ignoring him, Roscoe skated over to the players' bench and grabbed his water bottle.

Where did he even begin? In the three days since that fight with Ally, he hadn't slept more than a handful of hours, haunted by the image of Ally's face etched with heartbreak as Roscoe pushed and pushed and pushed. He knew she was in pain that night, knew she was having a hard time, and still he couldn't give her even a minute to take a breath.

Thing is, Roscoe knew she wasn't fucking her ex. Deep down, he'd fucking known that from the get-go. He knew *her*, despite all the secrets—knew all the parts that really mattered. Yeah, her story had a hell of a lot of gaps, but even as she'd stammered over his questions, she still hadn't looked like a woman caught cheating.

She'd looked like a woman who'd seen a ghost.

And instead of giving her a little breathing room, a little time to explain, he'd attacked her, lashing out like some damn wounded animal backed into a corner, all because he couldn't deal with his *own* fucked up relation-ship mistakes.

"I got pissed and said some dumb shit," Roscoe snapped, "and now I'm out on my dumb ass. So if you don't mind skating your pretty little face somewhere else, I'd like to sulk in private."

Dunn's eyebrows rose, then that pretty face broke into a grin. "I just want to state, for the record, that I fucking called this."

Roscoe chucked him on the shoulder. "You find this funny, asshole?"

"Nope. But I did just win a hundred bucks." Laughing, he said, "Eva and I bet Henny you were in love with her. And now I know my girl and I were right, Mr. Loverboy."

Roscoe shook his head, but he wasn't denying it. Just couldn't believe how fucked he was.

"To be fair, Eva called it first," Dunn said. "She's got a knack for this shit."

"Eva's planning a wedding. And women planning weddings want everyone else to fall in love and get married, too."

"She called it."

"That's not calling it. That's more like a disease, Dunn."

"Wedding disease?"

"Exactly. Probably all that cake testing. Sugars affecting her brain or something."

Dunn crossed his arms over his chest. "Sugars."

"You keep repeating everything I say."

"And you still haven't denied I'm right."

"You're..." Roscoe ran a hand through his hair, averting his eyes. "Not wrong. But what the fuck does it matter? I blew it the other night. Acted like a prime douche bag."

"If you want my advice—"

"I don't."

"Communication is really the foundation of—"

"Seriously? *Seriously*?"

"Good talk, bro." Dunn slapped him on the back, but then his eyes turned serious. Clamping a hand over Roscoe's shoulder, Dunn gave him a quick squeeze. "Hey. You'll figure it out." Then, with another sly smile, "You don't have a choice. Eva already included her in the final head count. And if you screw that up, there won't be a safe place you can hide."

That finally got a laugh out of him, blowing some of the tension away.

Dunn was right. He'd figure it out. This was Ally. He wasn't about to ghost on her after one fight. Yeah, they had some shit to work through, but who didn't?

Thing was, he knew Ally wouldn't make the move here. He'd watched her withdraw last night, curl up into her little shell. Then he'd asked for some space, and walked away.

So Roscoe could stand around holding his dick on principle, staring at his damn phone for the call that would never come, or he could march his ass over there and straighten this thing out.

The choice was obvious.

"You good?" Dunn asked.

Roscoe chugged the last of his water, then scrubbed a hand over his mouth. "Yeah. I'm good."

"Sweet. Let's go whip these ingrates into shape."

He played it low key for the rest of practice, letting Dunn and Henny take the offensive lead while he ran backup, helping the kids where he could. He paid a little extra attention to Nick Harper, hoping he hadn't done any permanent damage with his earlier call-outs, but Harper seemed pretty resilient. At the end of practice, the kid even fist-bumped him on his way off the ice, just like old times.

It was Reggie who threw Roscoe off his game.

"What's going on?" Reggie asked, skating over to him after the rest of the kids had vacated.

Roscoe folded his arms across his chest. "With?"

"Right." Reggie rolled her eyes.

"You know, kiddo, one day those eyes are gonna roll right out of your head."

"Oh, God. Now you sound like Mom."

"Because we're both right."

"Because you're both corny. Anyway, did something happen with you guys? Because I know for a fact we had two cartons of Cherry Garcia ice cream in the freezer, and now they're totally gone. She dogged them, Roscoe. And this morning I found an empty container of frosting in the trash, but did she bake a cake? Nope. And my Netflix queue is suddenly full of sappy eighties rom-coms."

Roscoe bit back a smile, marveling at her Sherlock-ian skills.

"It can only mean one thing," she said.

"Your mom had a slumber party and forgot to invite you?"

"More like a pity party."

Roscoe felt a little jab at his heart. As funny as it was to think about Reggie putting all the clues together, Roscoe hated the idea of Ally sitting home in bed, crying into her ice cream over the way they'd left things. The way *he'd* left them.

God, he was an asshole.

Thinking about it again now only made him feel like *more* of an asshole. He was no closer to knowing the details of her past relationship than he was the first time they'd gone out, but it was obvious the man had hurt her in some way. Maybe she'd escaped a bad marriage, leaving him in the dust. Maybe he'd left *them*, abandoning Ally with a kid to raise on her own. There were any number of fucked up possibilities—probably some Roscoe couldn't even imagine.

No wonder she was so hot-and-cold, so skittish. Here she was in Buffalo, keeping her head down, trying to build a new life for her and Reggie. Then along comes Roscoe, trampling in like the proverbial bull in a china shop, demanding answers about the very things she and Reg might be trying their damnedest to forget.

Then again, carrying around a photo of the guy wasn't the best strategy for forgetting him…

Roscoe shook it off. There was an explanation—had to be. And this time, he owed it to Ally to be patient enough, compassionate enough, and trusting enough to hear her out, no matter how hard it might be to swallow the truth.

"She picking you up soon?" he asked, ducking Reggie's all-too-perceptive gaze.

Reggie shook her head. "She had a meeting. I'm taking the bus home. And before you freak out, Mom is okay with it."

"Your mother is okay with the bus?" Shit. Letting her kid take public transportation? Now he *knew* Ally was avoiding him. "Tell you what. Give me ten minutes to clean up, and I'll take you home. But I need to make a couple of stops on the way. Actually, I could use your help with something, if you're up for it."

"Hmm. Can we get more ice cream?"

"Is this bribery?"

"You say bribery, I say fair compensation for services rendered." Reggie held out her hands, balancing them like the scales of Lady Justice herself. "You get me ice cream, I make myself scarce so you and Mom can kiss and make up. Preferably before my Netflix queue gets totally jacked."

Roscoe laughed. God, he loved this kid.

"Regina Heinz?" he said, clamping a hand on her shoulder. "Remind me never to get on your bad side."

CHAPTER TWENTY-SIX

"Reg?" Ally called out from the front hall, dropping her keys into the bowl by the door. "I'm so sorry I'm late! They had us in a last-minute meeting with the head of branding, and holy hell, that guy can *talk*." Kicking off her shoes, she finally caught a whiff of the saucy aroma wafting out from the kitchen. "Did you cook?"

"Delivery," Reggie called back. "Sort of."

"You're an angel."

"Can I get that in writing?"

"Do the dishes later, and you got it."

"Deal."

Ally smiled, taking a moment to steady herself before heading into the kitchen. Her encounter with Roscoe a few nights ago had left her raw and ragged, but she was determined not to let Reggie see her hurting. She didn't want Reggie to worry.

More importantly, she didn't want to have to tell Reggie how she'd singlehandedly ruined her relationship with Roscoe before it had even gotten off the ground.

A dozen times this week, Ally had picked up her phone to call him. To invite him back here so they could truly talk about everything. But a dozen times, she'd changed her mind. She'd made such a mess of things last weekend—the very least she could do was honor his request for a little space.

Roscoe would get in touch when he was ready.

And if he didn't get in touch again? Well, that was no less than she deserved.

Breathing through the pain in her chest, Ally squared her shoulders and headed into the kitchen to see her daughter, the one person guaranteed to put a smile on her face.

But to Ally's surprise, there wasn't just one person sitting at the table tonight. There were two.

Ally's heart leapt, a flush creeping over her skin. "Roscoe," she breathed, taking in the scene. The table was set with a whole spread—salad and bread, wine, something steaming in a baking dish at the center. He'd even lit candles. "What... What is all this?"

By way of explanation, Roscoe stood up and pulled out a chair for her, his smile so tentative she couldn't even find the dimple. "Hope you like eggplant parmesan, because my recipe is killer."

"I love eggplant parmesan," Ally said. It took a moment for her to process the fact that he was really there, sitting at her kitchen table with Reggie, waiting for her to join them, but eventually her lips curled into a soft smile, then finally split into a grin.

Roscoe sighed in relief. "I'm so glad you said that. I mean, it was a safe bet, considering you were a fan of the lasagna. But not everyone likes eggplant. Texture thing, I guess."

He trailed off, and Ally just stared at him, heart hammering wildly, her insides churning with a mix of relief and guilt and love and heartache. There was so much she wanted to say to him, so much she still had to explain, and none of it was going to be easy.

But for now, she sat down next to him and reached for his knee under the table, giving him a gentle squeeze.

"You did all this?" she asked.

Roscoe beamed, finally giving her a peek at the dimple she'd missed so much. It took every ounce of willpower she had not to lean over and press a kiss to that very spot. "I, uh… Yeah. I guess I did," he said, then thumbed toward Reggie. "With a little help from my favorite center forward here."

"Yeah, I'm *super* helpful." Reggie laughed, reaching for the salad bowl. "Now could you two *please* stop looking at each other like that? Some of us are trying to eat."

"You didn't have to go to all this trouble." Ally wrapped up the remaining eggplant and popped it into the fridge, already looking forward to reheating it for lunch tomorrow. "But I'm glad you did."

Dinner had been wonderful, the mood lighthearted and cozy as Roscoe and Reggie regaled Ally with tales from the ice. But Reggie had excused herself halfway through the meal, dashing off to her bedroom with her laptop and a carton of ice cream.

"I might've had ulterior motives." He stepped up behind her as she closed the fridge, grabbing her shoulders and gently turning her around to face him. She shivered at the contact, at the warmth in his eyes as his gaze swept her face. Leaning in close, he brushed his lips over her neck, just beneath her ear. "God, I missed you."

"Me too." She sighed in pleasure, her eyes fluttering closed. It would be so easy to give in to his magnetic pull. To put the arguments and the past and everything else behind them and just let herself fall right into his embrace. His kiss.

Maybe that's what he wanted, too.

But Ally couldn't do that now.

Gently, she pulled away, placing her palms against his chest and looking up into his eyes again. "There's so much I have to tell you—so much I *should* have told you."

"I hate how we left things the other night. How *I* left." Pain and regret clouded his eyes as he reached forward to cup her face, stroking her cheek with his thumb. "I knew it was hard for you... I should've given you a chance."

"You aren't the one who owes an apology here," she said. "I shut down that night, and I completely shut you out. And I'm so, so sorry. If I could redo it—"

"You don't have to. I get it." He pressed a kiss to her forehead, but Ally couldn't help noticing he'd avoided her lips. Even now, with Reggie tucked away in her bedroom, Roscoe still hadn't made a move to kiss her. Ally knew she didn't deserve his kiss—not yet. Maybe not ever again. But that didn't stop her from wanting it, the urge to slide her fingers into his silky hair and pull him to her mouth nearly overpowering her.

"Hey," Roscoe said, smoothing his thumb over the corner of her mouth. "No frowning. The night is still young! I haven't even given you your surprise yet."

Ally couldn't help but smile. "Another surprise?"

"Yes. Are you surprised?"

"Surprised that you're surprising me again?" Ally

laughed. "I guess I shouldn't be. Hopefully I don't need a smock for this one."

"You might." Roscoe's dimple deepened, mischief glinting in his eyes. He grabbed Ally's hand, leading her into the living room. "Now, close your eyes."

Ally obeyed, listening intently as he opened the French doors that led into the den—the room where she'd planned to set up her home studio.

"Okay," he said, flicking on the light. "Take a look."

Ally opened her eyes.

The room, which had served as a catch-all of empty cardboard boxes and bubble wrap from their move, had been completely transformed. The moving supplies and trash were gone, the room freshly vacuumed.

Two easels stood at one end, blank canvases set on each one, with more canvases stacked on a low shelf behind them. The built-in bookshelves along the back wall were lined with bottles—paints of every kind, brush cleaners, paint thinners, and a few things Ally didn't even recognize. On another shelf, glass jars held a huge assortment of professional-grade brushes, palette knives, charcoal, pencils, and any other tool she could dream of.

Ally's eyes filled with tears, the doors of her heart blasted clear off their hinges. The gift itself was extravagant and beautiful and completely over the top in the best possible way. But more than that, she felt like Roscoe had seen her that night at Wellshire—truly seen her.

Even through her own doubts, he'd seen the long lost sparks inside her and encouraged them into flames. Into fire. Into a raging inferno.

Speechless. She was utterly, completely speechless.

"Other than Candy's Canvases," Roscoe said, coming up to stand behind her at the easels, "all of my art knowledge comes from Bob Ross. I thought I could just walk in there and get some paint, right? Then the guy started throwing out all these names. Watercolors, gesso, pallets, fan brushes." He laughed. "Who the hell knew there was so much to making those happy little trees?"

"Roscoe," she whispered, still not trusting her voice. "It's so... It's beautiful. I don't even know what to say."

"It's not totally set up, obviously. But Reggie and I figured we could get it cleared out and started for you, then you could do what you want with it."

"Reggie was in on this too?"

"Of course. But she didn't really know what you liked, either. So I covered all the bases and got—well, everything."

Ally smiled, tears freely leaking from her eyes. The fact that he'd done this with Reggie touched her in ways she couldn't even describe. She loved that they had such a close bond. That they'd gone out and done this together. All for her.

"Acrylics were always my favorite," she said softly, turning to face him again.

"Yes! I got those!" Roscoe's eyes lit up as he rummaged through one of the shelves, picking out a few brightly colored tubes and holding them up. "Right?"

Ally nodded. "I can't... I can't believe you did this for me. It's perfect. It's..." Ally trailed off, emotion tightening her throat. "I don't know why you're so good to me."

"How can you say that?"

"Because there's so much you don't know about me. So much I keep screwing up. I'm a mess, Roscoe. A mess. One minute I'm laughing and joking around, happier than I think I've ever been in my life. Then I'm having a panic attack and running away from ghosts. I can't promise you it's going to get better. And that's a lot for anyone to take, let alone a man who's only known me a couple of months."

"Ally." He pulled her into a hug, pressing his warm lips to the top of her head. "Being with you... You light me up. That's all there is to it. From the moment we met, I felt it. Your passion. Your vibrancy. It comes through in everything you do—the way you love your daughter, the way you fight for her. The way you laugh. The way you paint. The way you make love. And yes, even the way you fall apart. I want to be there for all of it, Ally. Every part of it. Every part of *you*."

"Even the dark parts?" Ally pulled out of his embrace, looking up into his kind, compassionate eyes.

"The parts you haven't even seen yet, because I've purposely kept them from you? The parts so terrifying I haven't even found the strength to face them myself?"

Roscoe waited a beat, then nodded. "Well. Hit me with whatever you've got, Ally. I was upset the other night, made a huge mistake—and for that, I'm sorry as hell. I'll do whatever it takes to prove that to you. Because when it comes down to it, I'm not going anywhere. That's a promise."

"We haven't been seeing each other long enough to make that promise."

"By whose standards? Who made that calendar? Who decides what's long enough? We do. That's it. And if I say I can deal with it, I mean it."

"I don't want someone to have to *deal* with me."

"That's not—Ally, look. You think I don't know what it's like to be hurt by someone you love? My ex basically used my nuts for target practice, and even then, I couldn't bring myself to get rid of the damn ring until recently. We were totally incompatible from the start, but I didn't see it. So when she betrayed me, it fucking hurt. And yeah, I spent a good long while licking my wounds, screwing around... Hell, I probably have a few pictures of her shoved in a box somewhere. It just... Finding that picture in your purse took me by surprise, and I reacted badly. Horribly. That won't happen again."

"It's more than a few photos shoved in a box,

Roscoe." Ally gathered up the acrylics he'd taken off the shelf, rearranging them in color order before setting them back in their places. The room was so beautiful, the rainbow of colors calling to something deep within her, making her fingers itch to paint again. To recapture that same sense of otherworldliness she'd felt at the Wellshire. But she couldn't do that now. Couldn't let herself slip away into the comforts of this room, the kindness in Roscoe's eyes, the promises on his lips.

She needed to open her heart to him. To let him see inside, shine a light on everything that terrified her.

It would change everything. Who he thought she was, how he looked at her, maybe even how he touched and kissed her.

But it was time.

Setting the final tube of paint in its place, Ally finally turned to face him again. Roscoe smiled, dimple and all, and she blew out a breath, feeling as though she was about to leap off a cliff.

Ally reached for his hand, squeezed it gently.

"Come with me," she said. "I need to show you something."

CHAPTER TWENTY-SEVEN

Ally's bedroom had never felt so suffocating and small, but Ally knew there was no turning back now. She couldn't keep this from him any longer.

Opening the closet doors, she pushed aside her clothes, giving Roscoe a clear view of the boxes stacked neatly behind them.

"Still unpacking?" Roscoe asked, taking a seat on her bed.

"Not exactly." Ally ran her hand over the top of one of the boxes—Dan's old DVD collection. Mostly westerns and action movies, but he was also big on Disney, thanks to Reggie. He'd started collecting them when Reggie was about a month old, telling Ally he wanted to study up on princesses, just in case.

Ally smiled at the bittersweet memory.

"Everything my husband owned is in these boxes,"

she confessed. "These, and a few more in the garage. I didn't leave any of his things back in Colorado. I couldn't bear to part with them. I still can't, because parting with them means sorting through them, and all the memories associated with that, and I just... I'm avoiding it. I've been avoiding it for three years."

She heard Roscoe shift on the bed, but true to his word, he didn't leave.

"I want to hear about it," he said softly. "Anything you want to share. But whatever happened between you two is in the past, Ally. No matter how bad it was. Your divorce isn't—"

"We're not divorced." Ally grabbed a box of tissues from her dresser and joined him on the bed, tucking her feet up, her knees brushing against his thighs as she faced him. The room itself was silent, save for their breathing, uneven and sharp, and the faint sounds of Reggie's laughter floating in from her room down the hall.

Ally was glad to hear it. She hoped Reg was watching a fun movie, or maybe even talking to Nick on the phone.

Roscoe watched her, his brow furrowed, waiting patiently as Ally gathered her thoughts.

She took a shuddering breath, preparing to speak the words she hadn't uttered to another living soul in three years. "Dan died, Roscoe. Three years ago. Freak accident at work."

Roscoe gasped, the shock in his eyes plain as Ally held her breath, waiting for the panic to seize her lungs again. It didn't come this time, though, and she pressed on, determined to tell Roscoe everything.

"He died saving another man's life. They called me and said I had to get there as soon as I could—that there had been an accident. But I just… I knew."

Roscoe's shock gave way to compassion, then concern. He reached for her hands, holding them tight as he pressed a long, lingering kiss against her fingers. "I am so, so sorry, Ally. My God."

Tears streaked her cheeks, her heart lodging in her throat, but she had to get this out. "I didn't want to tell you at first. I wasn't sure how long we'd last, whether it would even go beyond a few fun dates. So why bring it up, right? And then things got more serious between us, and I knew I should say something, but I just… It never seemed like the right time."

Roscoe nodded, reaching to erase some of her tears with the gentle swipe of his thumb.

"And the more time we spent together, the more I… The harder I fell for you." She shook her head, swallowing through the tightness in her throat. "I was so, so scared it would change everything."

"Change?" he asked gently, confusion knitting his brow. "How I feel about you?"

"I thought you'd start treating me like this frail, fragile woman. Reggie, too. Like maybe you'd feel sorry for us. And then you wouldn't be able to be honest with me about anything—arguments, stuff I did that hurt you, even silly things like where we should go for dinner—all because you wouldn't want to upset me. It's happened before, Roscoe. Our neighbors, Reggie's friends at school. Everyone means well, but it doesn't always translate. After he died, after the parade of casseroles and sympathy cards ended, I felt like Reggie and I were stranded on this island. Clarissa was the only one who didn't change. She'd been close with Dan, too—we all went to college together. She was so amazing through all of it—despite her own pain at losing a good friend, she was there for us in a way no one else was."

Ally grabbed a tissue and told him the rest of the story, barely pausing to blot her tears as she went, leaving nothing out. By the time she'd gotten it all off her chest, she felt hollowed out inside, weak and drained and utterly exhausted.

"I'm sorry I kept this from you," she whispered.

"You don't have to apologize." Roscoe shook his head, looking into the closet again, his eyes skimming over the stack of boxes before returning to her face. "I... I don't know what to say, Ally. There are no words for this.

None at all." He kissed her hands again, then squeezed them tight, his gaze turning fiery and fierce. "The only thing I can tell you is that none of this changes how I feel, and I'd never treat you like you might break. You and Reggie *aren't* fragile, Ally. Far from it."

A laugh broke through Ally's tears. "Well, considering my kid actually *enjoys* skating around an ice rink at warp speed, *she's* not fragile, obviously. But I'm—"

"The strongest woman I've ever met. Just to go through something like this and come out on the other side... You moved across the country, started a new career, you're raising an incredible daughter... God, I wish you could see yourself the way I see you."

She smiled, but her heart was still so heavy. Three years had passed since the accident, and she still felt like she and Reggie had such a long, twisty road ahead of them. Of course Roscoe would be the first one to volunteer to help her along that road, but Ally didn't want that for him. Her grief wasn't something Roscoe could carry for her. All he'd be able to do was stand on the sidelines and watch her fall apart, and that wasn't a life she'd wish on anyone.

"Dan was a good man, Roscoe," she said, her lungs constricting again under the weight of this old pain. "An amazing father. He took care of us. And even though I can go through my days like a normal person—go to work, take care of Reggie, and even have the most amazing time with you—the truth is, I'm not over it. Sometimes I don't think I ever will be."

A flicker of hurt flashed through Roscoe's eyes, but then it was gone, replaced again by his compassion. His endless concern for her. "That's understandable. He was your husband."

"No, it's not that. It's..." Ally reached for another tissue, blotting her eyes as she searched for the words. She'd made it sound as if she were sitting here pining away for Dan, but that wasn't it at all. No, it was Death itself—Capital-D Death—that had gotten a hold of her, squeezing her heart until it was almost nothing but a shriveled black shell. The sudden, unexpected loss had hit her in ways she still couldn't process. It'd changed her entire worldview, shifted the whole planet on its axis. How could someone be there one minute—sitting at the kitchen table paying bills on the laptop, eating ice cream out of the carton in front of the fridge when he thought no one was watching, kissing Reggie on the top of her head before bed—and then just... not? He existed, and then he was gone. Just like that.

She'd lost people before—her mother had died of Alzheimer's, her father from heart issues. Both were younger than they should've been, but Ally was able to prepare, as much as anyone could in that situation. She had time to be with them, to say her goodbyes. When Dan died, she learned that life could shatter in an instant.

Other than Roscoe, Ally had never gotten close with anyone after that—no new friends, no dates, no real socializing at work or with the other hockey parents. Even with Roscoe, though, she still felt herself holding back. Every once in a while he'd slip behind her walls, but it never lasted. Some part of Ally would always be afraid of sudden loss, and knowing she could never survive that kind of pain again, she'd done her best to protect her heart from ever getting that attached in the first place.

It wasn't fair to expect a man like Roscoe—a man who loved so completely, who never did anything unless his whole heart was all in—to be with a woman who couldn't offer the same in return. No matter how much she wanted him to stay, to keep on promising her that this would never change how he felt about her, that he loved her, that they could be together... She couldn't let him make those promises.

"The woman that you think you see when you look at me?" Ally said. "She doesn't exist. And the longer we keep pretending otherwise, the harder it's going to be when you finally figure it out."

"You're wrong. She does." Roscoe shook his head, emotion clouding his eyes. "I meant what I said the other night. I'm in love with you—the beautiful, passionate parts just as much as the parts you think are dark and scary."

"I just… I rushed head first into things with you," she continued, ignoring the thud of her heart behind her shirt, the bubbles in her stomach at Roscoe's words. "And I liked you so much I tried to convince myself I could do it, you know? Just be with someone and have fun and not get so worried and hung up on the what-ifs. And for a little while, I did." She touched his face, fresh tears gathering in her eyes. "But when you found Dan's picture that night, everything came crashing down on me again. It brought up a lot of things for me—namely, that I haven't dealt with his death. Like, at all."

"Okay. So you start right now. You take one step—whatever you need to do. I'm not going anywhere. I'm with you, Ally. Through all of it."

"I don't even know what 'all of it' entails yet." She hadn't even finished going through the boxes. The material "stuff" that didn't even matter. How could she even begin to go through the psychological ones?

Ally rose from the bed and headed into the bathroom to toss out her tissues, grateful for an excuse to put some distance between her and Roscoe. She couldn't let herself fall under the spell of his kindness, his understanding. His devotion.

Keeping a safe distance, she turned back to face him, leaning against the bathroom doorframe with her arms folded over her chest. "I probably need to see a counselor, or at the very least a support group. I need to be there for Reggie, to share memories of her dad and help her process his death and our move and everything that happened in between. She seems so resilient, but deep down I know she's still hurting. She talks to Clarissa some, but I know she worries if she mentions her father to me, I'll break down again. I need her to know it's okay to talk about him again. To laugh, even. I don't know how long it's going to take, or what kinds of feelings it's going to unearth—I just know that I've been shoving all of it down for a long time, and there's a lot of work to do."

Roscoe scrubbed a hand over his mouth, his brow furrowed as he tried to process all of this. "What are you not saying?"

She took a deep breath, then another, thinking back to the other night, to the moment Roscoe had found Dan's picture. Roscoe might've called it surprise, might've tried to downplay it now. But the hurt and fear in his eyes that night would haunt her always. She would never, ever allow herself to put that look in his eyes again.

And letting him help her with this was like putting him on a collision course to heartache. How could she drag him deeper into this, knowing full well that something else might set her off at any time. Another picture? A song? A memory? One of those renegade socks in the dryer? It wasn't fair to him, and it wasn't fair to Reggie, either. Roscoe had become a mentor to her, a coach as well as a friend. Ally didn't know what would happen when the regular season started up again, but if Roscoe and Reggie had any shot at building their friendship and mentorship, the last thing Ally wanted to do was mess with that.

As difficult as it was, backing off from their relationship was the right call. Ally didn't want to hurt him, didn't want to subject him to the crazy ups and downs of her heart. Roscoe might volunteer for it, but she couldn't let him do it, no matter how much he loved her.

Ally frowned, her heart already breaking for him. But ripping off the Band-Aid was the best option. The *only* option. "I'm saying I need to work through this on my own. To face this. And I don't think I can do it without hurting you."

Roscoe rose from the bed, reaching toward her. "Ally—"

"I'm saying it's over."

He took another step forward, eradicating the space between them. Ally backed up against the bathroom wall, but he was right there, caging her in with his strong arms, his breath falling on her face in soft, warm puffs. In a whisper that damn near melted her, he said, "I don't believe you."

That's because I'm full of shit.

She was in love with him. And she saw it reflected in

his eyes, too, looking at her like she truly was the only other person in the world. In *his* world.

God, this was so hard. She hated hurting him like this, but it would only get worse the longer she tried to make this work. He deserved a woman who was strong and unbroken, one who wouldn't drag him into the darkness while she tried to claw her way back to the light.

Roscoe would never be the one to walk away from this—he'd said as much. It had to be her. Had to be now, before they got in any deeper.

"I made you a promise," she said, placing her hands on his chest and forcing out the words. "I told you that if I ever got to a point where I didn't want this anymore—didn't want us—I would tell you."

Pain flickered in his eyes, and his breath caught, but she couldn't stop.

"I don't want this anymore," she whispered, each word tearing through her heart like a hot blade. It was a lie, but that lie would set him free. "I don't want us."

"Ally—"

Ally shook her head, feeling as though she'd carved out her own heart and left it right there on the bathroom floor.

She might not survive this, but Roscoe would, and that was all that mattered.

"Please, Roscoe," she whispered. "Please just go."

CHAPTER TWENTY-EIGHT

The rink used to be the one place Roscoe could go to forget all of his problems. The swish of his blades against the ice, the snap of cold air on his face, the raw power coursing through his muscles as he chased that puck into the net—all of it made the rest of the world disappear.

But in the eighteen days since Ally had ended their relationship—yeah, he was counting every damn one—not even the familiar comforts of the ice could soothe the endless ache in his chest.

Not even tonight, mere hours before the youth cup tournament. The kids would be here soon, pumped and buzzing with energy, ready to run out here and give it their all. And Roscoe would give them the locker room pep talks, cheer for them from the box, call for the line changes to make sure every last one got some time on the ice. He'd tell them to get out there and kick some ass, and have all the fun in the world doing it.

But inside, he'd be waging the same old war, one side demanding that he march over to Ally's house, prove to her just how much he loved her, and refuse to let her go without a fight. The other side just wanted her to get through this okay, and if she needed him out of her life in order to be okay, who the fuck was he to refuse?

He squeezed his eyes shut now, shaking his head to dislodge the familiar loop. There was no war—not really. Ally had already beat him, and he'd walked away with his heart in his hands.

He hadn't seen her since.

"Roscoe! You ready for this, brother?"

Roscoe looked up to see Henny skating right for him, his grin both dopey and annoying. Dunn was right behind him, of course. After the breakup, they'd appointed themselves his personal fucking cheer squad, shouldering the bulk of the work at the youth practices, dragging him out for dinner and drinks every other damn night, and generally being giant pains in the ass, all in hopes it would take his mind off his woman.

Part of him appreciated them for trying.

The other part of him, well…

"I'm ready to punch you in the mouth, *brother*. Does that count?" He slapped the puck hard over to Henny, who caught it against his skate and let out a low whistle.

"I see you're just as sunny as ever."

"Sort it out, Roscoe." Dunn skated up behind him, clamped a hand over his shoulder. "We need you sharp tonight."

"You don't need me at all," he said, feeling immensely sorry for himself. "No one does."

"Aw, don't say that." Henny came at him from the other side, pulling him into a rough side hug. "Clarissa will always need you. Or at least your nuts. In a vice. And she'll be here in an hour, so that's all sorted."

"With the camera crews," Dunn added. As if Roscoe needed the reminder.

Scrubbing a hand over his mouth, he shook them both off. "I said I'm good."

"You sure?" Henny asked.

"Sure as shit." He gripped his stick and jerked his head toward center ice. "Let's go."

"Yeah?"

"Hell yeah." Roscoe grinned. "Nothing like beating both your asses to get me in the zone."

He zoomed over to the face-off circle, waiting for his men to follow. They got in a solid hour of ice time, pushing one another hard as they took turns passing, shooting, and defending. Roscoe didn't know if it was the anticipation of tonight's big game, or the fact that his friends had finally gotten through to him, but it wasn't long before he started to loosen up, to actually enjoy himself out there. With every crack of his big, hard stick against the puck, Roscoe whacked another chunk off his pent-up frustration, and by the time the media cavalry showed up, his head was clear, his mind completely in the zone.

For the first time in weeks, he was excited for the kids tonight. Pumped for the tournament, for watching them play in their first real game. Hell, he didn't even mind the fact that they'd likely be stuck signing autographs and giving media interviews half the damn night.

Roscoe was even smiling.

"There's the Mr. Sunshine we all know and love." Henny wrapped a meaty hand around the back of his neck, and for once he didn't bother shaking it off. "Welcome back."

Roscoe nodded. He felt good. Not great, but good, which was a vast fucking improvement from even an hour ago. No promises what would happen later, when he crawled into his cold bed alone, but for the moment there were no more thoughts of broken hearts and endings. For the moment, there was only the cup, and the kids, and the game he was absolutely born to play.

Until he caught sight of two familiar blondes at the edge of the rink, one blue-eyed and smiling, the other doing just about everything she could to avoid his gaze.

"Shit," he grumbled. He'd forgotten they'd made arrangements for Reggie to show up early. It wasn't just a matter of her enthusiasm, which was permanently off the charts, but of practicality—since the visiting team would be taking over her usual private locker room, Reggie needed time to dress and gear up before the boys rolled in.

Ally finally turned to look at him, but if he was expecting some big, emotional, movie-style reunion scene, Ally throwing herself into his arms and weeping about how wrong she'd been, well... He'd better ask for his money back. She kept her features neutral, offering a cool smile and a brief nod in greeting.

They might as well have been strangers.

How was that even possible? Had it really been that long since he'd made love to this woman, since he'd told her with words and kisses and hot, desperate breaths that he'd fallen in love with her?

A deep, fathomless ache bloomed in his chest, but he forced himself to shore up his heart, barricade it from this pointless pain. He had a job to do tonight, and he needed to stay focused. If not for himself, if not for the cameras, if not for Clarissa and the suits who'd no doubt be watching his every move, than for the kids.

Starting with Reggie, his badass super star.

"Forty-four," he said, waving her over. "Bring it in, kiddo."

Other than figuring out the locker room logistics last week, he and Reggie hadn't spoken much during the last couple of practices—Dunn and Henny had taken over most of the offensive coaching, and he didn't exactly go out of his way to make himself available. Part of him didn't want to overstep, figuring Ally would tell her whatever she wanted her to know. But another part of him—the bigger part of him—was simply prolonging the inevitable goodbye.

Roscoe sucked in a breath of icy air, clearing his head as Reggie scooted out onto the rink in her sneakers.

"You doing okay tonight?" he asked.

"Mostly. I might be a little nervous, though." She flashed him a big grin, shifting her weight from foot to foot, practically humming with unspent energy. "But otherwise good. I mean, I'm not worried or anything. I've got everything down, and our team is totally solid. But it's a big deal, right? A tournament, with kids from another town? And Aunt Clarissa told me all the local stations would be here, and more photographers and other media people… It's kind of a lot to take in. But I'm not nervous. Definitely not. Well, maybe just a little bit." She blew out a sharp breath, her cheeks puffing out.

"That's okay," he said, his brain still catching up with her mile-a-minute chatter. "I get nervous before games too."

"Yeah?"

"Totally."

She smiled at him again, so happy and excited it

made his chest hurt. Fifteen fucking years old… Roscoe still couldn't believe she'd been through so much in her life. Imagining what it must've been like for her when her dad died… It nearly gutted him.

"Reg," he said, resting his hands on her shoulders. Without her gear, she felt small beneath his touch, and he resisted the urge to wrap her up in a hug, to promise her that everything would be okay, that he'd always be part of her life.

But that wasn't his promise to make. Yeah, he'd been her coach—but that gig ended after the tournament. And as much as he cared for her, as much as he'd once seen a future with Ally and Reggie both, that's not how things turned out. He had no more claim on Reggie than he did on her mother, no right to stay involved with her hockey dreams, to teach her how to make eggplant parmesan, to hang out on a Saturday eating chips and playing *NHL 17*.

Tonight was *it*, he realized, swallowing the lump that had suddenly jammed his throat.

Tonight was goodbye.

Roscoe released her and stretched, looking around the arena in an effort to reign in his emotions. Somewhere in the distance, Clarissa shouted orders, her voice echoing throughout the arena as camera crews scurried into place. Soon the teams would be arriving, parents and spectators filling the seats, everyone eager to watch the rivaling teams battle for the cup.

Whatever happened, Roscoe knew his crew would give them a good show.

"Listen," he said now, forcing his tone to remain neutral. "Things might get a little crazy with the media after the game tonight, so in case I don't get a chance to see you later, I just wanted to say that it's been a real pleasure coaching you, Reggie. You are truly one of the most talented players I've ever seen. If you love the game as much as I think you do, I really hope you'll continue to—"

"Seriously?" Reggie put her hands on her hips, her eyes flashing with sudden fire. "You're giving me the farewell speech? Is this really happening right now?"

Roscoe blinked. "I... Well, I'm not sure how much your mom has told you about what happened between us, but things aren't—"

"I know all about that." True to form, Reggie rolled those big blue eyes. "But Mom said I can keep playing hockey this year, as long as I get good grades in school. And I know you have to go back to the real NHL soon, but she also said I could go to some of your home games with Aunt Clarissa, and Clarissa said she gets the best seats. So just because you and my mom are totally screwed up and don't even know a good thing when it punches you right in the mouth, that doesn't mean you have to get all weird on me." Tears leaked onto her cheeks, and she paused only long enough to smear her gloved palms across her face. "And you can tell me it's none of my business, or I'm too young to understand, or whatever other excuse you've got handy, but for the record? I think you and mom breaking up totally sucks ass."

Roscoe blew out a breath, slowly shaking his head. He'd finally done it—gotten on her bad side.

"For the record?" he said softly, offering a gentle smile. "Me too."

Reggie wiped her eyes again. "She won't admit it, but I know she wishes things turned out differently."

Roscoe's heart kicked up a notch, but he ignored it. Didn't matter what Reggie said. If Ally really wanted him back, she wouldn't be standing on the sidelines right now, pretending her own shoes were the most fascinating thing in the world. "I wanted things to be different, too, Reg. But sometimes wanting a thing just isn't enough."

Reggie shook her head, her eyes rolling again even as they glazed with fresh tears. "You and my mom are so full of shit, it's not even funny."

"Reggie—"

"No. You're standing here giving me, like, Instagram quotes. Wanting a thing isn't enough? Give me a break. If you really want something, you freaking fight for it. What else is there? If you're not willing to fight for it, then maybe you just didn't want it bad enough in the first place."

Roscoe pinched the bridge of his nose. Didn't want it bad enough? He fucking *burned* for Ally. Even now, even after all the heartache and the loneliness and crawling-the-walls insomnia, one genuine smile from Ally would've had him running over there, sweeping her into his arms, and kissing her until they both ran out of air. He wanted her so fucking badly that he could still feel her silky skin beneath his fingers, still hear her soft sighs in his ear, still taste her kiss on his lips. It was all he could do not to drop to his knees and crawl to her, beg her to let him back into her life, right here in front of all the camera crews and her daughter and his teammates and Clarissa fucking Finch.

That's how badly he wanted her.

But what Roscoe wanted simply didn't matter. Ally didn't want him back.

"Reggie," he said now, his tone darkening. "Your mother made her decision, and we both have to respect that. Even if it totally sucks ass."

"But—"

"But nothing. End of discussion. Are we clear?"

Reggie clamped her mouth shut, the muscles in her jaw ticking. After a beat, she finally gave him a curt nod, but she wouldn't meet his eyes.

"Good." Roscoe glanced up at the scoreboard clock.

"The teams will be getting here soon. You should probably get dressed."

Reggie nodded in silence. She started to walk away, but Roscoe reached out a hand, closing it gently on her shoulder. When she turned to look at him, he grinned at her and said, "You're gonna rock tonight, forty-four."

Reggie beamed, and Roscoe took a good, long look, memorizing that dazzling smile, tattooing it right over his shattered heart.

You, kiddo, were almost my family.

CHAPTER TWENTY-NINE

Reggie and Nick were on fire.

Along with their right winger, a stocky kid named Jordan Pulaski, they were an absolute powerhouse front line, damn near unstoppable. Rochester's defense was tough, but Buffalo was giving them a real run for the money.

"These kids are fucking amazing," Kooz said. He, Roscoe, and Jarlsberg were packed into the box with the rest of the kids, leaving the other coaches to sweat it out in the executive suite with Clarissa and the suits. Dunn and Henny had brought Eva and Bex, too. Originally, they were all supposed to go out together after the game to celebrate—triple date. But now that Ally was out of the picture, Roscoe was bailing on that plan.

Ignoring the fresh burn in his gut, Roscoe tracked his offense as they zoomed into enemy territory, their passing game tight as hell. They reminded Roscoe of his own starting lineup, so in sync it was as if they could read one another's minds.

"Take it home, Harper!" Jarlsberg shouted across the rink, on his feet as Nick slid into scoring range. Rochester's defense was tag-teaming Jordan and Reg, leaving no good passing options for Nick. Without missing a beat, he pivoted away from his own would-be attacker, then flipped back around, never losing track of the puck. Rochester was closing in fast again, but he pulled back to take the shot…

Damn. Shot bounced off the goal post, leaving it wide open for a steal.

Rochester swept in and nabbed the puck. Dude passed it to his teammate, who skated it almost to center ice before Jordan caught up and stole it back. Without hesitation, he tapped it over to Reggie, who passed it to Nick, who slipped around the approaching Rochester defense and sent it back to Reggie…

Who drove that bad boy right between the goalie's legs.

"That's my girl!" Roscoe pumped his fist, out of his seat with pride.

First goal of the night, and the crowd went fucking nuts. All around him, the arena flickered with the flashes of hundreds of cameras, parents and paparazzi alike. Even Kooz had his phone out, live streaming the whole thing to his social media fans. Reggie glanced up toward the box, and Roscoe pointed at her, his grin huge, throat tight with emotion. Reggie waved, excitement bursting out from every inch of her.

You deserved first goal, kiddo.

He called for a quick line change to give the kids a break, letting the second string take their turn on the ice. They weren't as strong as his starters, but they still put up a hell of a fight, refusing to give an inch. He continued rotating for the next period, making sure everyone got ice time, and everyone had a blast. More than anything, he wanted this to be a summer to remember for all of them.

Especially Reg.

By the close of the second, neither team had allowed another goal. It was one of the best, most intense games Roscoe had ever seen, with no clear winner in sight. The fans, evenly split between Rochester and the home team, were absolutely riveted.

"What is this thing called 'trending topic'?" Kooz asked suddenly.

"It means everyone online is talking about it," Roscoe asked. "Why? Did some celebrity post a butt-shot or something?"

Kooz flipped his phone around so Roscoe could see. "It says #TempestTeens is number one trending topic in U.S.A."

Roscoe shook his head and laughed. Clarissa would be supremely pleased—the Buffalo Tempest had finally done something meme-able.

A loud buzzer signaled the end of the second. Turning to the kids parked on the players' bench, Roscoe clapped once, giving them all a proud smile. "Great job, everyone. Grab some water, and let's regroup in the locker room."

Roscoe hardly recognized the man waiting for him outside the locker room, standing stiff in a brand new suit and tie, his gray hair gelled back.

Gallagher.

Other than a few brief check-in meetings, Roscoe hadn't heard much from the Tempest head coach this summer. After his supreme end-of-season fuckup, he'd done his best to stay off the coach's radar, and the feeling seemed pretty mutual.

But now Roscoe cocked a grin and went right in for the man-hug, slapping him hard on the back, genuinely happy to see the guy. "Damn, Coach. You clean up pretty good."

Gallagher grimaced, running a hand over his stiff hair. "We've got Clarissa Finch to thank for that. Woman strong-armed me into sprucing up for the cameras tonight. Now my wife wants me to dress up every weekend, take her out on the town. Christ, you'd think she never saw me in a suit before. I've got wedding pictures to prove *that's* a load of shit."

"Um. Haven't you been married thirty years?"

"Twenty-six and counting." Gallagher laughed, the skin around his eyes crinkling, the last of the tension between them obliterated. "Gotta hand it to you, thirty-eight. You've done a great job with these kids."

"I can't take all the credit. They're talented as hell, and they've worked hard for this."

"You know what they say, son. The best coaches make the best teams."

"Is that what they tell you at coach school?" Roscoe cracked up.

"Among other things." He held Roscoe's gaze a moment, then nodded, offering a final smile. To Roscoe it'd felt like an assessment—one he'd thankfully passed. "Alright, LeGrand. Don't let me keep you from your team."

"Thanks for stopping by. It was, uh... great seeing you."

"Yeah? Let's see if you still feel that way after I drill your ass in training camp." Gallagher clapped him on the shoulder, giving him a firm squeeze. "See you on the ice real soon, ready to rock 'n roll."

"That a promise or a threat?"

"Both. So until then, do us all a favor and stay the hell out of trouble." He winked at Roscoe, then released him and headed down the hall.

Heading in to join the gaggle of waiting teenagers in the locker room, Roscoe felt like he'd lost a hundred pounds of dead weight from his shoulders. Gallagher was a good guy, and Roscoe hated that he'd lost some of the man's hard-won trust last season. Getting it back was a definite win—one he didn't intend to take for granted.

Looking around at the kids all squished together on the benches, glowing and happy, Roscoe felt an upwelling of gratitude.

Sure, he'd hit some bumps in the road like anyone else, but generally, life had come pretty easy for him. He was blessed with natural talent and a career he loved, a tight family who never gave up on him even when he bailed on holidays and vacations and Skype dates, the best friends a guy could ask for, and these fucking kids he'd grown to adore.

The only thing missing is Ally...

Roscoe cleared his throat, forcing down the knot of emotion as he signaled for the kids' attention.

"You guys are absolutely fierce out there tonight," he said. "How's everyone holding up?"

They treated him to a chorus of *awesome!* and *great!* and something that sounded like *amazeballs!*, which Roscoe had never heard before, but kind of liked.

Drenched in sweat, their faces red with exertion, every single one of those kids beamed, their smiles brighter than all the lights in the arena.

"Let's keep this short and to the point," he said, gesturing for them to settle down. "You're kicking butt tonight, showing everyone out there what it means to be a real team. Hell, I might have to hire some of you to coach *my* guys this season."

That got a few laughs.

"Listen—we're up by one, but it's still anyone's game. Keep up the hustle, play smart, and keep looking out for one another out there. You're making us all proud tonight, guys." He put his fist out for a team huddle, and the kids reached in to join him. "Now. Who's ready to wrap this game up in a big, red, ass-kicking bow?"

Everyone cheered and whooped, totally pumped for the home stretch.

The final period of the game went by in a blur, Buffalo and Rochester locked in a rapid-fire battle that left every single hockey player exhausted on their skates. For a while it seemed as though they'd end in a dead heat, but then, with just three minutes left in the game, Rochester snuck in behind Buffalo's defense. Two quick passes and a slapshot later, they'd tied the game, one to one. Their center forward snagged the puck on the next face-off, passing it down the line with perfect precision, easily dodging Roscoe's team. Seconds later, the center swooped in out of nowhere and jammed another one right into the net.

Two to one.

"Dig in, guys. We got this." Roscoe called for a line change, clapping to keep their spirits up as he sent in his third stringers. Not ideal, given the score and the few precious minutes left on the clock, but he needed to save his superstars for the absolute final moments. "We're almost there," he called out. "Keep on 'em, keep on 'em."

"Let's go, Buffalo!" The chant started in the seats behind the players' bench, and it caught on like wildfire, spreading throughout the arena. Soon as the new line hit the ice, they were off, speeding after the puck, energized by the crowd, everyone on their feet and cheering them on.

Roscoe's second string right winger nabbed the puck, deked left, whipped back around, and shot it over to the center. Center scooped it right up, skated it on down to the zone, peeled back for the shot, and slammed it home.

The whole thing had happened in an instant.

"Holy fuck!" Jarlsberg nailed Roscoe in the arm. "You see that?"

"Damn straight," Roscoe said. "Here we go."

The crowd whooped and hollered, bouncing on their feet, taking up the chant with renewed vigor... "Let's go, Buffalo!"

With less than a minute on the clock, Roscoe sent his

starters back out to finish the job. Nick, Reggie, and Jordan skated harder and faster than he'd ever seen, going after that puck like nobody's business.

"Looks like the nitro-boost kicked in," Roscoe said.

"No shit!" Kooz panned his phone across the rink, jerking back and forth to keep up as Nick stole the puck from Rochester's right wing. He sailed back down to enemy territory, two opponents on his tail, Reggie and Jordan close behind.

Nick tried to pass to Reg, but he overshot, gift wrapping that puck for Rochester's center. Dude scooped it right up, but Jordan gave chase. Others joined the fray, blocking Roscoe's view.

Thirty seconds left.

Shit shit shit!

Seconds passed like hours until the knot of kids loosened up, one player finally emerging with his prize... It was Jordan with the breakaway, speeding down the center, Reggie just ahead...

Fifteen seconds.

"Come on," Roscoe muttered, "come on!" He clenched his fists, teeth grinding together as the kids approached the zone.

Ten seconds.

Jordan wound up for the shot, the goalie trying to gauge the angle, but no... It was a fake-out! Roscoe cheered as Jordan passed to Reggie, and the kid didn't

SYLVIA PIERCE

hesitate. She slapped that baby hard and true, launching it through the air, time slowing down as the crowd held a collective breath and the goalie dove high to block…

Clang!

Fucking bar down, baby!

Puck hit that top pipe, dropped right into the net.

Game over.

Final score: Three to two.

Buffalo won the cup.

The crowd went fucking *insane*. The roar was deafening, the echo of their cheers and pounding feet and clapping hands bouncing around the arena, straight into Roscoe's bones. He bolted out onto the ice and scooped Reggie into a spinning hug, falling on his ass as the rest of the team joined in the pile-on.

He was so fucking happy, he didn't even bother hiding his tears. The kids were crying too, hugging each other, fist-bumping, laughing their asses off, Kooz still streaming the whole thing. When the mayhem finally receded and everyone was on their feet again, Roscoe looked to the seats, scanning the sea of faces for Ally. The crowd had already started moving down to the main level, but despite the chaos he found her immediately, pumping a fist and cheering for her girl, grooving to the celebratory music blasting over the loudspeakers.

Their eyes met across the ice, and she flashed him a smile so big and genuine, it damn near stopped his heart.

She'd come a long way from stumbling onto the ice that first practice, shocked and dismayed that her kid had snuck onto the team without her permission.

If Roscoe didn't know any better, he'd swear she was happy. Truly happy.

She placed her hand over her heart, and Roscoe's fingertips tingled with the memory of her soft skin.

Thank you, she mouthed.

God, his ache for her in this moment was fucking *brutal*—for so long, he'd imagined they'd be celebrating the win together—but he couldn't be angry about it anymore. Not after tonight. Not after this summer.

Roscoe had so much fucking love inside him, and for awhile, he'd gotten to share it with her. Every single second of their time together—every damn heartbeat—had made him a better man.

So in the end, he simply nodded and returned her smile, keeping her locked in his sights until his vision blurred and the undulating mob swallowed her up, taking her away from him for the very last time.

CHAPTER THIRTY

Waiting patiently on the side of the rink, Ally watched in awe as Reggie soaked up the spotlight. She shone like a star, graciously accepting the accolades from her teammates, smiling for every media photo and fan selfie. She was truly in her element.

Ally blinked back fresh tears. To think she'd almost derailed this, that she'd almost let her own fears stand in the way of Reggie pursuing her dreams...

"Mom!" Reggie finally broke free of the crowd and made her way over, grinning up at Ally with that megawatt smile, her big blue eyes dancing with pure joy. Ally held out her arms for a hug, and sent another silent thank you to Roscoe as she pulled her daughter close. He'd made this moment possible—for both of them.

"You are incredible," Ally said. "Absolutely unstoppable."

"Did you see me?" Reggie was practically vibrating in Ally's arms, and when she finally pulled back, her smile was even bigger. "I can't believe I scored two goals! Roscoe says it's super hard to hit the bar like that. Even Nick was jealous. But he played awesome tonight, too. Everyone did. I couldn't have done it without them."

"You guys make a great team," Ally agreed. Then, with a wink, "But you're the best one out there for sure."

Reggie rolled her eyes. "You have to say that. You're my mom."

"Not true." Ally laughed, tucking a damp lock of hair behind Reggie's ear. "You might recall that even as your mom, I wasn't always the biggest fan of this hockey thing."

"Oh, I recall." Reg folded her arms across her chest, cocking a smug grin. "But then one day you fell in love with the coach and became the biggest NHL fangirl ever."

Ally opened her mouth to deny it, but of course she couldn't. No, she *wouldn't*—not after everything she and Roscoe had been through. She *had* fallen in love with him —that was the plain truth of it. She loved him still, and no matter how torn up she felt, she wouldn't disrespect what they'd had by trying to downplay it now.

"You're right," she said softly. Her voice was thick with emotion; she was grateful for the cover the noisy crowd provided. "And you're here tonight all because of him. It had nothing to do with how I feel about him. Roscoe convinced me to let you play because he believes in you, honey bunch. So, so much. Just like I do."

"You said feel. Not felt."

"I... did say feel. I care a great deal about Roscoe."

"No kidding." Reggie held her gaze a long time, narrowing her eyes as though Ally were some puzzle she might be able to figure out if she stared at her long enough.

Ally wouldn't give her the opportunity, knowing she'd never stand up to her daughter's scrutiny. Reggie was just too damn perceptive.

"I'm really proud of you," Ally continued, blinking away her tears as she tried to steer the conversation back to the main event—Reggie and her hockey. "You're so brave, baby. Really. I look at you and I see this spark, this drive. Whenever you set your mind to something, you just... You go out there and find a way to make it happen. I know I've been overprotective since Dad died —especially with hockey—but honestly, I've always admired that about you."

Reggie shrugged like it was no big deal. "Who do you think I got it from?"

"No idea." Ally laughed. "I keep hoping you'll find a way to bottle it, though. Until then, I've got Samantha Hart on auto-play, helping me find my inner warrior goddess."

"Yeah? How's that working out for you?"

Ally lowered her gaze, suddenly feeling like she was the child and Reggie the parent.

"Seriously?" Reggie said. "I can't believe you're actually making me say this out loud." She pushed the hair out of her face and blew out a breath. "Listen. After Dad died, *you're* the one who figured out a way to keep us going. You made sure I had food on the table and the bills got paid even when I know getting out of bed was the last thing you wanted to do. After we started running low on money, *you* decided to move us all the way across the country to a new city, and you went out and got a job, and you made it so we could be close to Aunt Clarissa because you knew that would help us figure stuff out. Even when you were deathly afraid I'd crack my head open on the ice, you still decided to set all that aside and let me play. And then out of nowhere, you started dating again, even though it scared you and even though it didn't exactly work out as planned. So pardon me in advance for the language, but sometimes there's only one word for the job." Then, with a wicked grin, "You're fucking *fierce*, Mom."

Ally laughed through fresh tears, offering a smile that was equal parts amusement, pride, and relief. Reggie never ceased to amaze her. How had Ally gotten so lucky to have such an incredible daughter? How had Reggie survived everything they'd been through?

When Dan died, he'd taken pieces of their hearts—pieces they could never hope to get back. In the immediate aftermath of the accident, Ally's soft, carefree, vibrant daughter had become hard and cynical, withdrawing into a world of darkness so impenetrable, Ally worried she'd never come back. Back then, Ally did her best to keep the two of them afloat, but she'd be lying if she said she didn't worry they'd both eventually drown, dragging each other into the deep until there was no more air to breathe.

But now she looked into Reggie's eyes and saw a ferocity there, a determination that could only come from staring into the mouth of utter darkness, facing your demons, and finding the strength to fight your way back.

For so long, Ally had felt weak and broken. She'd always felt like getting out of bed every day was the barest minimum—barely a step above complete neglect. But now, Reggie was helping her see things in a different light. Perhaps getting out of bed in those days was a greater act of courage than she'd realized. A small act, but an important one. One that had allowed her to keep going, one foot in front of the other, taking every moment as it came, all the way up to this one, right now.

Maybe there was some truth to Reggie's words, she realized. Maybe they'd faced some of those demons together, and come out stronger for it.

"Well. I don't know if anyone's ever accused me of

being fierce before," Ally said with a laugh, "but I guess I'll take it."

"You *guess*?" Reggie gave her the signature eye-roll. "Come on, Mom. If Samantha Hart were here, she'd tell you to own that shit."

"Hey!" Ally laughed. "I'll own that shit, but you've definitely burned through your curse quota for the month. Let's not push it."

"Okay, okay." Reggie looked out across the ice, where some of the team was still celebrating. Even some of the Rochester kids were still out there, goofing around with the Buffalo kids. Ally tried to imagine the Tempest and some rival NHL team doing the same thing. The idea almost made her smile, but of course it only got her thinking about Roscoe again.

God, what a mess she'd made. If she could go back to that night and do it all over again, maybe she'd—

"So," Reggie said, breaking into her thoughts, which was probably for the best. "Everyone from the team is going to Pasquale's for pizza and ice cream. I guess there's a Jack & Jill Java in the same plaza, so some of the parents are going to hang out there to wait for the kids. I mean, it's like literally right next door, so you could even spy on us if you wanted to. But I hope you don't want to. But either way, do you think I could go? Just for a little while? Like I said, it's right next to where tons of parents will be."

Ally bit back a smirk. "I see you've done your homework for this sales pitch, as usual."

"Please, Mom? I didn't crack my head open on the ice, so I'm pretty sure the pizza place is a safe bet."

"Is Nick going to be there?"

Reggie's cheeks darkened—a feat Ally didn't think possible, considering how flushed the game had left her—but there it was. "Um. Yes."

"You really like this boy, huh?"

Reggie bit her lip, her eyes suddenly dreamy. She looked around quickly to make sure none of her friends were within earshot, then leaned in close, whispering in Ally's ear. "I... I think I love him, Mom." When she pulled back, she was smiling again, shy but bright and beautiful. Ally had never seen that exact look on her face before. "I mean, I know it hasn't been that long, but we've spent a lot of time together on the ice, and texting and stuff, and sometimes you just... You *know*. Right?"

Ally nodded. *Yes. Sometimes you just know.*

"Should I tell him?" Reggie asked. "I don't want to freak him out, but I don't think he'll be scared. I'm pretty sure he feels the same way. But... What do you think I should do?"

Ally took a deep breath, preparing to talk her out of this. To proceed with caution, let things develop slowly, avoid jumping into anything too quickly, protect her heart at all times...

But when Ally tried to say the words, they wouldn't come.

Even as Ally's brain tried to convince her to spout out all those familiar warnings, even as the anxiety threatened to take hold, even as her own vivid imagination served up images of Reggie crying over a broken heart, Ally knew none of that was real. It was simply the aftermath of her grief, all those worst-case scenarios she kept on standby as if—just by spouting them off like a list— she could prevent Reggie or herself from experiencing pain.

It never worked, that old tactic. It was just her way of pretending she still had control.

Roscoe's previous words echoed in her memory.

"Let me tell you something about control, Ally. It's a fucking lie. Something we say to convince ourselves it's okay to get out of bed every day, because the truth is just too fucking dangerous to contemplate."

He'd been so right about her. Here she was, thinking she'd put up this brave front, this casual attitude, the walls that kept danger at bay, when all along he'd seen right through it, right down to her very core.

She'd never fooled him.

The only one she'd been fooling was herself. Thinking she could just end things, just walk away and pretend like it was for the best.

It wasn't going to be that way for Reggie. Unlike her

mother, Reg was brave enough to put herself out there, to open herself up to the possibility of love, no matter what the risks.

Everyone deserved a shot at their happily ever after.

Dan would've wanted you to be happy, too.

The thought came unbidden, so quick and unexpected it made Ally gasp.

"Mom?" Reggie's brow wrinkled in concern. "You okay?"

Ally smiled. "I was just thinking about Dad."

"I've been thinking about him all night. Do you think he's watching me?"

"Oh, I know he is. He'd be so proud of you, Reg. Unlike your worrywart mother, he wouldn't have hesitated to sign those forms." Ally laughed. "He would've rushed out and gotten you your own trading cards. And then he'd spend the rest of the summer telling anyone who would listen about his daughter playing with real NHL guys."

"That sounds like Dad all right." Reggie laughed, even as she fought back tears.

Ally cupped her cheek, sweeping away the tears with her thumb. "I think he would've wanted you to go for it."

"For Nick?"

Ally nodded. "For love."

Reggie gave her that penetrating stare again, but this

time, it ended with a grin. "Dad would've wanted you to go for it, too."

"You're right," Ally said plainly. She knew in that moment it was absolutely true, and hearing it come from Reggie felt like a reminder. A message she'd been ignoring for far too long.

What she'd had with Dan was real love, no doubt about it. He was her first, her husband, and the father of her child—the most important person in Ally's world. For those reasons and so many more, she would always carry him in her heart.

But Dan was gone, and he hadn't taken Ally with him. She still had a life to live. She still had love to give, however messy and imperfect that love may be.

And no matter how hard and fast she'd tried to run away from the impossibly inconvenient truth, it always seemed to find her.

Ally was in love with Roscoe. The big, epic, crazy kind of love that couldn't be pushed aside or shoved away in a box or forgotten.

She closed her eyes, the touch of him still fresh on her body. In her heart.

When she first met Roscoe, she was deathly afraid of getting close to him, knowing in her heart that he'd be taken away from her, just like Dan had been. But in the end, it had almost been worse. She'd had no control over losing Dan, but losing Roscoe? That was all her doing.

She'd caved into her fear. Whether it was fear of getting close and losing someone, or fear of letting him see her most raw, vulnerable pain, or fear of her own emotions, Ally had let that drive a wedge between them, finally shutting out the man who'd given her nothing but patience and compassion. The man who'd challenged her to find her passion again. The man who'd truly loved her.

Shame bubbled up inside her, hot and sticky as tar. She'd finally opened up her heart to him, showed him all the scars, and then forced him to walk away, assuming he couldn't handle her at her worst, even when he insisted otherwise.

She'd never even given him the chance to try.

Her throat tightened, tears burning her eyes. She glanced out across the rink, suddenly desperate to find him. Certain he'd be right there, looking up at her like before, waiting for her to come to this realization. She'd run out there into his arms and fall on her knees and pour out her heart, and he'd catch her and kiss her and promise her everything would be okay…

But Roscoe was no longer on the ice with the other coaches. She didn't see him with any of the camera crews or anywhere in the seats talking to other kids or parents. He was nowhere to be found.

Ally sighed, reaching way down deep for another smile. Tonight wasn't about lost loves and regrets. It was about her daughter. Her strong, amazing, beautiful, tough-as-nails daughter who'd followed her bliss right out onto that rink this summer, and fallen in love along the way.

Just like her mother.

"So I guess I'm telling him," Reggie whispered.

"Don't worry, honey bunch." Ally cupped Reggie's face again. "When the moment is right, you'll know exactly what to do."

And so do you, girl. So do you.

Ally tried to dismiss the nagging voice in her head, but despite Roscoe's absence, she couldn't. Because this time the voice in her head encouraging her to be brave and strong and honest wasn't that of Samantha Hart or saucy Paulette from the Wellshire or even her admirable daughter Reggie.

It was Ally's own voice, her own personal truth. And she could no more ignore it than she could stop the beating of her own heart.

An idea sparked suddenly inside her, catching on fast and spreading like wildfire until she was positively crackling with its energy.

Time to own your shit, girl!

"Um, Mom?" Reggie asked. "Why are you smiling like a freak?"

"Because I know what I have to do."

"Um… Okay. Does that mean I can go get pizza now?"

"What? Oh! Of course." Ally blinked back to reality, and returned her daughter's smile. Then, after a hug that was only slightly more tight than usual, she said, "Go change and catch up with your friends. Text me when you're ready to head home and I'll come get you."

"Aren't you going to the coffee shop?"

"Nope." Ally hiked her purse up on her shoulder, squaring off with renewed determination. "I'm going to find Eva Bradshaw."

CHAPTER THIRTY-ONE

Vacation's over, you bastard slugs. Where are you?

Roscoe sent another group text to his teammates, who were already twenty minutes late for practice and ignoring all his attempts to get in touch.

The longer you make me stand around holding my dick, the harder I beat your asses later.

I'm talking to you, ya bunch of sloths.

Are you guys planning to hump the bench all season?

Seriously?

You fuckers suck ass.

He'd given them the week off after last weekend's tournament, but with training camp starting soon, it was time to buckle down. That meant daily practices, proper nutrition, strength training, and seriously cutting back on late nights. Roscoe had made a whole schedule, hoping to kick it up a notch for all of them, especially the guys who'd taken more time off this summer. They'd been on board when he'd announced it, but here he was, first official day of practice, and the place was a damn ghost town.

Fuck it. He'd give them hell for it later, but he wasn't about to sideline his own workout to chase down a bunch of apes who should've known better.

Roscoe put away his phone and grabbed a stick and puck, lapping the rink to warm up. He was just curving around the back of the net when he heard another pair of blades entering the ice at the other end of the rink.

Stick in hand, he whipped around and charged forward, ready to give them hell. But the figure wobbling on skates was too small and uncoordinated to be one of his teammates.

It was a woman, actually, dressed in black workout pants and a light purple fleece, all of it weighted down with protective padding. She'd apparently covered all the bases—knee and elbow pads, wrist guards, even a helmet and tinted ski goggles.

Chuckling to himself, he watched her from a distance as she skated back and forth across the opposite goal line, her arms outstretched for balance as she propelled herself with one skate. She looked like she was riding a skateboard, and she was determined as hell.

He remembered that feeling as a kid, just trying to keep up with his older brothers, refusing to give up even when his whole body ached with cold and frustration. He gave her a few more minutes to play around, but unfortunately, he couldn't let her stay all day.

"Hi there," he finally called out, skating out toward her. She looked up at him and waved, then started making her way over, still pushing off from that one foot, wobbly as hell. "The rink is closed to the public right now," he said as they approached each other. "There's an open skate from three to five tonight, if you want to come back then."

Roscoe slowed to a stop at center ice, but the woman was coming at him fast, no signs of slowing down, no indication that she'd heard a word he'd said. Roscoe braced for impact, but at the last second, she cut her blades to try to stop. The maneuver shifted her trajectory, sending her spinning like a shopping cart with a broken wheel, her arms windmilling like crazy...

"Whoa. Whoa!" Roscoe lunged forward to catch her just before she crashed onto the ice. He grabbed her upper arms, but she slipped again, pitching forward against his chest, bringing with her a wave of lemon-sugar scented air.

No. Not possible...

Roscoe wrapped his arms around her instinctively, muscle memory taking over as he tightened their embrace. It was her. No one else had ever felt so damn much like home.

"Ally." It was barely a breath, his heart slamming up into his throat, choking off his voice.

After a moment that felt like forever, she finally straightened, reaching up to remove her helmet and goggles, a curtain of blonde hair spilling out.

"Hi," she said softly, tucking her hair behind her ears. She was winded, her cheeks and nose pink from the cold.

Roscoe blinked, not trusting his eyes. "You… You're on skates."

She bit her lower lip and nodded. "Yeah."

"On the ice."

"I know."

"You're ice skating."

Ally laughed, a musical sound that had been haunting his dreams for so long, Roscoe worried he'd never woken up this morning. Was he here on the rink, or still back home in bed? Was Ally really standing in front of him—on skates?

"I'm not sure I'd call what I'm doing *actual* ice skating," she said. "But I haven't broken any bones yet, so I'm calling that a win."

"But… I don't…"

Roscoe trailed off. God, there were so many ways to finish that sentence. *I don't know why you're here. I don't know why you ever left. I don't know how the fuck I'm supposed to survive without you…*

"Eva was kind enough to give me a few pointers."

Ally blew out a breath. "Okay, by pointers, I mean she brutalized me every night after work all week. God, that woman is ferocious. I never want to see another clipboard as long as I live."

Roscoe shook his head, still not trusting that any of this was really happening. "Do I have you to thank for my boys skipping out on practice?"

Ally lowered her gaze, her dark lashes brushing her cheeks. Roscoe fought the urge to touch them, to kiss them. "Eva helped me arrange everything."

"I see." He tapped his stick against the ice, nerves getting the better of him. Seeing her again, hearing her voice and her laughter, inhaling her sweet scent... It would be so easy to kiss her right now. To fall right back into her arms, if that's what she wanted. Fall right back into where they left off.

And set himself up for another round of heartbreak.

Fuck. There was no way he'd survive a second round of that.

But double fuck. He still loved her. More than ever.

He sighed, scrubbing a hand over his stubbled jaw as he took in her outfit. "So. You thinking of trying out for the team with all this gear?"

"No." She looked up at him again, her brown eyes glittering with tears. "I'm trying out for you."

Roscoe blew out another breath, tightening his grip on the stick. "Ally, I—"

"You don't have to say a word. It's all me. I'm here because I totally screwed up, and I need you to know how truly, deeply sorry I am." She took a shuddering breath and pressed on. "I never planned to fall in love with you, Roscoe. It just wasn't supposed to happen."

"Ouch." He ignored the burn in his gut and forced out a laugh. "You're not helping your case here, Al."

"But it *did* happen," she continued. "I fell in love with you. With the way you made me feel inside and out, the way you encouraged and cared for my daughter, the way you stood by my side, even as I was doing everything in my power to keep you at a distance. In your arms, my fears and anxieties dimmed, and I felt like I could do anything." In a whisper that damn near broke him, she said, "I really, really liked that woman, Roscoe."

Roscoe smiled softly, despite himself. "I liked her too."

She nodded, the silence creeping in again. She seemed to be gathering her thoughts, trying to put the rest into words without breaking the fragile peace between them.

"How's Reggie?" he asked.

"She's great. We've started grief counseling."

"Wow. Big step." Huge. He knew how hard that must've been for her. For both of them.

Ally nodded. "We've only had two sessions so far— one together, and then we each had our own. We've, um… We've started sorting through some of Dan's things for donation, and that's been surprisingly helpful, too. Just to talk about him again, remember his life. It's… It's been good." Ally smiled again. "Reg misses you," she said, then rushed to add, "I don't mean that in a guilt-trip kind of way. Just… You mean a lot to her, no matter what. She's excited to come to your games."

Roscoe nodded, but didn't speak. Couldn't. One word, and he'd fucking lose it. All summer he'd seen Reggie at least twice a week for practice, sometimes more, and then it was just… just gone. No eye-rolls or snarky comments or witty insights. He missed them both *so* much.

In the week since the tournament, he'd thrown himself into his training again, pushing hard all day and crashing at night, leaving little room for contemplating what could've been. What *should've* been. But now, Ally was right here. Telling him that Reggie missed him.

Fuck.

"Roscoe," she said, "you were right about me that night. The control thing? I was fooling myself. And instead of dealing with that fear, that reality, I freaked out and took away your control, too. I guess I just… I thought I could protect you, you know? Like I tried to do with Reggie's hockey. I went ahead and decided what was best for both of us without giving you a chance, and I was dead wrong." Tears fell freely now, streaking her cheeks, but Ally pressed on. "I don't know where you stand, and maybe I don't have a right to ask. Maybe I don't even have a right to be here after everything I put you through. But I never stopped loving you. Not for a second. And maybe I screwed up so badly you never want to see my face again, and I get it. But I'm here right now on these stupid ice skates risking a head injury and hypothermia because I wanted to meet you on your ground. I need you to know I'm in love with you, Roscoe. The timing kind of sucks and I'm still mostly a mess, but I'm trying. Every day I'm trying."

Roscoe remained pinned to his spot on the ice, hands still wrapped around the stick, his face giving nothing away as he tried to process all she'd said.

I'm in love with you, Roscoe...

How fucking long had he waited to hear those words again, to feel her warm breath on his lips as she spoke, to see the look in her eyes and know that she meant it?

"W-what..." he stammered, his voice sticking in his throat. "What exactly are you saying?"

Ally swept away the last of her tears with her gloved fingers, then met his gaze again, steely and determined as ever. "I meant what I said before—I have a long road ahead of me, and I would never ask you to put your life on hold for me while I figure it all out. But if you're able to forgive me, to consider letting me back into your life again, even a little bit... I know I've given you a hundred reasons to doubt me, and it would take a long time to earn your trust again—if that's even possible. But I want to try." Her voice broke as she spoke her final plea. "I am so in love with you, it hurts. I know it's messy and complicated, but I know it can be beautiful, too. Please, *please* give me another chance to show you."

Roscoe's heart ached all over again. Ally was right— the timing did suck. She and Reggie needed to focus on healing, on rebuilding their own relationship after their monumental loss. Roscoe was still hurting from their breakup, from the way she'd pushed him out. And soon the regular season would be starting, and he needed to focus on his team, on his performance, on the grueling schedule that came with a gig like this.

But despite the ache, Roscoe's heart was already healing, knitting itself back together with every beat, with every word Ally had spoken, every breath she'd taken. He knew how much it must've cost her to come here today, to open herself up again and bare her soul.

And she'd done it all on skates, besides.

"There's something you need to know." He dropped his stick and skated closer, gripping her shoulders, pinning her with his own fiery gaze. "I have no intention of putting my life on hold for you, Ally."

Her bottom lip quivered, but she nodded, her shoulders stiffening. "I… I understand. I'm sorry I—"

"No, you *don't* understand." He slid his hands down

to her arms, searching for her warmth beneath all the padding. "I said I have no intention of putting my life on hold. If we do this, I'm going all in. I'm walking by your side through all of it—your past, your present, your future—no matter how hard or scary or ugly things get." Roscoe tightened his grip. "I'm in *stupid* love with you, Ally Heinz. So when I say I want in, I fucking mean it. So yeah, if we do this? We're doing it all the way. I am never, *ever* letting you push me out like that again."

A smile broke across her face, her eyes glazing with emotion. "Really?"

"Really. I think you're…" Roscoe closed his eyes, trying to remember a phrase the kids had once used. "Amazing balls."

Ally burst out laughing. "Pretty sure you mean 'amazeballs,' and pretty sure no one over the age of eighteen is allowed to say it."

"Doesn't make it any less true." He opened his eyes and looked at her a long time, cataloging every one of the gold flecks in her deep brown eyes, the sweep of dark lashes, the soft arches of her eyebrows. This wasn't a dream. Wasn't wishful thinking. She'd come back to him. "You are worth it, Ally."

"You sure you want this? All of this?"

Roscoe nodded. "The whole messy, complicated, beautiful package. You?"

"Yes. The whole package." Ally bit her lip, her body

trembling beneath his touch, their mouths suddenly so close he could taste her sweet breath on his tongue when she spoke again. "Aren't you scared?"

"Absolutely terrified." He crushed her mouth in a bruising kiss, sliding his hands up to cup her head, fisting her silky hair. Ally parted her lips, and Roscoe groaned into her mouth, sweeping his tongue over hers, pulling her even closer as he drank her in. For weeks, he'd hungered for this kiss with a desperation of a madman, and now he couldn't get enough, the sweet, familiar taste of her mouth sending a current of raw desire straight to his cock.

He backed her up on the ice, keeping her balanced as he skated her to the penalty box, so fucking thankful the boys had bailed today. The bench was a cold, hard second to the pillow-soft comforts of a bed, but he'd waited too long for this moment already.

They stepped into the box, and Roscoe unlaced her skates, then kicked off his own as Ally removed all her extra padding and gear. He helped her out of her workout pants and freed himself from his, guiding her to straddle him on the bench. She was already wet for him, her heat radiating onto his cock, making him even harder for her.

"I missed you," he said, nipping at her lower lip as he rolled the condom over his shaft.

"I can tell." She slid closer, teasing him with a slow,

seductive roll of her hips, making him shiver. "Confession," she whispered. "I missed you, too."

He gripped her hips, lifting her up and guiding himself inside her. She was so fucking tight, so perfect, and Roscoe gasped at the feeling, his head falling forward on her shoulder as she slid her hands into his hair and whispered his name.

They stilled, each of them taking a moment to come back, to remember, to feel this closeness and hold it in their hearts. He lifted his head and looked into her eyes, then captured her mouth in another desperate kiss, sliding his hands up inside her layers of shirts, seeking the smooth, hot skin of her back. Grabbing her shoulders, he arched his hips and thrust inside of her, urging her body into a rhythmic pulse as she writhed in his arms, gasping for breath.

Neither of them would last long, but it didn't matter. They'd have plenty of time to make up for it later. Right now, he just wanted to feel her come, to hear her call his name as he brought her over the edge. As he made her his.

She kissed him harder, her breath shallow and hot, and he felt her body tightening around his cock, both of them pulsing with heat. Sliding his hand down to where their bodies met, his fingers teased her clit, urging her closer and closer to the release she'd gone so long without.

"Fuck," he breathed. "You feel so fucking perfect." He couldn't hold back. Not for another second.

"Let go," she whispered, her thighs tightening around him. "Let go, Roscoe."

And that was all it took.

He came with a shudder, slamming into her as she rolled her head back and shattered, both of them trembling as wave after wave of pure pleasure wracked their bodies, wringing out everything they had, leaving them spent and panting in each other's arms.

Right. It was just fucking *right*.

After minutes that felt like an eternity, Roscoe wrapped his arms around her and smiled, brushing a soft kiss across her lips, still trying to figure out how the fuck this all happened.

He couldn't explain it—how fast they'd fallen, how much they'd been through, how they'd found their way back to each other. And in the end, it really didn't matter.

Because here was their story—the part that mattered, anyway:

Once upon a time, this crazy hockey mom stormed out onto the ice and crash-landed into his arms. After a long and winding journey, she'd found her way right back into his arms, exactly where they'd started. Exactly where she belonged.

And this time? They would live happily ever after.

CHAPTER THIRTY-TWO

"Are we ready to show off some of that gorgeous artwork?" Candy, the bubbly owner of Candy's Canvases, grinned from the stage of the Wellshire community room.

"We're ready to try!" Paulette responded. "But there's no accounting for taste with this bunch."

"I disagree," John said, pulling Paulette into a side hug. "You have *excellent* taste. In men. Ha!"

"Don't let my husband hear you say that," she teased. "His head is big enough already."

Ally grinned at them both, enjoying their endless banter. They'd officially tied the knot a few months earlier, and since then, they'd grown too adorable for words.

Paulette had made a full recovery from her previous heart troubles, but John was on oxygen now, carrying a portable device everywhere he went. He seemed to take it all in stride, but for Ally, it was a stark reminder of how quickly life could change. How important it was to cherish those you loved.

"Come on up, Paulette," Candy called out. "Let's show your friends how it's done."

Paulette unleashed a put-upon sigh, but her eyes sparkled with delight. "If I must."

"Here she goes," John said. "Speaking of big heads."

Everyone at their table laughed as Paulette peacocked her way to the stage, holding her canvas in front of her so it wouldn't smudge. Tonight's gathering had been a free-for-all paint night, so rather than walking everyone through the motions of painting the same flowers or winter scenes, Candy had encouraged the group to let their muses out.

Ally was still putting the finishing touches on her painting—a silhouette of Reggie on the ice, skating under a moonlit sky.

It was the end of another summer and hockey clinic, and Ally, Roscoe, and Reg had just gotten back from a week in Maine with Roscoe's enormous family. After months of nothing but video chats and greeting cards, it was really nice to meet them all in person. Ally had been nervous—they were a big bunch, each one louder and more boisterous than the last—but just like Roscoe, they'd welcomed her and Reggie with open arms. By the end of the first day, it was as if they'd been a part of the family all along. Reggie was a bit older than the other kids, but she loved hanging out with them on the beach, helping the little ones build sand castles, and—of course —showing up all the boys who'd tried and failed to outshine her in their wave riding competitions.

Plus, Ally had finally gotten to hear Roscoe's infamous lobster voice, and that alone was worth the trip.

"That's just lovely, Paulette!" Candy beamed, directing Paulette to stand at the center of the stage. Her painting was simple but elegant—a black, calligraphy-style letter E, woven through with flowering vines. Ally didn't know what the E stood for, but the piece was pretty.

Karen Dunn went next. Lately she'd been having more bad days than good, her memory fading more every time Ally saw her, and now she walked with a bit of a shuffle. Walker said that she'd still surpassed the doctors' expectations, but he knew as well as Ally that it wouldn't last forever. It was yet another reminder at just how precious their time together really was.

Ally swallowed the lump in her throat, grateful that today was a good day for Karen, and that Ally had gotten to share it with her.

"Wow, Karen," Candy said, and Karen beamed. Like Paulette, she'd also painted a fancy letter. "Excellent lines on that M. Really clean and modern."

Other artists followed—Lorraine, John, Walker, Eva, and even June Higgenbottom, who'd made her peace with Paulette and John's romance in time to step in as a late-entry bridesmaid at their wedding, and had since become part of the gang. Each one of them had painted a single letter, all in different styles, and now they clustered together on the stage, comparing and contrasting while Candy commented on their creative techniques.

"What's going on with the letters?" Ally asked Clarissa.

"No idea, but it's super cute! Big, buff hockey players and sassy old women? Why are we not filming this?" Clarissa dug out her phone, climbing up on her chair to get a good angle.

Ally shot a questioning look at Roscoe and Reggie across the table, but they seemed just as confused.

"Probably some Pinterest trend or something," Reggie said dismissively.

Roscoe, who'd made Ally pinky swear not to peek at his painting for the entire night, simply shrugged his shoulders and winked, flashing her that killer dimple of his.

Ally's heart fluttered, a white-hot current buzzing through her veins. Roscoe was so damn cute, so damn sexy. How many times had she kissed that very spot, usually after he'd made her laugh until tears streamed from her eyes? How many ways had he continued to surprise her? Had he celebrated her artwork? Championed Reggie's hockey dreams? Held them both in his strong, protective embrace as they cried after their grief sessions?

God... Most days, Ally still couldn't believe how blessed she'd been. Standing here now, paintbrush in hand, surrounded by the people she loved most in this world, Ally felt her heart expand. When she looked out across the community room and saw her friends gathered on the stage with their paintings, all of them laughing as Paulette and John started making out in the middle of Candy's assessment, Ally's heart expanded again, blooming and blossoming in ways she never could've predicted when she'd first come to this city, scared and anxious, lost and scattered.

"Roscoe LeGrand," Candy called out now, and Ally felt her heart skip at the sound of his name. "Don't be shy, number thirty-eight. I'm sure I'm not the only woman dying to know what *your* muse looks like."

At this, everyone in the room cheered.

"Is it another letter?" Ally asked him.

Roscoe shook his head. "Not even close."

"Go on!" Ally bounced on her toes, making Reggie giggle.

"I don't know about this," Roscoe teased. He held her gaze for a moment, his face actually flushing. "We all know I'm not the artist in this operation."

"You're killing me," Ally said. "In the words of my daughter, I'm, like, *legit* dying over here."

"Please go, Roscoe," Reggie said. "Before she further embarrasses herself trying to be cool."

"I'll go if you go," he said, elbowing Reggie.

"You're such a man-baby." Reggie laughed. "Fine, fine. Let's go."

"Okay. We've got this." He blew out a breath as if he were prepping for a big game, then looked at Ally one more time, a hint of nervousness flashing in his eyes. "But don't judge me too hard. I'm a suck-ass painter."

"Yes, but you're *my* suck-ass painter," Ally reminded him with a grin.

"Always." He winked again, then picked up his canvas and headed up front, Reggie in tow. Candy rearranged the other artists to make room for everyone, settling them all into one long line across the stage, with Reggie and Roscoe at the very end. But in the confusion, everyone had managed to flip their canvases around, hiding their artwork.

"Well." Candy laughed, gesturing to the group. "This won't do at all. Come on, guys. Get it together."

One at a time, they flipped their canvases.

Karen had the M.

Lorraine had an A.

An R for June.

Another R for John.

Eva held the Y.

Ally gasped, her brain finally starting to figure it out.

Is this really happening?

Walker had another M.

Oh my God.

Paulette had the E.

This is... Oh my God!

Reggie had a question mark.

Ally's heart thudded in her chest, threatening to burst as she read the message again.

MARRY ME?

A murmur started in the crowd, everyone turning around to find the message's intended recipient. Ally's cheeks flamed, her eyes misting with tears.

And there, watching her from the end of the line with his beautiful hazel eyes, was her man. Her lover. Her champion. Her heart.

Without breaking their gaze, Roscoe got down on one knee and flipped around his canvas, revealing a painted diamond ring surrounded by pink and red hearts.

Time slowed to a crawl.

Even as the butterflies danced inside her, even as the tears finally spilled, even as her heart continued to drum its wild, untamed beat all for Roscoe, Ally still couldn't believe it was happening.

Slowly, as if in a dream, she made her way to the

stage, climbing up to stand in front of Roscoe, her legs trembling, her heart threatening to burst free.

"Is this real?" she whispered.

"It's real." Roscoe passed his canvas to Reggie and took Ally's hands, brushing his thumbs across her knuckles. The gesture was so familiar, so comforting, for a moment Ally forgot where they were. Everyone else faded away, and Roscoe looked into her eyes, speaking the words that healed the very last fractures of her heart.

"You're my best friend. My true partner. I know it sounds crazy, but I fell in love with you the very first time we met. I've loved you every day since. And I promise to love you for the rest of my life." He slid a ring onto her finger—a gorgeous platinum-set diamond surrounded by tiny rubies—sealing it with a kiss. When he looked up at her again, his eyes shone with love. With gratitude. With hope. "Be my wife, Allison Heinz," he said, raw emotion breaking his voice. "Be my messy, complicated, beautiful forever."

Ally didn't hesitate.

"Yes," she said, laughing through her tears as she dropped to her knees before him. "Yes!"

The room erupted in a chorus of cheers and whistles, Reggie and Clarissa loudest of all, but Ally paid them no attention, throwing her arms around Roscoe and kissing him until they toppled backward on the stage, consumed by love and passion and all the things bursting to life inside their hearts.

The good things.

The very best things.

By the time Roscoe and Ally came up for air, paint night at the Wellshire had turned into a full-on engagement party, complete with Champagne and food and music and dancing, all courtesy of Clarissa, who knew better than anyone how to throw a good bash.

There was celebrating. Cheering and toasting. Posing for selfies with Paulette and the ladies of Wellshire. Happy tears and hugs and laughter. Memories shared and made as Roscoe and Ally began the next chapter of their lives, surrounded by friends and loved ones.

But what Ally would remember most about that night was Roscoe. Always Roscoe.

Their time together had not been without its challenges, but that morning on the ice rink last year, Ally had promised she'd bare it all to him, never pushing him away or shutting him out. In return, he'd promised he'd stick by her side, helping her and Reggie through their hardest, ugliest, most rock-bottom moments.

They'd endured more than a few of those.

But here they were tonight, stronger together, bound by respect and friendship and a deep, devoted love that had transformed Ally from a woman living in fear to a woman living in peace. In joy.

For so long she'd assumed she'd never find love again. That her immense fear of loss and death would keep her locked in a cage until her heart shriveled and died.

But then she'd stormed out onto the ice and met-cute Roscoe LeGrand.

In the end, Roscoe hadn't *saved* her—not like some fairy tale prince on a white horse, slaying all her dragons. He'd simply given her the friendship, the encouragement, and the love she'd needed to find her own way out of the darkness, her own keys to the cage.

She loved him for that—maybe more than he even realized. And no matter what new challenges they faced, no matter what dragons still lurked in the deepest, darkest dungeons, she'd love him through all of it, and he'd love her, standing by her side for all the days of their messy, complicated, crazy, wild, amazing—and yes—beautiful forever.

Thank you so much for reading BIG HARD STICK!

If you enjoyed this book, I hope you'll consider sharing the love and leaving a review! Reviews are one of the best ways to help new readers discover my books, and I truly appreciate each and every one.

More Sexy Reads!

Have you read the rest of the Buffalo Tempest series? If not, find out how Walker and Eva fell hard and fast on the ice in NAUGHTY OR ICE, and then get to know Bex and Henny in DOWN TO PUCK.

If you're all caught up with the Tempest boys, how about trading in that cold hard ice rink for a scorching hot beach? Ex-Army ranger Asher Burke is waiting for you in BAD BOY SUMMER! Read on for an excerpt...

BAD BOY SUMMER

First day back at Starfish Cove in a decade, and Asher Burke couldn't decide what he'd missed more: hot, beautiful women sunning themselves on the beach, or wet, beautiful women splashing around in the ocean.

It was a damn tough call, one that would require serious hands-on research. He stripped off his T-shirt, sticky with sweat from the daylong drive down, already tasting the salty blue ocean on his lips. But before he could officially kick off his work boots and dive in, he had to do a little recon.

Ash dropped his gear in the mudroom and stepped into the kitchen at Summerland, the Southern California beach house where he'd spent every summer for twenty-two years. A pang of longing twisted his heart, but he stowed that shit quick. He wasn't there to reminisce or beat himself up about his piss-poor decisions. He was there to do a job.

Ash had made that absolutely clear on the phone with his old man last week. He'd heard from his sister Lizzie that their father was planning to sell the beach cottage at the end of the season and needed some repair work done, but didn't have the cash to make it happen. So after a ten year estrangement, Ash had swallowed his pride and made the old man an offer he couldn't afford to refuse.

His father hadn't invited him down to the house in San Diego, which was just as well—Ash wasn't ready to go home yet. But they'd managed to find some common ground: the old man was upside down on the Summerland mortgage, needed the work done fast and cheap. Ash had just finished out his lease in Seattle, then coasted into town on fumes, needing a gig and a place to crash for the summer.

Right now, that's all they had to offer each other.

Course, that was before Ash had seen the place. Now

that he was here, he couldn't believe what the fuck he'd gotten himself into.

FUBAR didn't even begin to describe it. He'd seen better construction on huts in the damn desert.

The back door was missing a hinge, and the screen had a hole big enough for a roadrunner to jump through. The kitchen faucet was leaking. The baseboards under the sink were warped to shit, and the floor was starting to buckle, too.

Ash opened a few cupboards, still stocked with chipped and mismatched dishes. They might be able to get away with the original cabinetry, but the shelving inside was shot, and most of the doors needed to be rehung with new hardware and knobs. When he turned on the faucet and flicked the switch for the garbage disposal, the thing made a sound like a car wreck.

He flicked off the switch and shoved his hand into the hole, pulling out a twisted hunk of metal that used to be a fork.

Pressure built up behind Ash's eyes, threatening to blow up into a headache. When he and Lizzie were kids, Summerland had been his mother's heart and soul. The Burkes had never had much money, but his mother had always wanted her kids to have a special summer place growing up—a place where the stresses of real life didn't exist.

"Summerland is magic. When you're here, you get to be whoever you want to be..."

Ash shook his head, clearing away the echo of his mother's voice. She'd been gone ten years now; it wasn't that he wanted to forget, it just hurt too damn much to remember. And now his father was getting ready to sell the very thing that had once brought his mother so much joy—that had brought the whole family joy.

Ash tossed the mangled fork onto the counter. When he'd first heard about his father's plan, he didn't think much of it. The old man was getting, well, old. Lizzie had her own life now, living out in Huntington Beach, teaching English at some tough-as-nails high school. Summerland had fallen into disrepair and wasn't being used—selling it made perfect sense. In fact, he was surprised his father had held on to it for this long.

But now that he was here, Ash couldn't shake the feeling that they were selling off a piece of his mother's heart, the one thing that had meant more to her than any other possession, including her own home in San Diego. It was the place where she'd given her children those happy summer memories, just like she'd always wanted.

By this time next season, they'd be someone else's memories.

Ash yanked open a few drawers, peeked inside the oven. In his mind's eye, the place had never been particularly fancy, but he'd always remembered it being in good shape. Solid. Homey.

Now everything was falling apart.

What the hell happened to this place?

Blowing out a frustrated breath, Ash braced himself against the chipped countertop and looked out the cracked window over the sink. *Hell.* He knew damn well what'd happened—he just wasn't ready to face those demons yet.

Avoiding the refrigerator—more specifically, the collection of family photos plastered across the front of it —he rummaged through the junk drawer for a notepad and pen.

So much for a day flirting at the beach. Ash had hoped he'd be able to pick up supplies in town, but if the state of the kitchen was any indication, that plan was shot to shit. He had his own tools in the truck, parked in the beach access lot up the hill, but supplies were another story. Unless a Home Depot had sprouted up in the Cove while he was away, he'd need to hit the lumber-yard out in Jackson Bay, and probably that kitchen-and-bath place he'd passed on the drive in. Not to mention grocery shopping.

Jesus Christ. The old man was lucky Ash wasn't charging him for labor. Even the cheapest parts would just about wipe out the budget. How had his father let this place get so out of control?

A fresh wave of guilt crashed through Ash's chest. Everywhere he turned, he saw his mother's face, felt the touch of her hand on his cheek. She was so weak by the end, it had taken almost all of her strength to hold up her arm, yet she'd always managed to find a smile for Ash. Right up until the last day.

"I'm sorry," he whispered. But they were just words, and in the ten years he'd been saying them, not a damn thing had ever changed.

Get your shit together, asshole.

Ignoring the stab of pain in his heart, he jotted down some more notes, trying to figure out how he could minimize the number of county lines he'd have to cross to get all his supplies today, but it wasn't looking good. He tossed the notepad onto the counter and yanked open the fridge, hoping against the odds that fate would smile on him with a beer left on the door. What he found instead almost made him a true believer: the entire bottom shelf of the fridge was full of wine and Corona, and the rest was stocked with enough food for a party.

Before he could even guess whose stash that was, a pair of female voices floated in through the kitchen window, just outside the mudroom.

"I can't believe you didn't go with him," the one said. "He was totally into you. And totally hot."

"He didn't respect my boundaries," the other one said.

"The boundaries you so clearly established by throwing your arms around his neck and mashing your boobs against his chest? Or the boundaries where you shook your hot little ass against his crotch."

"I was just leaving him wanting more."

"Judging from the bulge in his shorts," the first one said, laughing, "mission accomplished."

Ash swiped a beer from the fridge and was about to head out and introduce himself, but they beat him to the punch. At the sound of the screen door creaking open, Ash plastered on a grin, turning on his heel toward the mudroom.

And then he almost lost his shit.

Two women wearing nothing but sand and bikinis—one hot pink, the other black. Both of them staring at him with shocked, open mouths, water dripping from their hair all over the floor.

Time stopped, then rewound, and suddenly he was twenty-two again, his baby sister standing in the kitchen wearing too much makeup and not enough clothing, pleading with him.

"Just two beers, Ash. One for me, one for her."

"No way. You're underage."

"We're eighteen, dickface. Next year we can totally drink in Canada."

"Oh yeah? If you start walking now, you'll hit the border right on time."

"Come on, Ash! Mom and Dad won't know. Pleeeease…"

"Ash?" pink bikini said now, her eyes glazing with tears.

Jesus. Like so many things in this house, Ash wasn't ready to face those tears. But unlike the ghosts he'd been wrestling with, these two women were real. Flesh and blood. And nothing like the teenagers he remembered.

Pink bikini was his baby sister, Dizzy Lizzie.

Black bikini? Lizzie's best friend, Pam Diederman. Deeds. Also known as the woman who'd fueled every last one of his sexual fantasies from high school to—frankly—last night in the shower.

Ash hadn't spoken to her in ten years. The night he'd said goodbye was supposed to be for good, and he'd made damn sure of that—never once stalked her on social media, never called, never asked about her the handful of times he'd talked to Lizzie after their mom's funeral.

Yet there she was, standing there like a Victoria's Secret model in that bikini that hugged her every curve, her innocent Blue eyes wide with shock, mouth frozen into a tiny pink "o."

Ash's heart banged against his ribs as memory after memory crashed through his skull, jerking him in a dozen different directions. Pam, laughing on the beach year after year as she snapped pictures of their childhood summers. Pam, giggling with Lizzie—Deeds and Dizzy, or D-squared, as their parents used to say—as they played Marco Polo in the water.

And that last summer... Pam, naked beneath the press of his hard body, her eyes dark with pleasure as she arched her hips and whispered Ash's name again and again and again...

He lost the ability to think, to breathe, to fucking speak in complete sentences.

There was only one phrase he remembered at the moment, and it pretty much summed it all up.

"Well fuck *me*."

It's not long before Ash and Pam get up to their old tricks, sneaking around for another red-hot, wall-banging, toe-curling summer. But what happens when secrets come to light and Ash puts his heart on the line? Find out in BAD BOY SUMMER!

ACKNOWLEDGMENTS

My dear, sweet, amazing readers! Thank you for loving my hockey boys, and for inspiring me to keep on telling these messy, beautiful love stories.

Speaking of love stories… There aren't enough heart-eyed emojis in the world to show my appreciation for Kara Schilling, Janice Owen, and the lovely ladies of the Boneyard!

And finally, all my love and in-person heart eyes go to my husband, who is the best research partner a romance novelist could ask for. (I'm talking about *hockey* research, ladies. Hockey! ;-))

ABOUT THE AUTHOR

Romance author Sylvia Pierce loves writing about kick-ass, headstrong women and the gorgeous alpha guys who never see them coming. She believes that life should be a lot like her favorite books—smoking hot, with happy endings and lots of temptations, twists, and trouble along the way. She lives in the Rocky Mountains of Colorado with a strong, sexy husband who appreciates her devious mind, loves making her laugh, and always keeps her guessing. Like the heroes in her stories, Sylvia's man didn't see her coming... but after nearly twenty years together, he's finally figured out who's boss!

Visit her online at SylviaPierceBooks.com or drop her an email at sylvia@sylviapiercebooks.com.

facebook.com/sylviapiercebooks

twitter.com/xosylviapierce

goodreads.com/SylviaPierce

amazon.com/author/sylviapierce

bookbub.com/authors/sylvia-pierce

Manufactured by Amazon.ca
Bolton, ON

24504781R00231